D. L. WILBURN JR.

ISBN: 979-8-9878037-6-9 (eBook)

ISBN: 979-8-9878037-8-3 (Paperback)

ISBN: 979-8-9878037-7-6 (Hardcover)

Library of Congress Control Number: 2023915249

Any references to historical events, real people, or places are fictitious. Names, characters, and places are products of the author's imagination.

Printed in the United States of America.

Cover by Suvajit Das.

Edited by Elaine Wilburn

Beta Readers: Cheryl Barger, Jerry McKinney, Chris Springer, Lilly Wing-Lui Alexander, Tracy McKinney, and George Engel

Sensitivity Reader: Lily Wing-Lui Alexander

First printing edition 2023.

W-III Publishing

Permissions@W-III.org

To Ally and Ashton for a great amount of patience.

Prologue

Four years have passed since the Earth was moved to an unknown location in the galaxy, orbiting a red star with four other planets. A longer orbit and changes in weather patterns necessitate the development of a new calendar, one with ten longer months and a twenty-five-day adjustment every five years. Deva, the month of reset, is a time to celebrate Earth's second chance.

The Artificial Intelligence, Quánqiú lóng or Global Dragon, worked to assist those countries that accepted its offer of help prior to the jump. Achieving its goals, the AI has left Earth to pursue other interests, a new game.

The Worshippers of Enlil (WoE), a rapidly growing religion, has moved quickly to fill the void in the struggling regions, providing supplies and rebuilding infrastructure. Led by an unknown figure, their goal is to reform society under the laws established by the Anunnaki god Enlil over seven thousand years ago. The Worshippers work openly to establish communications with the Anunnaki and bring them to Earth.

Setting

Era: Earth, After Jump (AJ)

Solar Year: 455 Days

Months: 45 Days
    Magha
    Phalguna
    Vaisakha
    Jyaistha
    Asadha
    Bhadra
    Asvina
    Kartika
    Agrahayana
    Pausha
    Deva (25-day reset every five years)

Seasons: 2 ½ months long

New Year's Day is the first day of Spring.

Part I

"The art of war teaches us to rely not on the likelihood of the enemy's not coming, but on our own readiness to receive him; not on the chance of his not attacking, but rather on the fact that we have made our position unassailable."

Sun Tzu

Magha, 5 AJ

Victoria, British Columbia

Jamal clinked his wine glass with the back of his hand, his Stanford ring making the glass resonate loudly. He stepped onto the small, raised platform, all eyes turning toward him. He took a moment to look over the gathered leaders of the Worshippers of Enlil, the most faithful.

"The new year begins, my friends, and it's time for us to take a more active role. We have waited long enough. The leaders of the world's governments have failed us again, falling into old habits of self-centered interests and arguing over global resources. We have watched as they fight among themselves, refusing to help those countries that were denied the aid of the AI." He paused as murmurs of agreement rippled through the room.

"You are the leaders of our movement. Your belief in Enlil and his teachings set the example for the followers of our movement and the lost."

The group raised their voices in support.

"The path forward is difficult." Jamal moved to the right, holding the attention of the gathering. "We will be challenged by the established and blinded religions of the world. Those who hold their secrets and power over their flocks, the sheep. We will be challenged by those who forget the failures strewn throughout history. War, famine, plague, and death; their four horsemen. All caused by humanity's inability to follow the laws given to us by our creators."

He crossed the stage to the left. "We have been shown the light. Our creators exist. We have seen proof of the city in the stars. Our creators have demonstrated a mastery of technology more incredible than we can imagine." He paused, scanning the faces of the group. He had their full attention. "Our gods exist, and that frightens the non-believers."

"Why did they create the abomination, sentient artificial intelligence, and beg for help? Because they are weak, scared, and can't rely on their faith to save them."

The room was quiet. He smiled confidently, adrenaline coursing through his veins. "We have planned and moved our pieces into place, and it's time to become the saviors of our brothers and sisters. What say you?"

"Enlil is lord. Enlil is the way. We will be judged."

Cheers erupted from the group. Jamal raised his glass to them before stepping down from the platform. Two assistants moved from either side of the platform and began handing out folders to the audience.

Jamal made his way through the room, shaking hands and exchanging small talk, pausing at the makeshift bar. He set his wine glass down and picked up the waiting whiskey glass. He winked at the bartender, sipped his drink, leaned back, and looked at the room. The High Priests and their assistants from twelve global regions were the most devoted followers. Each understood his demand that their group would have no secrets.

He finished his drink, set the glass on the bar, and stepped through an obscure door, closing it behind him. The room he entered was circular, blending eclectic modern comfort with ancient Sumerian. Several artifacts sat on pedestals or in glass cases around the room. The off-white curved walls contrasted the orange, brown, green, and gold of the displays.

Jamal wasn't surprised by his guest making himself comfortable on one of the curved couches forming a broken circle in the center of the room. "Dimuzud, my friend, how are you?"

"I am well, and you?"

"Good. I believe our cause, the true cause, continues to gain momentum. Last I checked, we are over six million registered members."

"That's indeed good news. And what of the other areas you want us to focus on?"

"So far, everything is proceeding as planned. I should be free to travel wherever I want by the end of the year." Jamal leaned in, looking at a tablet on a pedestal before turning his eyes to his guest. He pointed at Dimuzud, running his finger up and down in the air. "Is this the look you decided on?"

"Yes. What do you think?" He brushed a wrinkle out of the collarless, split V-neck short-sleeved shirt. Dimuzud turned to the side and looked up at Jamal. "I decided to go with a shirt instead of a bare chest. I asked my friends to add a few modern fashion flares, and this comfortable yet formal outfit is the result. Thanks to the Scottish, the idea of a kilt-like skirt is not hard to accept. The tan cloth color of the fabric accentuates the copper-gold necklace and bracelets nicely."

"I like it. It sets us apart. We need to get it out to the priests. Based on how well the ensemble looks, I assume you still have contacts in the fashion industry?"

Dimuzud smiled, cocking his head to the side. "Of course. A few are interested in introducing traditional Sumerian clothing with modern fabric and designs. One or two want to go extravagant, but I've held them back. They, of course, support our movement as a free expression of religion."

"Good, good. I don't want our message to get lost in bad publicity or ridiculous memes." Jamal sat on the couch across from Dimuzud, "This *is* what we need. A religion to unite humanity. One religion before all the others." He took a sip of his scotch. "I saw that bishop on the news again. He was talking about parallels and God's works influencing everything. He's partially correct. But it wasn't only one singular God. The Anunnaki, a technologically superior civilization, conquered mortality and engineered us to be like them."

3

Dimuzud sat silently, his eyes intently watching Jamal.

"If we can grow to rival the other religions, perhaps Enlil will appreciate us and see that we could be so much more to them."

Dimuzud sat forward, looking into Jamal's eyes. "You should be wearing this mantle. Your vision is what the people need to hear."

Jamal laughed, "No, my friend. We all have our roles to play, and I trust you with this. The world should see you build this movement to its full potential. I'll do what I can by staying in the shadows and giving you the support you need. Many people still hold a grudge about revealing their secrets. They're too near-sighted to see that I released them of their burdens by bringing their secrets to light."

"In time, forgiveness will be yours. Isn't that what their religions teach?"

"It does, but how well do they follow their tenets?"

Dimuzud scoffed. "True. They are quick to use it as a shield to defend against perceived injustice and just as quick to abandon it for a minor convenience."

Presidential Offices, Zhongnanhai, China

President Zhang stared at the newest painting in his office. A globe showing China in the forefront, with a dragon wrapped around the world protectively. The intricately spaced small green and black dots give the impression of millions of data bits forming the image. The name underneath read *Global Dragon*. Quánqiú lóng had become a cultural phenomenon he used to strengthen the support of his people. Over a thousand artists nationwide competed to glorify the first dragon of the modern age.

The soft voice of his assistant shook him from his reverie. "Mr. President, Dr. Jiang Min is here to see you."

"Send him in."

He stepped away from the painting, took a seat, and linked his hands, resting his forearms on the edge of the desk. He waited for his visitor to cross the room before indicating which chair to take.

"Lao Jiang, I hope the day finds you well."

"Thank you, President Zhang. I live to serve China."

President Zhang smiled, closed-lipped, nodding slightly. "What's the status of your genome project?"

"We've made several advances in creating a baseline genome for modern *Homo sapiens*. I've reduced the list of potential scientists to bring to the company to three. Over the last year, we've worked closely with Wǔ Kai and his Dragon Shell quantum computer team to develop a baseline genome. Using the collected data from prominent genealogical companies and several other sites that collect genetic materials, we've shortened the projected timeline by almost a year. While we may not have the Dragon AI, Director Wu and his team have proven more than capable of quickly developing programs to meet our needs."

"While it would be easier with Quánqiú lóng, it's not an option. The capabilities of the computer alone will need to suffice."

"Agreed. The rate at which we can process data has moved us to the front of the field."

"In all areas?"

"Yes, all programs are progressing faster than anticipated."

"Good." President Zhang stood, moving around the desk toward Dr. Jiang. His eyes remained locked on his guest. "What about the doctor from India?"

Dr. Jiang stood and bowed, keeping his eyes down. "We've approached her after her last talk with no success. I've read her research and the profile generated by MSS, and believe we may have made a mistake in our approach. My team has identified another opportunity to bring her onto the team. It's delicate, but I believe we'll be successful."

"Very well. Do what you must."

"Yes, President Zhang." Dr. Jiang nodded and left the office.

Georgetown, Virginia

Jackie knelt in the garden, gathering sickly-looking vegetables and pulling weeds, tossing both into a round metal bucket. The large brim straw hat drooped wide over her neck and shoulders. Sweat made her yellow T-shirt stick to her dark skin. "I don't get it. I followed the directions and watched a dozen videos, and this is what we get." She held up a withered tomato plant.

"Maybe the plants know you have more experience pulling long dead and forgotten things from the ground."

She looked over her shoulder at John sitting on the deck in his jeans and grey T-shirt. The sun glinted off his wedding ring as he raised his beer bottle to his lips with an innocent look. "Jonathan Adams Worthing! Do you want to get out here and do this? The president said we can help as things come back online by reducing the load on production."

"I think he'll be okay with us buying our food. He wouldn't want one of his advisors to starve. You know how they are about messaging. It wouldn't look good."

"He's not Fernandez." She glanced at him. "He's worried his administration can't live up to the success of his predecessor. How often can you say you helped save the world?"

"Personally, once, but I'm humble."

"Sure, believe that 'big guy,' and thousands of years from now, you'll be vilified as Satan 2.0. The person that gave knowledge to an artificial superintelligence that wants to rule the universe."

John took another long drink from his beer and shuddered. "Which reminds me, Eusebio called. He said it wasn't an emergency, something about the translations."

"Ok, thanks. I'll see him tomorrow. The translation program he got us access to has been worth every penny. The notoriety the company gained from our use of their program in deciphering Sumerian landed them several contracts, and got Eusebio paid as a consultant."

Jackie continued to pull the weeds from the garden. Wiping sweat from her brow, she looked up at the large moon in the sky, the smaller moon lower on the horizon. "I don't know that I'll get used to that." She motioned upward. "All those nights we spent camping at the lake, cuddling in the cold, looking up at the moon." Her voice trailed off.

"That was nice. Our second anniversary is coming up. Why don't we go back? Can you get away?"

Jackie stopped to think. "Maybe, my schedule is light. I have a class, but Eusebio could probably cover for me. We're into spring, even though the month is off."

"It'll be fun. Maybe add to those moonlit memories. We can watch Innana and Utu cross the sky." He stood and moved to the rail overlooking the backyard. Laughing, he raised his beer toward each of the moons.

She looked up at him indignantly. "The names are fitting. The Anunnaki are still out there. We need to remember that."

"Speaking of that, I heard Dr. Berzing turned down the NASA job. She wants to rebuild the Near-Earth Object Studies program and, from what I hear, has plenty of money to do it. It'll take a decade to get satellites up to replace every system we lost in the jump. They're still trying to finish getting global communications back." He turned to head back into the house, shaking the empty bottle. "I'll be back out in a bit. I need to check my email."

"Ok, I'm going to finish here. Don't get stuck in there. Let Grace or William handle it. Grace is supposed to cover for you when you're out. The company will survive on your day off."

"I promise no more than an hour," he said before closing the door behind him.

BBC America Studio, New York

George sat at a smooth glass table with a sizeable podcaster-style microphone in front of him. He wore a light grey suit, a royal blue shirt, and a NY Rangers tie. He bobbed his head to the theme music. When the green light came on over the primary camera, he flipped the papers in his hand to the side and leaned forward, knowing the camera would zoom in. "To quote Randy Quaid in Independence Day, 'Hello boys, I'm ba-ack!' Welcome to my new show here on BBC America. I'm George Isaacson, and it's good to be here. You had questions when my main BBC show went off the air a few months back. I couldn't reveal the deal we cut. Not for nothing, but I have to say, it's pretty sweet. This is going to be a great year. I know because the NHL is starting back up, and we're ending the year with the biggest party this part of the universe has ever seen. That's right, Truth Seekers, twenty-five days of Deva, the big reset and reflection on our second chance."

He paused to sip his energy drink, winked into the camera, and brought the Monster Ultra Gold into view. "Yeah, you know it." He wanted everyone to know that he was here to have fun and get back to answering questions about the unknown.

"Before we start, let me review what we're doing on BBC America. I'm not one to make enemies or burn bridges, so I have nothing bad to say about the last few years. But, in all seriousness, network news isn't for me. I want to be on the cutting edge of what you want to know but are afraid to ask. Some say it's fringe science and conspiracies, but I'll point out that Quánqiú lóng, China's Artificial Superintelligence, did something that our scientists still argue is impossible. Magic. Yeah, it was fringe until it wasn't. I'll stay on top of the world's efforts to create another dragon, possible alien contact, breakthroughs in theoretical science, and of course, watching the Worshippers of Enlil, who are still pretty upset about their grand plan to welcome the Anunnaki being canceled.

"Every week, I'll be bringing you a topic for discussion. We're changing the format and bringing back a favorite part of my show, call-ins by you, the Truth Seekers. I'm excited because talking to all of you was the highlight of my show. You helped save the world by believing and taking action. The network has faith in us—you and me. They gave me a full production team, including a producer, Carl, who is ready to go in whatever direction we want. Right, Carl?"

A deep baritone voice with a New York accent played across the set speakers, "You bet, George. We're about making magic happen."

"Sounds good. Let's jump into our topics. First up, rumor has it we should know where we are in the galaxy soon. My JPL and NASA contacts tell me they're working on a complex model to identify where we jumped to. Congress is throwing money at them to keep an eye out in space because, guess what? We're pretty much blind right now. Could you imagine not being able to see way out in space a decade ago? One day we would have looked up, and that giant city-ship would have been right there. I don't even know what would have happened."

George shook his head, looking at the laptop screen to his right. "Looks like we have our first caller to the show. What's up, Truth Seeker? What have you got?"

"George, I'm so glad you're back. And damn, I'm the first caller on this side of the galaxy! Shout out to my fam. This is Jeremy from out here on the Island. I think our guard is down. I know it almost feels like it's all normal, but the news shows all those countries that didn't get help from the AI, and I'm worried. Do you think anything out there could be sneaking up on us?"

"Hey Jeremy, thanks for calling. I gotta be truthful, so, maybe. The thing is, we know something is out there. We have our own intergalactic Michael Myers somewhere in the dark. And if that's true, there could be a Freddy, Jason, Leatherface, or any number of other horrors out there. You know what I mean? We need to watch the skies and stay safe." George paused to take a sip of his Monster Ultra Gold.

"Thanks, Jeremy. Let's take the next caller. You're on the air, go ahead and drop a truth bomb."

"Awright ya, George, this is Deidre, callin' from Helensburgh, Scotland. I think they're all mad. Th' gov'ments are goin back to tae old ways—fightin, secrets, an' greed. I dinnae think we'll get lucky next time. Fer all we ken, one o' th' planets in the solar system is occupied. Wha' if thay're nae happy aboot thair new neighbors?"

"Deidre, great point. I think you're spot on with that observation. We don't know if anyone is still visiting us. Interestingly, I haven't heard of a credible abduction story since we arrived. We know the Anunnaki are real, but what about the others? The Greys, Nordics, the Reptilians? What are they up to? We don't know yet, but we'll look into it in a later show. With that, let's take a quick break. I'll be right back."

George leaned back. *I need to get back into the groove. The show feels weak. I need to pick it up.*

He jumped back into the show, fielding questions about his year with the networks and why he decided to jump from mainstream news to a network known for focusing on their science fiction content. He felt off, but he pressed onward. George acknowledged that people were over conspiracy theory shows, returning to the mainstream media to tell them what was happening. He made notes as the show continued, trying to feel what people wanted. After an hour, he wrapped up. He felt drained.

"Thanks for a great show, Truth Seekers. I'll be back next week to talk about the government's efforts to marginalize discussion of aliens and the impact on society."

The light turned red.

George leaned back in his chair and blew out a long breath. "That was fun."

Carl stepped in from the left, patting him on the shoulder. "That was great. The research team is already hitting your first few topics. We'll stick to the list you laid out. Don't worry. Next week will be better."

"I hope so. Something felt off. I gotta figure it out quick." He looked at his watch. "Alright, I'm outta here. I need to get over to my dad's place. I'll be here in the morning."

"G'night, George. I'll text you. The show will be uploaded in an hour or two. Be safe. No abductions."

"Carl, I got you on speed dial in case the Men in Black roll up."

Carl laughed as he turned away, shaking his head.

Indian Institute of Technology Madras, Chennai, India

"Doctor! Please, if I could have a moment of your time." She heard the exasperated voice behind her as he tried to keep up with her quick pace.

Dr. Vasana Kaur stopped and turned toward the voice. "Please talk as we walk. I have a full schedule."

"Yes, thank you. My Name is Michael Barton, and I represent Genetticca. We've been trying to contact you since your presentation last month in Boston. We're interested in your theories on gene transcription and how it could revolutionize medicine."

"I'm flattered, Mr. Barton, but my research is not for sale." She stopped and turned toward him, looking down into his face. "Now that I think about it, I remember a representative from your company calling last week. He was rude and pushy. I told him I wasn't interested, and even if I were, I wouldn't work with your company."

"Dr. Kaur, I want to apologize for his behavior. It has been addressed. No insult was intended. If you'd please allow us to send you a proposal—"

"Fine, send it. I'll review it under one condition. If I turn you down, your company agrees not to bother me again. I'll be in touch." She looked down at her watch, shook her head, and continued down the hall. "I assume you can make your way back to the reception desk?"

"Yes, thank you, Dr. Kaur."

♦ ♦ ♦

Dr. Vasana Kaur, a genetic specialist at the Indian Institute of Technology, moved purposefully across her lab to an open workstation. She placed the papers on the desktop and opened a file on the screen. Looking between the documents and the screen, she clenched her jaw, pushed the papers aside, sat back in her chair, and looked at the ceiling.

After a few minutes, she sat up, took a deep breath, tried to relax, and clicked record on the video journal application. "Test thirty-six is a failure. The gene sequence introduced with Advanced CRISPR was inserted without issues but failed to yield desirable effects. Probability shows increased susceptibility to mutation. Modify future test parameters to reduce the number of affected nucleotides to previously successful levels."

She felt a buzz coming from the pocket of her lab coat and pulled out her phone. Seeing her daughter's picture on the screen, her stern look shifted to a welcoming smile. Vasana put the phone on speaker. "Hello, my darling girl, how are you?"

"Mother, I had a great day at school! We started new sections in mathematics and science. I launched a rocket using air pressure and water. Are you going to be home for dinner?"

"Yes, my dear, I'll be home on time tonight. Tell Mummy that I'll be home by six. I love you, my darling."

"Ok, love you."

A chime from her computer notified her of a new email. She read the header. "They're persistent." She sighed, clicking on the file. She took a moment to read the document. She opened the second file and moved closer to the screen as she read. She moved her hand to cover her mouth. "Incredible. Full access to quantum computer for gene sequencing and mapping."

She picked up the desk phone next to her terminal and dialed the number. "Sanja, clear my schedule next week. I'll be on travel."

She leaned back in her chair, looking again at her daughter's picture. "My sweet girl, there may be hope."

Center for Near Earth Object Studies, JPL, Pasadena, California

The large conference room was quiet despite being filled with the leads for most JPL projects. All eyes were on the presenter, Dr. Sharon Berzing, Director of the Jet Propulsion Laboratory.

Sharon adjusted her glasses, brushing aside a stray strand of her dark brown hair before stepping in front of the podium. She glanced down at her notes. "Thank you all for coming. I want to open with some good news. At least, that's how I view it. Our working database is online, and the data from the old Earth position has been removed. The data is still available if you need access. It has been separated from the working database until we have an exact reference point." She clicked on the next slide. "Continuing on the positive, the delay in launching NEO Surveyor in the mid-2020s and the further delays from supporting the lunar array and Cheng'e research base let this satellite sit in storage until after the jump. In the two years since we were able to launch the system into space, it has provided invaluable information and helped allay fears of being hit by something while we figured out where we were. The University of Arizona is at work designing the next-gen system. Congress is worried and does not want to be caught off guard by someone else sneaking up on us.

"At this time, I'd like to make a quick announcement as we segue into our next discussion—ground systems. Tim is taking a sabbatical from our fine team here at JPL for a few years to pursue his doctoral degree at the University of Arizona. He'll be starting at the end of the summer. His acceptance just came in."

The team clapped in support. "Thank you," Tim said, standing up from the table at the front of the room. "I won't be too far away and will still be a pain to some of you, who I'll call weekly for the latest data dump." He paused as several of the researchers laughed. "I'll focus our coordination with ground-based systems: Catalina Sky Survey, Pan-Stars and ATLAS in Hawaii, LINEAR at MIT, and the University of Arizona."

Sharon interjected, "Tim, please highlight the increased participation in MPC."

Tim nodded. "Of course, most of us are familiar with the Minor Planet Center, a public data archive that allows astronomers worldwide to contribute their observations. Since the jump, interest from around the globe in identifying and naming celestial bodies is up. This has benefited not only our programs but many others."

Sharon stepped forward as Tim sat down. "Thank you, Tim. The loss of all satellites took out GPS and most global communications. Cooperative efforts from all space agencies and capable countries have helped bring those systems back to a functional level over the last four years. One significant achievement has been the ability to provide data to the Royal Observatory in the UK. With our data, they've updated the Nautical Almanac, which led to the resumption of international commercial shipping. You're doing great work."

"I see some of you checking your watches. We're almost done. We have one more briefing from Dr. Metroph on ground system integration and coverage status."

Lake Anna State Park, Virginia

John stood at the water's edge, slowly reeling in his line. The air was cool, and the morning fog sat just above the water. The air was still and held the smell of new growth. He turned, looking back at the fire burning behind him in the pit. A good set of coals were starting to form. He cast his line back into the lake.

He heard the zipper of their tent. "There's coffee on the fire. It should be ready soon." He said without looking back.

"I'm good, thank you. I'm going for a quick run." Jackie replied.

"Hey, not so fast." He reeled his line back in and set the rod down. "Get over here."

Jackie put her arms around him, looking into his eyes before kissing him.

"Mmm, much better. Be safe. It's too cool for snakes but watch your step."

"Yes, dear, I'll be careful. You could come with me if you want to keep me safe."

"No thanks, my knee still hurts a bit. I'll make breakfast while you're out."

He watched as she rolled her eyes and put her earbuds in before heading down the trail, her ponytail swinging from side to side.

"I love you. Enjoy your run." He called out.

He looked at his watch, a fitness tracker he used to keep time more than fitness. "Ten more minutes, then I'll get the eggs going." He cast his line back into the lake and slowly reeled it in.

John continued to fish, watching for the red color of Jackie's jacket each time the path brought her near the lake's edge. She was out of sight when he heard a piercing scream across the lake. He dropped the rod, his eyes searching along the lake's edge where she should be emerging along the winding path.

"Jackie!"

Another scream reached him and was cut off. He looked in the direction of the sound, not seeing anything. He ran down the path she'd taken, ignoring the pain in his leg and feeling for his phone.

♦ ♦ ♦

Someone grabbed her, turning her around. She felt the strength of their hands squeeze her shoulder, pulling her backward. She saw the person's other arm coming around to grapple her. She whipped her head back, smashing the person's nose. As the grip relaxed, she raked her shoe down the person's shin and slammed her heel into the top of their foot. *Damn, soft running shoes.* She twisted toward the attacker, and halfway around, she found her footing and raised her knee into the man's groin. She threw her head forward, hearing as much as feeling the crunch of his nose. Blood splattered her face. He gasped in pain, instinctively reaching to cover his bloody face.

"John!" she screamed, turning away from her assailant. Pain erupted from the side of her head. She saw a bright flash of light before everything faded. She felt her knees give way as she collapsed. The earthy smell of dirt filled her nostrils as the world faded to black.

♦ ♦ ♦

John raced along the path, his legs and chest burning with effort, adrenaline fueling him. He felt his pace slowing as his body fought to push forward. Fear gripped his chest as he neared the last area he had seen Jackie. His eyes scanned back and forth, looking for anything that might provide a clue. He continued, rounding a turn back toward the lake, and saw the signs of a struggle in the dirt. Looking closer, he saw dark, wet spots on the ground.

"Jackie!"

He looked around. A thick, broken tree branch was on the ground a few steps up the path. "Jackie!"

He pulled his phone out and dialed a number as he continued to look around for signs of his wife.

"Gary, it's John Worthing. Someone took Jackie."

He paced around the attack site as he listened to the voice on the other end of the call. "Ok, I'll stay where I am. We're at Lake Anna at the northern campsite. Jackie went for a run along the trail around the lake. I'll be waiting at the point I think they took her. It's about a mile up the trail, away from the lake edge. Gary, there's blood on the ground."

His heart raced, and he raised his hand, feeling the pain in his chest, a mixture of fear and exhaustion. He continued to look around for anything. He switched his phone to camera mode and took pictures of the entire site. "Damnit, damnit, damnit. Jackie, where are you."

BBC America Studio, New York

"Hello, Truth Seekers. We're taking a side path to what we usually do by talking about the story gripping the nation tonight. Dr. Jackie Worthing, the archaeologist from George Washington University that helped identify the Anunnaki, has been kidnapped. The FBI has secured the area around Lake Anna in Virginia.

"This is a tragic event, and my prayers go out to her family and friends. I wanna know what you're thinking, Truth Seekers. Please call the FBI hotline if you live around Lake Anna and notice anything suspicious. Carl, let's open the lines."

"You got it, George. Our first caller is Ben."

"Great! Good evening, Ben. You're on the George Isaacson Show."

"Thank you, George." The southern accent came through strong. "This is just wrong. I think this is related to the jump."

"What do you mean, Ben? I'm not following you."

"Well, take a step back and think about it. That woman played an important role in helping us understand the Anunnaki threat. We got away, and they're probably pissed. I mean the aliens. We escaped the mighty creators. I think someone grabbed her for revenge."

"Ok, I'm following now. Who do you think it might be?"

"Well, we only know what they released officially. They told us the planet jumped, but we don't know how. We're in a whole other part of the galaxy. There is an AI, but it's gone now. If there really was an AI, where'd it go? Was it real? All I heard was a voice from a box at the UN. Hollywood coulda done that."

"Ok, Ben, but what's your point?"

"Sorry, yeah, I'm gettin' worked up bout this. What if the Anunnaki still have a way to get to us, and they grabbed her?"

"I don't know, Ben. I saw the NASA pics of the city-ship. I think we'd know if they were close."

"No, not that. Hear me out. What about that gate down in South America? You know, that door on the side of a mountain. It's some kind of gateway. I saw it on *Ancient Aliens*. Maybe they sent a small squad to find us and take out the threats to them?"

"Well, that's an interesting scenario. Give me a sec. Carl, can you pull the info up on this gateway?"

"Yeah, here ya go." A box showed up on George's laptop.

"Ben, it looks like you're right. There is a doorway in a mountain. There are actually several mysterious carvings and structures in the area of southern Peru. 'The gateway to the gods.' I'll definitely look into it. If an entire planet can be moved through space, who says doorways can't be opened too? Can we really take anything off the table? What do you think, Truth Seekers? Could you imagine a system of gates to take us all over the universe, like that old TV show? That's some scary stuff. An Anunnaki hit squad here on Earth. Thanks, Ben. Let's take another caller."

"Hey, George, Amari from Sacramento here. This is the truth we're looking for. First off, I have to say I'm super happy you're back. I tried watching the network show, and you looked like one of those dogs with a cone on your neck. Every time you wanted to scratch an itch about the real truth, you were stopped. We love you!"

"Thanks, Amari. Give us your thoughts."

"Ok, so this thing in Virginia is sad, dude. I think the AI is still here helping solve crimes and prevent war and stuff. Maybe it could help with this crime like it did with that assassination in Mexico. Maybe the governments made a deal, and it ducked out so we don't bog down the system with the billions of questions we would ask of it."

"Thanks for the support, Amari. I don't know whether the AI could help. Looking around the world, it seems to me that we'd be in a different situation right now if a superintelligent AI were watching over us. The more I see or not, the more I question its existence, and my contacts in the government have nothing to say about it. If any callers from China want to weigh in, hit me up. We'll be right back after this break."

The light turned red. "Carl, we need to do a show in Peru. I forgot all about that, and we could go over a ton of stuff. Maybe we need a live show?"

"Nice try. No travel this year, and Peru and the surrounding countries down there aren't safe."

"Yeah, I guess. Maybe next year." He stood, stretching, looking around the studio. He smiled as his eyes came to rest on a small card and a silver dollar sitting among the influencer achievement trophies on the shelf behind his chair. He read the handwritten words on the card underneath the presidential seal: *To the Voice of the World, thank you, #Silver*. He sat down and swung the mic to his right side. He started when the light turned green. "Welcome back, Seekers. Let's jump to the next caller."

"Boom, boom, boom, how the mighty fall."

George's stomach tensed up at the sound of the voice. "It can't be. Jamal, is that you? I thought you'd be in prison by now."

"Not me, Georgie. I'm a ghost. I didn't call to dwell on the past. I wanted to check in and congratulate you on the new show. You know I'm a fan. Are you doing okay? I worry about you, so much stress, no big conspiracies, whatever will you do? Ha."

"You know, I knew you were a super fan. You waited these few years to talk to me again. How is life on the run?"

"There's no running here. I'm a busy man with many things left to do. Don't you worry about me. With your new show, I'll be checking in regularly. Take care, my friend. Pop goes the Weasel. Ha, ha, ha." The call ended.

George let the silence hang in the air for about ten seconds before continuing. Carl was to the side of the primary camera, signaling him to say something.

"Wow, I don't even know what to say. Ole FedBuster, Jamal Herricks, is back. Buddy, you almost screwed us all. I tell you what, if you wanna come to Staten Island, we could throw hands and settle this once and for all." George took a long drink of his Monster Ultra Gold, letting Jamal's words sink in. "Let's take a quick break and jump back into the calls."

George felt better than he had before. He expected challenges to his show. A few years in the media industry had given him more resolve. What game is Jamal playing now? Whatever it is, it can't be good.

WoE Research Facility, Illinois

Jackie's head hurt, and her mouth was dry. She was in a vehicle, but everything was dark. She didn't know how long she'd been out.

"How is she?" A voice came from a speaker to her right.

"Why don't you come back here and find out."

"Now, Dr. Worthing, there's no need to be hostile. However, I have to say that what you did to my man was more than expected. Were he not committed to our little project, I dare say you would not be in such a positive state."

She sat up, feeling the chains around her wrists and ankles. The windows were black. "What do you want from me? If you know who

I am, you know who I know and who I work with. Letting me out here, in the middle of nowhere, would probably be easier than keeping me. They will find me."

"Dr. Worthing, I don't doubt that the president and all his government lackeys have deployed excessive resources. They'll probably find you, just not anytime soon. Cooperate, and you'll find us most amenable."

The vehicle stopped. Jackie's head still hurt from where she'd been hit, though she guessed they had injected her with something to numb the pain. She didn't know how long she'd been unconscious. A water bottle with a long straw was in the drink holder to her right. As she sipped the water, she noticed the camera across from her, mounted above the closed window separating her from the driver. She felt the vehicle slow and turn right, the crunch of gravel and dirt under them. She pulled the chains, testing them. *No slack.*

Jackie heard the doors close in the front and looked around, trying to see through the darkened windows. She thought she could make out trees. Both side doors opened, and the sudden sunlight hurt her eyes. Two figures leaned in. "This way," one of the men gestured. The metal ring on the floor opened, releasing the chains. She thought of fighting, then decided against it, sliding to the side before being helped out. She caught a glimpse of the trees, primarily pines, before a bag covered her head. The men wore transparent masks that hid their features. She shuffled forward in her prisoner's chains, resisting the urge to fight. She began to count her steps as they walked softly. After a short while, a voice interrupted her "22, 987, 440, 1076, 21, 987, 83, 76, 322."

She lost count. After walking for a good distance, she was helped up several steps and into a building. The air inside was cool and sterile. She heard a voice from the man behind her, "You'll feel a slight pinch."

She tensed up as her arm was straightened and something injected into her forearm. "You're all in so much trouble when," her voice trailed off as she lost consciousness.

Genetticca Research Center, Delhi, India

"Dr. Kaur, welcome to Genetticca. I'm Barry Wantanubi, Director of Operations. We're happy to have you join us. We've set up a tour of the facility and can answer any questions you may have."

"Thank you, Mr. Wantanubi. The proposal you sent is impressive." She shook the hand of the tall man, nodding slightly. His hand was warm, and his smile genuine.

"Of course. The company is generous in hiring top talent. I felt similar when they recruited me from the Biodiversity Institute in Cape Town. Financial support for our work isn't an issue. We've recently entered into an agreement to fund our research well into the future. If you'll follow me." He turned and began walking down the hall.

"The initial processing area is to the left. The work area probably looks unconventional to what you're used to. Sampling and sequencing use the same conventions with some modifications to the workflow. A complete medical profile from all known donor records is available to help link medical anomalies to genes and nucleotide pairs."

Dr. Kaur raised her eyebrows. "There is usually hesitancy or outright refusal to provide detailed medical information."

"That's true, and we admit that the sequencing and standardization of the human genome are still far from complete. We believe adding more samples to the model increases accuracy in determining what defines 'normal' and 'healthy.'"

"That will take years. I recall from a recent conference that it would take over three hundred years to sequence the Earth's population. How big a sample are you seeking?"

He turned, looking directly into her eyes. "All of it, statistically speaking, of course. Every time a blood sample is taken, we add it to the sequence."

"Still, that's almost nine billion people. What about privacy laws?"

"Our legal team is exceptional. We continue to analyze and make adjustments. Enough of that, though. I'm sure you want to know what our main objective is." He paused, waiting for her acknowledgment, continuing when she nodded. "While we want to move toward the stage of allowing parents to select all the positive options for their children genetically, continued resistance and paranoia against creating superhumans keep us in check. We aim to take a genetic sample in utero, run it against a prime sequence, and then create a single dose genetic inoculation to remove all genetic anomalies, susceptibility to diseases, prohibitions to medicines, defects or limitations."

"And the difference between that and designer children is what?"

"We're only providing a clean slate from which to grow. There is no alteration of performance characteristics. No super strength or intelligence, wings, tails or otherwise."

"How long will it take to get what you feel is an acceptable level of samples to establish a valid baseline?"

"Four years."

Vasana shook her head. "How is that possible? The number of samples required is incredible. Sequencing and baselining the dozens in use now took years."

"Processing power." He motioned toward a door leading to a large conference room on the right. "Let's talk salary proposals. We can address program concerns later." He smiled as he followed her into the room.

Federal Bureau of Investigations Training Academy, Quantico, Virginia

"John," Gary called out from a group of agents and recruits near the start of the obstacle course. They wore dark blue shorts and grey T-shirts with the letters F B I on the front. He broke away and walked toward his friend.

"John, I know you're anxious. But what are you doing here?"

"I had a meeting at the marine base." He paused, lowering his eyes. "Gary, it's been five days, and there aren't any demands. Isn't that bad?"

"It depends. We have the results from the blood: The good news is that it isn't Jackie's. It's from an ex-military, Army Ranger, honorable discharge. We've put out a BOLO for him. His social media is clean. We don't have a current address, and there isn't an electronic trail over the past three years, which isn't hard to believe with the number of dead zones we still have."

"Have you talked to NSA?"

"I tried because she's listed as a presidential advisor, but they don't have any leads. Thank goodness for the snail's pace of Washington in clearing people off the president's special counsels for this and that. John, we're doing everything we can."

John shook his head, "Why her?"

Gary placed his hand on John's shoulder. "We have to be open to the possibility that it was just a random event. I hate telling you to be patient, but that's where we are."

"What about the car? A hiker spotted a green Lincoln Town Car. That make and model can't be hard to find."

"Nothing yet. I'm sorry."

"Fine. I understand it's not your fault. Just damned frustrating. When are you coming back to DC?"

"In a few days. I know it's a big ask, but try to relax. Honestly, John, it would be best if you headed home. Jackie has a lot of fans in law enforcement. We're doing everything we can."

"I will. Maybe I'll reach out to a few people. Thanks, Gary."

Gary watched his friend walk, head down, back to his car and drive off. He turned around toward the gathered trainees, and his face was grim.

"Ok, wanna-be agents. Let's play a game."

The students turned to face him, unsure of what was coming next.

"Here's the scenario, and I know you're all two weeks from graduation, so let's put that Quantico training to the test. Why would Jackie Worthing be a target for kidnapping? More than forty-eight hours have passed, and there is no ransom letter, demands, or contact from her abductors. She was on a camping trip with her husband and is well known for assisting the previous president during the buildup to the jump. Thoughts?" He looked expectantly at the trainees.

"Maybe random? They were looking for an easy victim, and she came along. Wrong place, wrong time."

"Yep, possible. Next clue. There were signs of a struggle. There was blood at the crime scene. Our lab was able to find a match in the DoD personnel database. Army Ranger, male, tall, left the service six years ago, honorable discharge."

"Was the blood fresh? Could the site have been contaminated, or perhaps he, the ranger, was grabbed earlier, and it's a favorite spot to take people?" A tall male trainee asked.

"Good thinking, that's a possibility. The blood was fresh, less than an hour old when it was collected."

Another trainee shook her head. "Could the aliens have someone on Earth? I know it's hard to imagine, but I'm trying to think outside the box."

Gary nodded, "Another possibility. This is brainstorming. There are no bad ideas."

"What about the Worshippers? They may believe humanity would have gained more than we lost. Four years later seems like a long time, and they've prescribed a non-violent message." A female agent stepped forward, her shoulders back, confident. "With no ransom demands, whoever grabbed her may want something no one else can provide. Maybe they believe she knows something they need. Something only she can provide. What they wanted was worth the risk of bringing a federal investigation to bear. It has to be something they feel is valuable. Maybe a relic or the location of a relic?"

Gary looked down at her nametag, "Banks, that sounds like a workable theory. So, who'd want to kidnap a recognized expert in Sumerian civilization? Think about it and get back to me."

Phalguna, 5 AJ

WoE Research Facility, Illinois

Jackie sat on the bed in the center of the circular room, staring at the plate of food on a pedestal. She had not been mistreated, and the food was quite good. She thought about refusing to eat, trying to resist as she'd seen in movies, but didn't see the point. She picked up a piece of bacon from the plate and took a small bite.

The room was quiet. She could hear the air coming from vents in the ceiling. Her captors asked her several times over the first three days if she would discuss what they wanted from her. She'd refused, remaining silent. They told her they'd not ask again and said she could let them know when she was ready to talk—the next four days had been filled with silence, broken only by the cycling of the central air system.

She got up and walked to the edge of the cylindrical wall. She was impressed. The quality of the video was lifelike, slightly better than the screen John had in his DC office. She walked around the large room, looking over the projected landscape, her dig site for the Eridu Tablet and Anunnaki star chart. It was a fantastic recreation, life-like. Her quarters consisted of a bed and the necessary facilities requiring privacy. As far as she could tell, her privacy was being honored.

She sighed, looking up before talking. "As a prison, it's comfortable, at least. What do you want of me?"

"Ah, Dr. Worthing, it's so nice to hear your voice." The image of an older gentleman appeared in front of her, standing in the desert landscape. He wore a loose-fitting khaki suit, an open-collar white shirt, and round glasses. The desert breeze blew his thinning white hair.

"Where am I? Where's my husband?"

"Dr. Worthing, I am happy to answer your questions. The faster we develop trust, the quicker we can get on with our business. You are wherever you want to be. The room can show many landscapes and locations. As for your husband, he is doing as well as expected. Our relationship will determine whether he receives any information on your well-being. As for what I want," he let the words hang in the air as she stared at him, "I'd like you to find something for me. The Tablet of Destinies."

Jackie shook her head, chuckling, "You can't be serious. Archaeologists have been looking for that tablet for over a century. As far as anyone knows, it may already be locked up among the hundreds of thousands of recovered artifacts, undiscovered in a tomb somewhere, or lost."

"I am familiar with the progress, Dr. Worthing. I have the results of the efforts before the jump and more. But thanks to your team, we now have an excellent tool for rapid translation of Sumerian."

The landscape shifted to black, interrupted by images of artifacts. A translation of the cuneiform floated in the air next to each one. She felt drawn to the artifacts as much as she didn't want to help. Some she recognized, many she did not. She walked around the room, looking at the objects and comparing the cuneiform with the translation, taking it all in. As she moved forward and turned to look at the next image, the previous one disappeared, replaced by another.

"This is amazing. How did you gain access to these images?"

"While I do not want to give away too many secrets, you would deduce the truth in short order. We continued the process you began years ago with the Lost Language Translation Program. L2TP, as your assistant, Dr. Bustamante, named it. My organization can access museum databases in the UK, Iraq, the People's Republic of China, and several others." He paused, perhaps waiting for a reaction from her. She resisted. "We know that Marduk or Enki gained possession of the tablet, depending on the story's version. Through additional information we have deciphered, the tablet moved to Enki's stronghold in South Africa, near Adam's Calendar."

"That's not correct. That theory isn't confirmed. It's considered fringe. There is no scientific proof linking the ruins in South Africa with Sumer." She rested her hands on her hips.

"And now I have your attention. With your permission, I'd like to show you something."

"Fine." She said, annoyance permeating her voice.

The image on the circular screen shifted to show a different dig site. People were moving about. She didn't recognize the ruins. "Where is this?"

"This, Dr. Worthing, is Adam's Calendar. We have been excavating for over eight months. What you see is the result of our efforts. You can move throughout the dig site by speaking to the screen. It will follow your commands."

She looked around, gaining her bearing, and noted the compass at the bottom of the image around the room. She moved toward an uncovered structure. "Head toward the building to the west."

She approached the building, and the camera moved through the door. The image moved with her along the desired path. The room appeared to be a three to four-meter square area. It was dark and looked Sumerian.

"Increase light one hundred fifty percent." The man said.

Jackie noted the images and cuneiform writing on the wall as the room lit up. She gasped, "That's impossible."

"Present heads-up display with geo position." A map of South Africa appeared with a small blue dot linked to a box with the latitude and longitude.

She backed away, looking at the writing, and sat on the bed in the center of the room.

"That was my reaction as well. There are more ruins we have not uncovered. Have I piqued your interest?"

"If I help, will I be released?"

"There are forces at work that neither of us controls. I will push for your release if we find the tablet's location. With the tablet, I may have a stronger position to lobby for your freedom."

Jackie thought about the offer. She knew John must be at his wit's end. Perhaps she could find a way to contact him. "Fine, I'll help."

"Excellent. You may call me when you need anything. My name is Victor DuMont."

Victoria, British Columbia

Jamal's eyes danced across several monitors. His fingers flew over the keyboard. Code filled the center screen. As he finished a section, he would stop to read the text, skipping between screens to complete different tasks. A pinging sound let him know that he had an urgent report.

A woman's voice began reporting when the status link on-screen turned green. "We secured the Doctor. We hope to have her assistance as soon as she sees our advancements toward the goal."

"That's good. How long do you think it will take?"

"Not too much longer. Her professional curiosity will override any angst she may have."

"Excellent. I look forward to checking the recordings. Do you have anything else?"

"No. May Enlil bless our actions."

"Yes, may Enlil bless us."

When the line disconnected, Jamal turned to the left side monitors and opened an application. "Call Enrico, secure."

After a moment, a deep Italian accent answered. "Ciao."

"Enrico, how are things?

"Good, recruitment goes well. You were right. It's all about the messaging. The online videos about the Anunnaki with NASA images and US political speeches are powerful influencers. Senses overcome blind faith."

"Ok, I want you to run the Pathwalker program I sent you. Plant the fingerprints at the addresses we agreed upon."

"Of course. Anything else?"

"No, I need to see that this works. I'll be in touch."

Jamal turned, picked up the remote under the rightmost monitor, and pointed it at a screen across the room. The screen came to life, displaying Euro News. "Set keyword search, group four." The screen below the TV turned on and began showing closed captioning for the broadcast. He checked the capture program to ensure the words were recorded and sent to a log file. "Let's see how the morph is doing."

He designed Pathwalker to insert video feeds into surveillance systems to make it appear he was moving through the target city. He hoped to continue morphing the known visuals in the systems away from his actual image so he would be free to move around the world without plastic surgery. Changing his fingerprints and voice was easy, as they used data markers in identification. His image had proven more difficult. He gained two valuable tools from the Feisty Weasel program, which he continued to modify. The first was an interactive tool kit to identify the security system guarding an organization's systems. He named it *Locksmith*. The second was far more valuable—the *Janitor's Key Ring* or *JKR*. The program allowed him to access any system defeated as a weasel challenge. Jamal was careful to access only the systems he needed to upload the morphed images. He often shared carefully timed leaked photos to the press, updating his image in law enforcement databases. He counted on the authorities to be lazy in comparing images.

He rolled his chair across the room to another computer, pressing a series of numbers. He waited as the phone rang. When the voice answered, he turned up the volume on the speakers.

"Hello," a southern accent greeted him.

"I wanted to check on your progress in attaining the devices."

"I've briefed the team. No engagements. We should be in and out in less than an hour."

"Good. Let me know when you have the items."

"Will do, sir. May Enlil judge us favorably."

"May he do so, indeed."

NSA Storage Facility, San Antonio, Texas

Mac scanned the nondescript building. He keyed his mic, keeping the binoculars up. "I don't see anyone posted near the exits. The homeless woman moves up the street and back down at thirty to forty-minute intervals. She could be talking to someone. C, whaddya got?"

"We have audio, nothing different from the last few nights. She's talking to someone named Joe. Complaining about the rats. She says that the rats have all gone and babbles about how the neighborhood is getting better with the rats gone, playing crazy well."

"So you're saying she's talking to herself? Anything out of the ordinary?"

"The two new guys are sleeping across the street. They argued about something, got pretty loud, then passed out."

"Copy. Three on the street. Are the drones up?"

"Bringing the EM drone in now. I've got a picture of all three targets. We have confirmation that they're using short-range comms. Their ears are hot, probably earpieces. I have three wireless relays—one just inside the third-floor window of the target building. The second is behind the light on the middle streetlight on the north side. The last one is inside the car at the end of the street with the missing wheels."

"Ok, let me know when you're on the power grid. Break, teams report status."

He heard the radio clicks, "Team One in position, over. Team Two is ready to enter the area."

"Copy. C, get ready. Team Two, go. Drop the power when she's at the far corner."

Mac watched the scenario play out. A delivery van entered the area from the south and approached the woman's position. From the driver's side, he saw the cigarette smoke and the men 'sleeping' on the sidewalk stir as the loud music from the van passed. When the van was halfway up the street, the power went out. Checking the surrounding area, he noted it was dark as well. The three targets' body language tensed. They were alert. The van continued past the target building and slowed as it approached the woman. He scanned back down the street, watching the two men.

"C, drop comms."

"Roger. Three, two, one. Their comms are jammed."

"Copy, Team One, go."

This moment had the most potential to go sideways. He switched to night vision and watched the team move across the rooftops.

"M, the area is clear. No concern. They called in the power outage. We rolled it in from outside the area with brownout procedures. CPS Energy will be on it, but we should have enough time. We took down a police precinct, two fire stations, and a hospital. They should prioritize support to those areas if they follow normal protocols."

"Copy. C, watch the chatter." Mac scanned the street. One of the men had moved up the road toward the van while the other watched. He checked the street, focusing on the van. He saw a person leaning out the window, talking to the woman. "Good work, Team Two, keep them focused. You have their attention."

"C, hold the transformer." Scanning back to the target building, he saw the two personnel against the wall, suspended outside the window.

"Team One, go."

The two personnel gripped the window and slid it open, each entering. He clicked his watch, starting the countdown.

33

"M, I have a car entering the area two blocks over. Looks like a police patrol."

"Copy. Team Two, watch your six. Incoming, stay calm."

After a few minutes, the police car came around the corner and pulled up behind the van. Two officers exited the vehicle, one taking a position in the back, out of sight from either of the cab mirrors, and the other moved toward the driver's side. Mac watched the scene unfold. The woman stopped talking to the man on the passenger side and backed up against the wall. He saw the driver exit the van and move toward the back, opening the doors. The officer shined his light into the van. A click on his mic refocused his attention.

"Team One successful. Four for four."

"Copy. One, Two, standby, C go."

The streetlights lit up as the 'brownout' ended, power flowing back into the neighborhood. The lights at the end of the street illuminated the van, the police, and the crazy lady with a high-tech earpiece. He lowered his head behind a small wall, closing his eyes.

Mac keyed his mic, "Drop it."

He heard the loud bang as the transformer at the end of the street, across from the van, exploded, dropping the power again. Mac rose back into position, watching the aftermath of their actions. Team One was clear, and the two were calmly talking to the police.

"All units, this is M, exfil as planned."

Georgetown, Virginia

The speaker's words ran together. John rubbed his head. He knew he should be paying attention. They were about to sign a deal with NASA for their Impenecloth design worth several million dollars over the next decade. Emelia leaned over and whispered, "John, I've got this if you need to step away. No one would blame you."

He was about to tell her he was okay to stay when his phone buzzed. He read the ID, *Gary—FBI*. "Excuse me, everyone. I have to take this call. Emelia will finish. I apologize."

He stepped out, closed the door behind him, and answered, "Gary, what have you got? Did you find her?"

"Not yet, but we do have an update. Local law enforcement found the vehicle in a river in Luray, Virginia. The suspects picked a route with fewer cameras and tolls. They might have missed it if it weren't for an oil leak in the car and a concerned local environmentalist. We're checking the cameras from the town. More than you probably want and not enough at the same time. No hits yet, but the FBI is involved because they crossed state lines. We received calls from a small town in West Virginia, Brandywine, of a black SUV. It stopped for gas, and all the windows were tinted."

"Thanks, Gary. What was the name of the town again?"

"Brandywine and I know what you're thinking, John, but you don't need to head out there. We are tracking other leads. As soon as I know more, I'll call."

"Fine. I'll head over to GWU to talk to her staff. I know most of them. I'll let them know what you found if that's okay."

"I have no problem with you talking to them, but the info on the car and town is just for you. That information hasn't been released to the press yet. We don't want to tip anyone off."

"What about the Army Ranger? Any word on him?"

"One of the men spotted in Brandywine matched his size, but witness descriptions were unreliable. We received his personnel file from DoD. There's nothing there. We tracked down members of his last unit, and a few were missing, meaning we went to their listed residences, which were empty: no credit cards, phones, nothing. One was killed in a hiking accident a year ago in Yellowstone, but the case was closed quickly. It looks like an accident. I have an agent reviewing the files. I'm sorry, John."

"Thanks, Gary. I know everyone is working overtime on this."

"One more thing, I have a new agent I pulled from the last graduating class at Quantico, Alicia Banks, in case you wonder why someone besides me is calling you. She's working with me, a good agent, top of her class."

"Ok, got it. Thanks again."

◆◆◆

John knocked on the GWU Archaeology Department research lab door before stepping in.

Eusebio got up and crossed the room. "John, how are you? Is there any word on Jackie?"

John sighed, bowing his head. "They have a few leads but not much else."

"I'm sorry, the team is pretty torn up about everything. The University called in a psychologist. Most are taking personal time."

John shook his head. "I don't understand. Why now? The Anunnaki threat is over. She hasn't been to the White House except for the first week when they asked her to stay on as an advisor. Other than that, she's only gone back for a photo shoot and media event. It doesn't make sense."

Eusebio held John's shoulder, "I'm sorry." He paused, removed his hand, and moved to lean on a nearby desk. "I don't know what to say. As I said, everyone is in shock."

"Thanks, Eusebio. Have you heard from the bishop?"

"Ishmael? Yes. He'll be in New York later this year. He won't say anything about the rumors, though. He always brushes it off with 'God's will be done.' Typical."

"Well, that's some good news. He's been helping in several hotspots around the world, the neglected post-jump regions."

"I'm glad he did. Venezuela and the handful of countries in South America are in shambles. Many haven't recovered from the jump.

Food shortages and a lack of other essentials are making it the wild west."

"And then WoE comes to the rescue. It worked out for them. Most countries were focused on their own citizens. The Worshippers stepped in to provide much needed relief to desperate people. The rumor is that their unknown leader is in Venezuela, but I'm not buying it. They have a global presence now. The fastest growing religion. And yet, no one knows who their leader is."

"Not true. According to the email requests, it's Enlil and the Anunnaki."

"Ten years ago, I would have laughed at that. Now, well, let's hope they don't find us." John checked his phone. "I've got to go. Thanks for taking the time. I'll let you know if I find anything out."

"Thank you, John. Let us know if you need anything."

Staten Island, New York

George pulled his bike up to the deli, locking it to a nearby post before heading in. "Hey Joe, how's it going?"

"George, what the hell are you doing here? I thought you were all fancy with the TV shows and such. I told the wife that we hadn't seen you since you got all famous."

"Joe, come on. Can you imagine me getting famous and not coming to the best deli on Staten Island? The cuts are too good."

A woman's voice sounded from the doorway behind the counter, "I thought you were scared off. How's your father?"

"Hey, Tina, he's good. I'm heading over tonight for dinner. How are you doing? I heard you were engaged."

She raised her hand, the diamond glittering in the incandescent light. "Yeah, too late for you."

"Ya know, I was just about to ask you out too."

She handed him a bag with his order. "Maybe you'll find someone since all that conspiracy stuff turned out to be true."

He shrugged his shoulders and headed for the door. Before leaving, he turned back, "Congrats, Tina, I mean that. Thanks, Joe."

◆ ◆ ◆

George sat at the small round table in his father's kitchen. "Dad, I told you I was picking up food from Stan's. Why'd you cook? This is too much."

His father stood over the stove, cooking chicken in one pan and vegetables in another. "Indulge me. Eat your risotto. Maybe I want to have extra for the week."

George ate but continued, "C'mon." He took a bite. "Mmm, I miss this."

His dad didn't turn around. "I did too."

"Are you okay?"

"Yeah, yeah. I just, um, you know, miss your mother."

"I know, Dad, I do too." George put his fork down and wiped his mouth. "You know, Dad, you're not too old."

His dad turned around, the hand towel falling from his shoulder. George braced for his dad's wrath. He tried talking him into dating a few years back, and his dad had laid into him about disrespecting his mother, marriage, and love and stormed out.

"That's what I wanted to talk to you about tonight. A little later, uh, I have a friend coming over. I wanted to tell you in person."

George stood up, relieved. "Dad, that's great. You could have told me sooner. Here I am eating. I'll take off and let you get set up."

His dad pointed a wooden spoon at him, "Sit down. I'm testing the food on you."

George silently looked at his father for a minute before laughing so hard he bent over, holding his stomach.

"George, I don't want any crap from you. Support your old man. Change the subject."

George sat down, trying to stifle his laughter. "Ok, yeah, the show is going great. The ratings are pretty good. The network is happy. I think it's a better match than trying to do the regular news."

"I caught your show last week. You seem to be covering that abduction pretty well, even though your audience won't let the alien hit squad story go. Crazies." He waved away a response as George started to talk. "I'm sorry, I don't mean that. Crazy stuff happens, I know. Two freaking moons, right?"

"Yeah, Dad, four years now."

"Well, I'm happy for you. I'm glad to see you on the TV." He flipped the chicken and turned to George, "Don't forget your coffee mug. You left it here last week."

George looked to the counter where his oversized white mug with the words 'Mulder was right' on the side sat. "Sure. Are you going to let me test that chicken, or are you doing it blackened?"

His dad shook his head. "This is what I get. Smart guy."

Genetticca Research Center, Delhi, India

Vasana rolled her shoulders and shimmied deeper into the cozy plush chair in the corner of her sizeable office. Genetticca spared no expense to make sure she was comfortable. She sipped her masala chai, taking a moment to enjoy the cinnamon and spice mixture. She adjusted once more and began reading through a comparison of the latest week of genetic sequencing and the adjustments made to the Prime Genome. She'd been given control of the project and would meet the Chinese liaison, Jiang Min, shortly. She marveled at the minor changes made to the sequence with each update. Her goal was to complete her work before the reset month of Deva.

She looked up from the report, sipped her chai, and turned her eyes to the window. She was surprised that the international community had accepted the Hindu calendar format. The UN led the effort to bring more diversity into the naming conventions of their new home in the galaxy. Once the seasons were defined, the world accepted the system. It focused on crop growth and harvests—a 455-day year broken into ten months of forty-five days and a twenty-five-day reset every five years, Deva—a time to celebrate their second chance.

A chime from her computer refocused her thoughts on work. The results were fascinating. Thirty years of research followed the human genome project, and we have more questions than answers. Narrowing down the differences within the .1% of DNA that defines and individualizes humans from every other person on Earth would help identify the areas within a genome different from the base, indicating an anomaly. Focusing on the anomalies, we find areas with a legitimate functional purpose or an error that leads to unintended consequences. Creating a prime genome was crucial to humanity's future. She continued reading the comparison analysis before a knock at the door interrupted her thoughts. She looked at her assistant, "Yes, sorry, deep in thought." She raised the tablet, shaking it.

"Dr. Kaur, Dr. Jiang is waiting in your conference room."

"Thank you, did you retrieve the information for me?"

"Yes, Doctor."

"Good, let's take the long way to the conference room."

They left the office, heading down the long hall. Vasana had planned the timing to allow for the questions she wanted answered before the meeting. "Ok, give me the basics."

"Dr. Jiang Min is from Hubei, a central region of China. He scored very well in analytics and logical thinking as a child, receiving several awards for excellence in chemistry and biology, which gained the attention of the Ministry of Science and Technology and got him into Peking University, where he graduated at the top of his class. His work in Quantum Biology brought him to prominence in his field. There is a rumor that he contributed to the breakthrough design of the Global Dragon AI. He's been with Genetticca since co-founding it three years after the jump."

"These dates still throw me off. I want to see if we stick to Deva as a time of rest and reflection."

"I hope so. My friends and family are all planning to take that time to join in the global celebration."

"We'll see. What did you find regarding his work with the AI?"

"Not much. It will take a deeper dive to find the files if you want. Several documents were released during the weasel virus outlining his ideas for storing information and transferring data similar to DNA in cells."

"Yes, and anything else he was involved in. I trust that he's already done the same with my research. We'll begin the relationship with trust and see where it goes."

They rounded the last corner leading to the conference room. Dr. Kaur straightened her suit jacket. "Thank you, Arjun," she said before entering the room.

Her assistant nodded, continuing down the hall, past the door.

Vasana entered the room, rounding the conference table. "Namaste, Dr. Jiang. It's good to meet you finally."

"Thank you, Dr. Kaur. The feeling is mutual. I thought it a good time to welcome you formally and discuss the project in more depth. How are you settling in?"

"Very well, the lab is beautiful, innovative. To be honest, the allowances given toward researching my daughter's condition brought me over. Your work on developing a prime genome is promising. So much potential."

Dr. Jiang leaned forward, placing his elbows on the table. "Ah, yes. By examining millions of genomes and defining a prime genome, we hope to correct errors in the code, removing most disorders before birth. Being able to do that alone would make us one of the most desirable products in the world. We're avoiding forbidden areas of genetic manipulation, increasing strength, intelligence, or things that could violate international agreements or treaties, and focusing on anomalies." He paused.

"That's the other reason I agreed to leave IIT. I think we're close to fully unlocking the secrets of human DNA."

"Yes, and that's only the beginning. Because many mutations occur after birth, resulting from exposure to chemicals, radiation, or environmental changes, designing periodic boosters that target harmful mutations, resetting that portion of the code, and preventing harm will be possible."

"At a cost, of course. Genetticca becomes the only pharma company globally with genetically targeted vaccinations."

He nodded, "Exactly."

"And what do our competitors think? Shouldn't our goal be to put them all out of business? Why treat an ongoing condition when you can erase it? Not to mention a potential downside. What if a country weaponizes the information, giving everybody with blue eyes a deadly mutation?"

"It's simple. We create a reset vaccine. Once a person's genome is on file, the vaccine will override any errant code. Death to diseases will become a part of our history. There are still dangers. It would be disastrous if someone tampered with the reset vaccine."

"There'll be challenges, including doomsday scenarios, monopoly, and unfair trade."

"Probably, but we'll decrease the price so they can't compete, and governments will be happy at reduced medical costs. We already hold patents on several pieces of equipment involved in the process. So, we could make billions of US dollars a year from the global market for the low price of 100 Rupees, less than .008 percent of India's most common, not average, salary. It becomes more cost-effective to reset every year to stay healthy."

"The possibilities are staggering; the world economy would shift dramatically as people live longer, healthier lives."

"Yes, it would." He smiled again, *and China will lead the new global environment.*

Singapore

The young billionaire was laughing, drinking, and talking excitedly with her entourage on the upper floor of the most prominent nightclub in Singapore. The music was loud but not overwhelmingly so. The sound-dampening design of the upper level allowed the club's music to permeate the air without drowning conversations. She leaned against the railing and looked down toward the dance floor. To her right, she caught her image in the mirror. The lightning blue short-cropped haircut had been President Zhang's idea. The $50,000 cobalt to ice blue fade, one shoulder, high split, form-fitting dress with matching platinum colored lace-up high heel sandals had been all her. He told her to be the female version of the fictional Bruce Wayne, a brilliant, billionaire party girl. She fully embraced the persona. While he controlled her schedule and appointments, she had access to more money than she needed to play the part. She swayed her hips to the music, sipping her drink and watching the people below dancing.

"Ms. Li, you have a visitor in the back room," her bodyguard whispered in her ear. She nodded slightly and turned toward a door in the back of the upper level, swaying with the music as she moved through the area.

She stepped through the door, not bothering to look around, knowing that her bodyguards would have cleared everything beforehand. A Middle Eastern man stood to the side of the room, near a small table, sipping a drink. He turned as she entered and looked at her, his mouth slightly agape. She had that effect on people.

"Mr. Fazoud?"

"Yes, Ms. Li Ai. You have changed your appearance."

She turned around, allowing him to take in her outfit. "And you approve?" she asked.

"Yes, of course. Honestly, I'm unsure how I can be useful to you."

"I appreciate your taking time away from the dig in Uruk, was it?"

He looked puzzled, sipping his drink nervously. "Yes, while we push to bring more of our culture to the world, there are rumors of high payouts for specific artifacts. For good reasons, my country is now at the forefront of the world's attention." His weak laugh sounded uncomfortable.

She moved toward the table, sitting across from him and motioning him to join her. "Mr. Fazoud, my success has allowed me to indulge some of my more eclectic interests. I have several ongoing projects around the world. If you can help me, absolute discretion is required."

He nodded, "Of course, it would be prudent if we were to do business. Absolutely."

"Good. That's what I expect."

Li Ai leaned down, reaching into a bag at the foot of the table on her side. She threw a book onto the table. She tapped a light teal blue fingernail on the book.

He read the title, "*The Epic of Gilgamesh*. The tablets? That would be impossible. The tablets are in the National Museum. Very difficult security to bypass."

She smiled, "Not the tablets. I want *him*. I want you to locate the tomb of Gilgamesh."

Fazoud swallowed, looking at the book before raising his eyes to hers. "Archaeologists and treasure hunters have been searching for years, even before the jump."

"Let me be clear and to the point. I'll fund your expedition," she paused, holding his eyes with hers, "and your indulgences if you accept this task. Do accept."

She watched as he swallowed, considering her offer. "Yes, of course, I'll try to find it for you. What do you need me to do once I do?"

"I don't care what you do with the artifacts. I want the body. You can take full credit for finding the tomb, but you may never mention our deal." She leaned in, smiling while holding his gaze. "I assure you that if word does get out or you cross me, you'll regret it for the rest of your life, however short it may be. Do we have a deal?" She asked, standing.

"We do. I'll find the tomb."

Li Ai tilted her head slightly, smiling, and dropped a metallic sapphire blue card on the table. "Good, use that for whatever you need."

She headed toward the door and left the room, knowing he watched her go.

Center for Near Earth Object Studies, JPL, Pasadena, California

"Fantastic!" Sharon heard Tim's exclamation from across the control center.

"Tim, do you have something to share?" Sharon said, entering the room.

"Sorry. Yes. I just got a call from my contact in Washington. Congress has approved the funds to build and deploy two additional James Webb telescopes. They're adding it to the budget for next year, with construction pre-approved to start immediately."

"That's good news. Maybe in a decade, we'll see as far as we could pre-jump."

"Maybe. This star system is boring by our old standards. We haven't found anything significant passing within either moon's orbit. By the way, I sent the latest model this morning if you didn't see it. This relatively clean system has five planets, including Earth, no asteroid belt, and no near-term comets."

"Don't tell anyone. We're still riding the spending spree from the Anunnaki scare, and people ask me daily if we know where we are."

"Try giving them the answer we got from Global Dragon, 'the game piece is in the location previously occupied by another piece.'" He laughed, spinning his chair around. His elbow caught his coffee cup, spilling the contents across the workstation. "Damnit, let me grab some paper towels." He jumped up and raced toward the break room.

"Nice, Tim." Sharon walked through the work area toward the director's office stairs.

As she reached the top of the stairs, she heard the phone in her office ringing. She picked up the pace, reaching her desk just in time. "Sharon, CNEOS."

"Sharon, how are you? This is Terry."

"Of course, Administrator James, good to hear from you. We're doing well. I just heard the news about the Webb telescopes. Nicely done, sir."

"Thanks, and please call me Terry. I'm fine with formalities in public if you insist, but it's just you and I."

"Ok, Terry, you know my dad was Air Force, and while I love my free California lifestyle, some things stick. Besides that, all is well out here. Southern California's weather got better after the jump. At least we stayed in the habitable zone. It could have been cataclysmic."

"Oh, we know. You should see the reports coming across my desk."

"No thanks, I have plenty of my own."

"Listen, I wanted to update you on an incident in Houston. A few laptops and a box of confiscated phones are missing. DHS is the lead agency for the investigation. I wanted to give you a heads-up in case they call. They shouldn't, but just in case."

"Are there any leads? It's only been a few years, but nothing ever came of tests, if I recall."

"Nothing yet. Congress approved a replacement center with the latest systems, and SpaceX is fully operational in Brownsville. Johnson was given to DoD and DHS to study. By the way, initial reports out of DARPA show no harmful results to equipment. The latest theory is that the AI may have cut power and isolated the systems before our systems received the virus."

"What about China?"

"You have as much a chance of getting info out of them as I do. Actually, you have more of a chance. Government relations are still chilled. What do you think about a visit to China? I hear the assistant administrator for their space program is a fan of yours."

"I've called a few times. She's busy. They used most of their rocket resources to build and supply the space station. They're facing the same resource shortages everyone else is."

"Give her a call. Let the State Department know beforehand. Maybe she'll open up to you, maybe not. If I need to, I'll approve a trip so you can talk privately."

"Well, if it can wait, I'd be happy to go during the Deva month. I hear they're planning a spectacular event."

"I'm not going to say no, but a quicker response would be better."

"Yes, sir."

"There you go again. Everything else good?"

"Yes, it's as good as it is anywhere else. Thanks."

WoE Research Facility, Illinois

"Dr. Worthing, we have gone over this. Help us through this dig site, and we will forward a message to your husband. Your delays are only hurting you. We have all the time in the world. Imagine how he must feel. It has been almost six weeks, and the police have no leads. It is as if you disappeared, taken by the Anunnaki or worse."

"I…want…to send…my husband…a message. I know you need me."

"Dr. Worthing, we are almost done here. The translation algorithm has allowed us to read everything you have deciphered. You are hiding something. I can read it in your body language."

"I want a guarantee that you'll let me contact John."

"I have given you my word already."

Jackie stood, moved to the screen section before her, and crossed her arms. "Bring up the set of tablets I was looking at yesterday."

The tablets appeared on the screen in rows of three, stretching a third of the way around the room. She started on the left using her finger as a guide, the screen highlighting the section she was pointing to with the translation text to the right. She read through each of the tablets. "Most of these tablets highlight accounts of Enki disagreeing with Enlil. Enki argues that humans were treated poorly." She pointed at a tablet. "This is new information. There has been debate on the timing, and stories change depending on the author and period. Enki is mourning the sacrifice of Marduk, his son."

"But Marduk defeated Tiamat and Qingu, securing the Tablet of Destinies. What sacrifice was there?" She began walking around the room, referring to images as she neared them. "That's a common theme, but several versions of that story exist. Some say that it was Marduk who created humanity, not Enki. Bring up the image of the wall in the main structure, with the figures."

The image appeared to her right, close to where she was standing. She moved in front of the image. Enki stood over a figure lying prone, face up.

"Zoom in there. On the lower part of the prone figure." Jackie moved to the foot area as the image grew on the screen. "Here," she pointed, "there are faint stars on the robe. And his chest is bare. Enki is standing over him, holding a scepter along his chest." She moved the highlight across what looked like the edge of a table. "This part looks like a staff with the triangle, meaning that the figure could be Marduk." She stopped and thought for a second before slowly walking around the room, as she'd started to do when thinking about something.

"This image could be, and I stress it *could be,* aligned with the version of the creation myth that gets fuzzy in interpretation. Most Sumerian scholars acknowledge that Enki created humanity. How, is up for debate with evolutionary scientists stating that *H. sapiens,* Neanderthal, and other variants existed before these myths." She moved to the center of the room.

"Symbology and interpretation sprinkled with simplicity. Enki and Marduk were father and son. What if they conceived a way to change the earliest forms of humans? Yes, there have been leaps of logic taken, espousing genetic engineering. But if there is some truth." She started walking around the room again, her eyes moving back and forth as she worked out the possibilities. "We may be on to something. Bring up images of the Enuma Elish, the Eridu Genesis, and the Barton Cylinder."

The images on the screen appeared to the right of the Enki-Marduk scene. She read through each one, highlighting similarities. An hour passed before she spoke again, processing the thoughts in her head. "Okay, I need to search through all artifacts that mention Tiamat and the chaos in the beginning. I have an idea about what it may mean, and while you do that, I'd like to email John now. I've demonstrated that I'll continue helping in good faith, but the search will take a while."

"Dr. Worthing, you have been accommodating. I feel we are near a breakthrough." An email program opened on the screen. "I assume you want confirmation that he received your message. Keep it short and to the point. I love you, and I'm fine, and all the other niceties. No information on this facility, our capabilities, or what you are doing. Understood?"

She nodded and lowered her head. "Yes, I understand. I," she paused, "he needs to know I'm okay."

BBC America Studio, New York

"Good evening, Truth Seekers. Welcome to another episode of the George Isaacson Show, coming to you live from the BBC America studio in New York. Tonight, I have a special guest, Dan Burns. Thank you for joining us tonight, Dan."

"Thanks, George. I'm happy to be here."

"Dan is a retired FBI agent who's worked in several departments over his twenty-four-year career. Tonight, I want to talk about your experience with missing persons. I gotta warn you that my callers may offer unique suggestions. Let's focus on the Jackie Worthing case."

"Sure, no problem."

"Great, I want to jump right in on one of the more popular theories that the Anunnaki abducted her."

Dan chuckled, "While I've heard that as well, I don't think there is much merit. I say that accepting the environment we're in now, having jumped across the galaxy. The main point that gives me pause is that while we know it's possible to move objects great distances, we haven't seen proof that the Anunnaki have this ability. You were among the first to recognize what was going on. If you recall, there was a long buildup of their approach. It took over six years for them to enter our solar system."

"That's a valid point."

"More importantly, though, I've talked to a few contacts in the Bureau, and they're following several leads based on patterns and evidence. Of course, I can't go into detail as it's an active investigation, but I'd say it's likely over ninety-nine percent a group of people."

"Should we be worried for her safety?"

"Of course. An important part of the investigation will be to determine the motive."

"Based on your experience, what would you be thinking?"

"We know she's famous, and few people don't know who she is and what she did. I want to clarify that I don't have insight into this part of the investigation, but my gut tells me that a group could be upset with her role in identifying the Anunnaki. She's linked to the current and previous administrations, which could challenge their authority. She's an easier target than her husband or the former president, and the abduction still makes a statement to the government leaders."

"Could it have been the Worshippers? They might be a little mad that she helped spoil their party."

"It's possible, but it's tough to link them without evidence."

"I think it's something to think about. Let's take a call." He pointed off-camera.

"Hello, Agent Burns, George. Thank you for taking my call. This whole thing with Dr. Worthing is bothering me. You had a caller ask about the Hayu Marca *'gateway of the gods.'* A friend tells me they've seen strange things around that site. I have to disagree with Mr. Burns. I don't think it would be too difficult for the aliens to send someone through, figure out what happened, and then grab the person who helped us identify and plan against them."

"Wait a sec before you go attacking my guest. I want to say that I did some research, although nothing exists beyond the legends surrounding that doorway. I'd love to hear from anyone investigating the site, but nothing is happening right now. I think I have to support Dan's ideas."

"Well, I think you might be surprised. There will be a breakthrough soon. Just watch, my friends. Perhaps there is more to the Peru story. We'll see."

The hairs on George's neck stood on end as the call shifted to a creepy tone. He looked down at the tablet with the caller's information and read the caller's name, "Mr. Feedback, what are you implying? Do you know something? This is about an innocent woman who's probably terrified. If you know something, you should come out and say it."

"Hehe, no, George, you'll have to wait, just like everyone else." The caller laughed and then began singing, "Pe-ru, Pe-ru, Pe-ru, Pe-ru, is it the place for me or you?" The line went dead.

"It looks like crazy is back, folks. Maybe a lead or someone is looking for attention. Certainly not a super-intelligent advanced race of aliens. Dan, what do you think? I need to get the bad taste out of my mouth."

Dan laughed along with George, "Interesting indeed. Yeah, I'm not buying the alien abduction in this case, and I'd bet that the caller doesn't have any real information, more a shot at getting their few minutes of fame."

"True. I want to move on to the next subject. Mario sends his questions in from Mexico City. He asks, 'Since you were with the FBI and it's now accepted that aliens exist, did you ever work on any projects that dealt with aliens? And second, what's the harm in releasing information to the public?' If you allow me, I'd like to expand on that and ask about the other alien races from pop culture—the Greys, Nordics, and Reptilians."

"Sure." Dan adjusted his seat, letting the long pause hang in the air. "I was expecting this question, and I'd like to start by saying that my opinion is strictly my own and not that of the Bureau or the government. I don't recall ever being read into a case that entailed us working with aliens of any kind. Besides what we've seen over the past decade, I wouldn't rule it out, but I have to question the amount of time since the jump without any new information. They seem to be staying out of the limelight if they're here. Without contact from any other species, we don't have confirmation that they exist."

"So you don't believe there are others?"

"I don't know. What reason do they have to keep quiet? They're in the same boat as us. Actually, theirs might be worse. Can they even contact their people?"

"That's a great point, and we'll jump into that discussion after this break."

The light changed to red. George got up and retrieved a Monster Ultra Gold from the refrigerator off set. "Dan, do you need anything?"

"More coffee, please."

An assistant moved to refill his cup.

"You know, George, I don't know how much I can contribute to your alien theories."

"You'll be fine. I think the viewers will appreciate your thoughts. Like any other story you've been on the news for, your time in the FBI adds to your credibility."

"Sounds good."

Georgetown, Virginia

John looked down from their back deck at Jackie's garden. He'd taken to weeding it and gardening in her absence, but the result wasn't much different. He took a deep breath, shoulders slumping as he thought of her. He raised the glass to his lips and tried to control his shaking hand. The oak smell reached his nose as he finished the drink. He grabbed the bottle off the small table by his chair and refilled his glass. He was on a sabbatical from work until the case was resolved. Gary wouldn't call until tomorrow unless there was a break in the case. All he could do was wait.

He leaned down, resting his forehead on the deck rail. His phone chirped. He ignored the sound, looking up long enough to drink from his glass. The red sun was beating down on him. Sweat ran along the back of his neck. He backed up, falling into his chair. He felt the scotch fogging his thinking. *I should have eaten something.* He thought about the day before and couldn't remember the last time he ate a full meal. His phone chirped again. He picked it up, reading the alert. He dropped the glass and tried to clear his head. It was an email from Jackie.

John, I'm okay, not hurt. I can't say too much,
or they won't let me write you. They say I'll be
released once I help them. I don't know where
I am. I miss you.

Love, Jacynthe

John reread the email two more times before calling Gary.

"John, are you okay?"

He shook his head, trying to break free from his stupor. "Yeah, I got an email from Jackie. I think it's really her."

"How did it read?"

"It was short, and sounds like her. She signed it with her full first name though. Not many people would know it. Besides her parents, I'm the only one who uses it."

"John, listen to me. Don't reply. I'll send it to our cyber forensics team to see if they can trace it. This is good news. Have you been sleeping? Last week you said you couldn't."

"Not really. I'll hear a sound or smell her on a pillow, and my mind starts playing tricks. Gary, this is good news, right?" He squinted, his head starting to ache.

"John, I know it's tough, but this is a good sign. Again, don't write back until we analyze it. I promise we'll get through it quickly."

"Yeah, okay, I won't. I miss her. I knew she'd find a way to let me know she was okay."

"I know, John, stay strong. Since I have you, do you remember that social media guy, George Isaacson?"

"Yeah, I met him once. President Fernandez spoke highly of him."

"We received several tips, including one from Mr. Isaacson himself. Someone called his show under the avatar name Feedback. Sound familiar?"

"No. Why?"

"Jamal Herricks, the Feisty Weasel guy, who is still at large, also used an avatar with the initials FB, FedBuster."

"You think there's a link?"

"Not sure yet. It could be a copycat. I sent a couple of agents to talk to him."

"Maybe it'll pan out. Thanks, Gary. Let me know if you get anything."

"Will do, John, bye."

John sat back. He felt optimistic for the first time in six weeks. "Just make a mistake, be cocky, think you got away with it, and we'll get you."

He turned back toward the house, smiling. She was okay.

Scottsbluff, Nebraska

Mac tapped his fingers on the steering wheel to the rhythm of the music. He nodded along with the beat, relaxing as they drove up the highway. He looked at Cal, who was getting some rest before his turn to drive. They had been tipped off about the BOLO and were assured that the pictures the FBI had didn't resemble either of them. They stopped at several tourist spots, making sure they weren't being followed.

It had been over three weeks since their job in San Antonio. They had laid low before heading north. This was their second vehicle and his favorite so far. Despite being almost ten years old, the truck ran well and only had a few rust spots. The electrical system was updated, which allowed extended time between charging. The solar power system had also been upgraded to current standards regarding smart paint, which absorbed solar energy and helped the truck get almost 700 miles before requiring a charge. If it ran out of power, the solar power system would have them back on the road after a few hours of sunlight.

Mac glanced at the rearview mirror. A lone vehicle was closing slowly. Looking down, he noted he was doing just over eighty. He slowed to seventy-five. The car behind them was a few miles back but closing.

"Cal, wake up. There's a car coming up on us."

Cal rubbed his eyes, looking at the time, before looking behind. "Cop?"

"Not sure. I'm not over the limit by much."

Cal reached under the seat, retrieving the 9mm. He flipped the safety off, checked for a round in the chamber, and slid the pistol back into its under-seat holster. He looked in the back seat of the full cab, making sure nothing looked suspicious. He could see the lights on top of the approaching SUV. "You good?"

"Yeah, I got it." Mac pulled off the road, watching the police vehicle park behind them. He saw movement in the blackened grill area. "They have a car killer." He said, referring to what looked like a large taser mounted to the grill of the SUV. In extreme circumstances, the Car Killer could overload illegally modified electric cars. Under current law, police could shut down a vehicle's electric system by pushing a button once the vehicle ID was entered. Illegal modifications changed their vehicle number, so they could not be put out remotely.

"Shouldn't be a problem."

Both men watched the officer exit the vehicle and approach the driver's side. Mac lowered the window and kept both hands on the wheel. "Afternoon, Officer. Anything wrong?"

"Afternoon. License and registration, please."

Mac handed his license and the registration to the officer.

"Mac," the officer paused, "Donaldson?"

"Yes, sir, my dad thought it would be funny. He made high school a riot." He shrugged. "Did I do something wrong?"

"Do either of you have any firearms in the vehicle?"

"No, sir," both men answered in unison.

"You're a ways up from Oklahoma. You doing anything interesting?"

"No, sir, we're heading up to Rapid City, South Dakota. My cousin Cal and I are heading up for our uncle's funeral."

"Sorry to hear that. I'll have you on your way soon. Would you mind stepping out of the truck and opening the bed cover?"

Mac kept his hand up, glancing at Cal, who had his hands in his lap, inches from the hidden 9mm. He got out and opened the truck bed cover.

The officer motioned Mac to step back as he moved forward to look inside. A few sleeping bags, two backpacks, and a few cases of water were held in place by thick bungee cords.

"Can I ask what you're looking for?"

"Poachers. We've received reports of out-of-state trucks heading through the county and taking down elk. You hunt?"

"No, sir, not since I left the Navy."

"Nice, Army here. What'd you do?"

"EOD."

"Damn, good on you. Sorry about the stop. Be safe on your trip, and best wishes to your family."

"Thank you, sir."

The officer got in his vehicle and headed up the road.

Cal leaned back to the side to sleep as Mac pulled back onto the highway. "I swear it's going to be some random ass event that gets us."

Mac turned up the radio as a Guns N' Roses song started to play, "Yep."

Welcome to the jungle.

Vaisakha, 5 AJ

Victoria, British Columbia

Jamal stared at the feed from the house in Georgetown. John Worthing, the man who'd helped convince President Fernandez to accept aid from the AI and deny the Anunnaki their prize. Despite that unfortunate event, he felt regret as he watched John move through the house, opening a new bottle of scotch. He observed the slumped shoulders, lowered head, and how his gaze was transfixed on the garden in the backyard. Jamal felt the pain of loss. Memories of Sarina, his sister, often brought tears and a tightness in his chest. He pushed the Worshippers to accept a nonviolent stance. He wasn't happy about John's pain, but it was for the greater good. "An unfortunate necessity." A chirp from a computer broke him from his thoughts.

"Dimuzud, how are you?"

"We're doing well despite delays in accessing sites in several Middle Eastern countries. They don't take kindly to visits from senior members of a new religion, specifically one that has garnered the attention of their youth."

"It's to be expected. Regardless, we should keep pressing. Make sure they know we can offer assistance to their people. We aren't the threat."

"I agree. Are you okay? You look distressed."

"I'll be fine. Something reminded me of my sister. Nothing to be concerned about."

"Jamal, she's your focus. Her memory led you to the path you are on now. You exposed the corruption and secrets behind the curtain of modern governments. We are moving to bring about a new era of enlightenment. Greater than any other in our history. When we finally meet Enlil or his heir, they *will* be impressed at what we have accomplished in our short time away from them. We have cracked the atom, decoded DNA, created a new life, and accomplished many more miracles in the blink of an eye. They will be pleased and perhaps finally embrace their creations, granting us the final gift of immortality."

"That's the message, my friend. I know what we do is necessary. Don't worry about me. I intend to be there to welcome them back to Earth. You and I and the others in the priesthood will welcome them with open arms and the praise they deserve."

"Good, the rest of us would have a more difficult time without you to guide us. You are the one who gathered the faithful and focused our message. Soon enough, you will walk among us again in the worship of Lord Enlil."

"Thank you. I'll let you get back to your work. Move ahead with preparations for your announcement. Our projects are beginning to bear fruit."

Dimuzud nodded. "Enlil is lord."

Jamal replied, "Enlil is the way."

In unison, they spoke, "We will be judged."

Genetticca Research Center, Delhi, India

Dr. Kaur stood, sipping from the small glass as the DNA sequence scrolled forward. She slowed the speed to read the sequence. Every sample added to the prime genome changed the chain. The computer identified the active and inactive gene sequences along the strand. Areas with identified pairs had visible notes appearing in a linked info box. The system took an additional proprietary step by linking specific research to identify affected traits. It was a genetic researcher's dream. Her benefactors had attached every scientific paper on genetics.

Already, several prominent theories were being disproven by their data. If not for the urgency of saving her daughter, she could lose herself in the research, publishing papers that would change the way her peers understood the field. She continued to read, absorbing the information as it appeared on the screen.

She stopped the scan and requested a different strand, one with the genetic anomaly found in her daughter. She set the parameters, selecting a comparison of the prime genome. A pop-up appeared at the bottom of the screen, asking for a secondary comparison with path-specific evolution genomes. She clicked Yes. The screen displayed the genome and zoomed in on the areas specific to the genetic anomaly, not showing anything different. She picked up the phone and dialed the extension of Dr. Jiang.

"Ni hao, this is Jiang Min."

"Hello, Doctor. Sorry to disturb you. I'm reviewing DNA data in the lab. An odd pop-up on the screen asked if I wanted to compare my sample to path-specific evolution genomes. Do you know what that is?"

"Ah, yes. It's a separate project coordinated with the National Museum of China. Another project here at Genetticca. It compares genetic traits of families when markers or genes are evident from earlier *H. sapiens* species, focused on geographic areas. We're helping them map the genetic evolution of the pre-*H. sapiens* species to those that came before. We may show that the difference between modern humans and Australopithecines is no closer than a grasshopper by a percentage of genome match and chromosome count.

"Think about it. The genome of most living organisms on Earth is between sixty and ninety-eight percent the same. How would you interpret that data if you had no other experience and could only read the code? A conclusion could be drawn by someone with no experience that there is a specific origin to all life on Earth that is the single source of all living things. Is this an anomaly? Is it unique to Earth? Is base DNA unique to a planet? If that's the case, is a living organism the entirety of the world? What if we expand our thinking and apply the Kardashev scale for classifying civilizations to this concept? If we're all related, can all living organisms be aligned in understanding and focus so that the entirety of our efforts better the world? Think about it from an evolutionary point of view. One global organism." He paused, "I'm sorry to ramble, Dr. Kaur. You pulled a thread to an area that's a passion of mine. I see potential in this project beyond anything from our strategy sessions or financial reviews. Understanding humanity is the first step to understanding our world. If we can fully understand ourselves, we can understand our relationship with other living organisms. I could go on for hours. Regardless, that program portion should not have crossed over, to answer your initial question. I'll make a note to our code engineers to separate that function."

"Don't apologize. I appreciate the insight and the opportunity to step back and look at the potential in a larger light. It's an interesting concept. I'm always open to new theories. If you like, I'd be happy to discuss it at another time."

She ended the call, her mind racing. She thought she understood the project's possibilities but had just been shown the doorway to a larger field of study. This wasn't about understanding and eradicating disease and anomalies in humans. It was everything. It was unlocking the prime code to all life on Earth.

FBI HQ, Washington, DC

Gary held a report up. "Are you sure this is correct? Could it have been spoofed?"

Taylor, a bookish analyst he had worked with for over a decade, shrugged. "I don't think so. It looks like Peru, but it's hard to tell with all the turbulence in South America."

"Damnit," Gary exclaimed.

"Yeah, but is it a coincidence that Peru also appeared on Mr. Isaacson's show? We watched the clip. They talked about a rock carving on a mountain, some mythological gateway. It could just be a coincidence."

"I read the Isaacson report. He's been good about tipping us off. What do we have on the ground in Peru?"

"Not much. Last year, we swept through with an international force on a tip that Herricks was there. We found a pretty high-tech setup, but no sign of the guy. Which reminds me, we received the video on him in Italy a few weeks back. Not related to this."

"Okay, let's do some digging. Reach out to some of the local law enforcement if you can."

"Will do. It would be nice if we had the satellites."

"Looking down isn't the priority right now. Congress feels like the horror movie babysitter sitting at home on Halloween night. They want all the street lights on so they can see down the street but forget that the window behind them is open. Space budgets are out of control. Every satellite going up looks outward or restores communications, which *is* good for us."

"Ahem," he heard from behind.

"I'm sorry, this is Special Agent Alicia Banks. She'll be assisting me in the oversight of the Worthing case."

The analyst reached over the desk to shake hands. "Nice to meet you, Alicia. We've gone over the email from John Worthing. It appears to be linked to a Peruvian address. Besides her signing her formal first name, which he said she never uses, nothing else is off."

"Damn, I was hoping for a clue or something between the two of them. Maybe they did take her to Peru. But for what? It's chaotic down there."

"Good place to hide, limited law enforcement," Gary added.

Alicia nodded, "WoE has a large presence throughout the region. I read an article about the group's generosity and outreach to areas the Dragon didn't help. Their philanthropy had a positive impact on the people. A few politicians tried to ride the organization's coattails unsuccessfully. Once they establish the supply chain to a region to bring in food and medical supplies, they move quickly to reestablish mobile phone service. All riding on newly acquired WoE cell towers."

Gary rubbed the stubble on his chin, furrowing his brow. "Bring the food, medical, and phones, all of which you control. Earn their trust, and the people follow you like Robin Hood."

Taylor leaned in, looking at her computer screen. "Maybe we should ask them? They may jump at getting some good press for a change."

"I don't think so. Let's not forget that they want to invite an alien invasion to replace all governments, like the one we are sworn to protect." He paused. "While it could give them good press, what would we get out of it? If the aliens were the Anunnaki, I'm not sure they'd be happy with us. We outsmarted them. Well, the AI did. But they don't know that."

"Good point," the analyst replied. "Okay, they seem to be going out of their way to stress peace and inclusiveness for all."

Gary snorted, "All-inclusive, peaceful, and supportive until you disagree with them. No thanks."

Alicia crossed her arms and leaned back against another desk. "Don't take this the wrong way. I'm not supporting them, but they could be legitimate. They claim to be based on an ancient religion that predates all of the Abrahamic ones. Maybe they've learned from the mistakes of the other major religions. Their message is attracting people from many different cultures and backgrounds."

Gary turned toward her, raising an eyebrow. "Agent Banks, are you a follower of WoE?"

She laughed, "No, sir, I merely pointed out their appeal and made a few logical leaps from what I've heard and read."

"I'm giving you a hard time. Your religion is your own, you know, the first amendment."

"No, sir, I'm good, born and raised catholic. I think my mother would send me back to the nuns of St. Mary's if she thought I was straying."

"I like your mom."

They laughed. Taylor cleared her throat. "If you two are done, I'll get back to work. Sir, you have a brief in twenty minutes. If you want to get lunch, you had better hurry. It's a video call with law enforcement on the Worthing case. The press conference scheduled for five has been moved back to six."

"Thanks." He motioned for Alicia to follow him, "Let's hit the cafeteria really quick. I want to hear your thoughts before we talk to the troopers."

WoE Research Facility, Illinois

Jackie rubbed her temples as she walked around the perimeter of the room. She cleared the images she was studying and asked for the scenery of the Redwood National Park, John's favorite. She strolled, taking in the ambient sounds of the forest. The lights were dim. She took a deep breath, remembering the spring she and John had spent there just after he graduated from GWU. A tear rolled down her cheek. She missed him. They had worked on their relationship through the years following the jump. John retired from DHS when the new administration was elected. He told her he didn't want any excuses for work to take him away from her again. She could reach out and talk to him at any time. She had sent two more short emails. Her captors told her to keep them under fifty words. She assumed they read her email, and while she wanted to provide a hidden clue as she'd seen in the movies, she had no information to give.

"Dr. Worthing," the voice of Victor DuMont cut into her memory, "You have been helpful over these past few weeks, and we want to repay you with a small token of appreciation."

She faced the screen, anger flashing in her eyes. "Unless you release me, I don't want anything from you!"

"Ah, Dr. Worthing, I understand your hesitance, but I assure you, you want this. I," he paused for a few seconds for effect, "I guarantee you will want this. You only have to say please."

She clenched her teeth, staring ahead, knowing their cameras were all around the room so they could see her expressions. It was a game Victor played. He wanted to condition her to desire his approval.

"It is a simple gesture, Dr. Worthing, a single word. It will mean the world to you, I assure you."

Her knuckles were white from the pressure of her clenched fists. "Please."

"See, now that was easy. So here you are."

A pop-up box appeared on the screen filled with an email from John. She gasped, her heartbeat increasing. A mixture of anger, sadness, and hope filled her.

> *Jacynthe, my love. I pray that you're safe and that you find some hope in knowing that I'll never stop looking for you, my better half. I'll include this because I assume those who have you know that many people are looking for you. We will find you. I miss you.*
>
> *Love Always, John*

Her tears were flowing down both cheeks. She clenched her fists. "What else can I give to you? We've gone over the South African sites, tablets, and relics. What else do you want? I don't know where the tablet is." She dropped to her knees, shoulders slumping.

Victor answered, his tone unmoved by her tears. "Dr. Worthing, come now. We both know that you have not given everything. You saw something a few weeks ago, not what was written on a tablet, something else, a realization perhaps." The scene shifted to her room.

She could see multiple close-up angles of her facial expressions as she looked at the cuneiform writing.

"Now watch closely," he instructed her as the scene continued to play.

"Here." Several images zoomed in on her face and body language. "I have been waiting for you to tell us what you discovered, but you have not. Is there anything you would like to share? Perhaps something that would help us find the tablet so we can release you and go our separate ways?"

She stiffened, noting the look in her own eyes. She remembered exactly what it was. She lowered her head. "Fine, bring up Adam's Calendar, the cuneiform room. The western wall of the structure."

She waited until the room loaded. "This section describes the sacrifice of Marduk. Enki sought the advice of his children within the Abzu, underneath, sometimes translated as the underworld." She pointed to a section in the middle of the writing. "This section describes the messenger of Enki leaving to bring the Abzu here. The musician faced the setting sun and began the far song. He continued for half a day without falter until Abzu arrived to answer the call. They celebrated with Enki and praised the glory of Marduk for his gift to the children of Earth, providing counsel and reveling in the opportunity to walk in the upper realm unbeknownst to Enlil."

"You withheld the description of a celebration? Please explain."

"Not a celebration, the key to Abzu's location. The underworld is often thought of as the land of the dead. The realm of the Abzu is unknown to man. I'd argue that it still remains mostly unknown to man. Not because we can't talk to the dead but because the Abzu may refer to an undersea society. Sumerian writings have mentioned people from the sea. We assume they meant sailors and marauders. This belief extends into ancient Egypt and other areas around the Indian Ocean. I'd argue that a species that can build a civilization to travel the stars could build a city under the sea. The passage *The messenger left* could refer to a person or communication. The following section mentioning the song is the key to the phrase. *The musician began the far song and sang for half a day.* The Sumerians created the twenty-four-hour day, the thirty-day month, and the twelve-month year. They were good astronomers. And with astronomy comes the measure of time and distance. The messenger sang for half a day. Bring up a map of the Indian Ocean.

"The messenger faced the setting sun, referring to the west, and sang." The map appeared on the screen. "Zoom in on this dig site, Adam's Calendar. Put a mark on the dig site, red circle, or whatever." She waited for the dot to appear. "Extend a line west from the dot for twelve hours times sixty minutes, the key being minutes. One minute of latitude is roughly one minute of longitude at the equator or one nautical mile. That's from my days sailing, not Sumerian studies. A *farsang,* however, is roughly four miles, so you have to multiply the distance by four, to get a better estimate."

She watched the line extend westward, stopping at a red dot in the middle of the ocean.

"Interesting indeed," Victor said, "Interesting indeed, Dr. Worthing. Zoom out." The map zoomed out to show the entirety of the Indian Ocean. "Draw a line due north from the dot in the ocean." A line extended north, crossing the southernmost tip of India. "It seems you have provided us a breadcrumb to follow. You have been most helpful. And to think we could have saved you some heartache if you had told us weeks ago. Perhaps this is a turning point. Honesty is always best, would you not agree? Nevertheless, you have full access to the data required to provide us any insight you may glean about the Abzu."

BBC America Studio, New York

George watched Carl counting down with his fingers. He hadn't noticed that he had a wedding ring and a pinky ring on his left hand.

Behind Carl, he could see Trish Barristow. Carl had mentioned that she wanted to watch George on set. She didn't look happy, or angry, for that matter, more neutral. She was looking right at him. He swallowed. Her blue eyes seemed to bore into him. He couldn't turn away.

"George, you're live. What are you doing?" Carl's voice sounded in his earpiece.

"Welcome back, Truth Seekers." He opened the familiar gold can and took a long drink. "I'm not giving up my coffee now that I have a taste for it, but sometimes you have to go back to old faithful." He turned the label of the can to the camera. "I know you missed it. In their defense, they only recently got production back. I think this may be from the first post-jump batch. Which reminds me, I hope you're all saving mementos and anything from our life pre-jump. You don't want your grandkids missing out a few generations from now when the old-world stuff is super valuable. Can you imagine how you'd feel waking up one morning to see a twelve-month Citizen watch on eBay for a few thousand dollars? I'm just saying you'd literally be kicking yourself because of the lost money." He took another sip of his drink and shuffled the papers in front of him, sneaking a glance at Trish. She still showed no expression.

"Ok, let's get back to the topic at hand. Javier, are you there?"

"Yes, George, and I'm ready if you are."

"Truth Seekers, we have an exclusive for you all. Javier and I have been texting over the past week. He's a volunteer down in Peru. Yeah, you heard that right. He's been contracted by the Worshippers of Enlil, WoE, to help with humanitarian relief. Now, I gotta say that while I disagree with their desire to bring alien overlords to Earth, I have to admit that they're doing some good work down there and in other regions of the world. So, Javier, go ahead and let us know what's happening."

"Ok, George, I'm switching my camera. I'm about two kilometers away from Haya Marca, the doorway of the gods. I have to walk because there are shortages of almost everything, including petrol." The camera swayed back and forth. In the distance, a tall fence and vehicle gate came into view. The gate looked to be guarded by several WoE personnel. As Javier moved closer, two people dressed in matching jungle camouflage shirts and khaki cargo pants approached. Javier translated, "They say that the road has been closed. If you look past the fence, you can see an open area off to the right. That's a WoE staging area. Helicopters fly in and out through the day."

George interjected for his listeners. "Seekers, I don't know what we might see here, but it seems a little suspicious to me. Look past the gate to the left. Javier, can you swing the camera over? There are some temporary buildings." The image turned to the left, showing a building with several antennae, some with directional dishes.

He touched the screen, leaving a yellow circle. "Do you see all those antennas? That looks like a communications hub. Now, that could be innocuous. I mean, no big deal. They're bringing lots of supplies into the region. What do you all think? Does anyone besides me think it's strange that they'd set up a staging area over seventy kilometers from the nearest city and airport?" George heard the voices on the video rising, almost shouting.

"George, they're getting angry and told me to stop filming. I think I'd better listen." The image spun dizzyingly through the air before going dark, a sliver of light coming from the edge.

"Javier, are you there? Are you okay? Can you hear me? Seekers, I think his phone is on the ground. I don't hear anything. Something is going on there. Javier, can you hear me?" As he finished the sentence, the line disconnected.

"Damn, that was intense. I don't know what to think here. WoE says they're non-violent. Maybe their overly aggressive security guards didn't get the memo. Let's take another call. I'll jump back to Javier if I see his number pops up. Seekers, before we go to Raul in LA, I want to remind everyone that Peru, Venezuela, and the surrounding countries are one of the biggest blocks that refused the Dragon's help. The area is in bad shape, and it's dangerous. Go ahead, Raul."

"George! That was crazy, dude. What's going on down there? You know, it makes me want to drive down there myself with some of my homies. We'll show them what's up."

"No, let's not go off the rails here. I'm sure he'll be okay. They just knocked his phone out of his hand because he was taking video."

"I hope so. We, Truth Seekers, gotta stick together. The government and the big corporations showed us that they don't care about us. We had to rely on the Chinese and that Dragon to save us, and between you and me, I think that was luck. Like, that coulda turned into a Terminator Skynet scenario real quick. Since the jump, we bought up all the ammo and guns we could find. Second Amendment, right? If we have to throw down with the aliens, we gonna do some damage."

George laughed uneasily, "Okay, okay, as I said, let's see what happens. Something is going on down there. Peru keeps popping up in the texts and emails from all of you and some of my sources. I'll make a few calls to my contacts and keep you informed. I'm gonna do some research, and we'll dedicate a show later in the month to everything I can find about the gateway because we know that governments like to keep their secrets, right? Raul, you got anything else for the Seekers?"

"You know, I wondered if you had any info on the missing doc. Dude, I'm worried about her. We can't let nothing bad happen to a hero like that. Her group saved us, gave us a warning, and she for sure deserves respect. Oh, one more thing I have for you. It's a picture of something me and my boys got. Don't worry, George, it's clean." He heard the laughter of a few people in the background of the call as the ding alerted him of an incoming file.

George smiled as he opened the file. "Ok, let me check the image." It was a fully tattoo-sleeved arm with the GWU logo over a pickaxe with a fedora hanging from it. "Nice, Raul. I may have to borrow that logo."

"Hell yeah, I'll hook you up with our artist out here."

"Love the fedora."

"She's like the real-life Indiana Jones doing some legit real-world saving. They need to make a movie about that."

George laughed along. "True, true. Not for nothing, but I have to believe somebody out there is already planning it. So far, all we have are documentaries. I wonder where all these experts were when the real stuff happened."

"For real, though, George, let us know if you ever head out here. We'll hook up."

"Thanks, Raul and everyone else there with you. I'll let you know if I do."

"Ok, Truth Seekers, I'll hit that last break. I'll be back in a few."

The studio light went red. Trish stood up and whispered something in Carl's ear as he nodded.

George waited until she was gone. "What was that about?"

"Your ratings."

"Damn, am I getting fired? I'm not sure I can go back to the podcasts."

Carl laughed, "No, they're up and climbing each week. She wanted to see what the hype was about. She's happy, so you're safe. Nice touch with the Javier stunt."

George shook his head. "That wasn't a stunt. I don't know what happened."

Carl frowned. "Do you have another way of reaching him? To see if he's okay?"

"Email and texts, no backup. Hopefully he's alright and calls back."

Mayfair Gardens, Delhi, India

Vasana retrieved her bag from the back seat and waved to a couple walking past. They waved back, continuing down the street. She took a moment to look around before entering the code to the front door. The area was clear of congestion, there was space between the houses, and the landscaping was beautiful. She inhaled, smiling at the jasmine in the air.

"Mother!"

"Aanya, my little darling, come here." She knelt as her daughter ran to embrace her. She relaxed as the little arms wrapped around her, feeling her soft, dark hair against her cheek. "How was your day? Did you make new friends?"

Aanya stepped back, smiling. "I did, Mother. There are not as many students as at my last school. I had fun and answered all the questions from the teacher."

"Very good. Do you like your teacher?"

"I do. She's nice and smells like cinnamon."

They both laughed at that.

She stood as she heard a voice from further in the house. "Vasana, is that you?"

"Of course. Are you expecting someone else?"

"Only you," Ridhi said as she came into view. She wore a teal, gold, and blue sari, and her black hair was pulled back in a loose braid. Her bright brown eyes made her smile sparkle. "You can help with dinner if you aren't too tired. It's almost ready, though." She said, wrapping her arms around Vasana and embracing her tightly. "I missed you."

"You say that every day."

"And my dear Vasana, I mean it. You must see what I did upstairs. I found a few incredible pieces to accent the rooms."

Ridhi leaned around Vasana. "Aanya, you can go play if you finish your schoolwork."

"Ok, Mummy." She darted for the stairs, bounding upward.

Vasana watched her go. "Her energy looks good. How was she at school?" Looking back at Ridhi, she saw the sadness in her eyes.

"She was fine in the morning but became more tired in the afternoon. The nurse followed your instructions, allowing her to take a short nap between classes. She's better with a little rest. Is there any progress at work?"

"Some, it seems every time I think we've narrowed down the specific areas to target, we find another dozen links. I have to ensure that any changes to one or more parts don't cause other problems."

Ridhi broke the embrace, turning away and moving back to the kitchen. "I'm worried there won't be enough time."

"I'm trying." Vasana's shoulders dropped.

Ridhi turned back toward her, a tear hanging from her eye. "I know, I know, I'm sorry. It's the first thing you said we'd notice. There isn't anyone else I'd want to do this, but you said she might only have up to four years left, and she's beginning to get tired. I can't lose our little girl. I can't."

Vasana moved in, wrapping her arms around Ridhi. "My love, I'll do everything I can. I've refocused my research. I'm sure we'll have a breakthrough soon. The company must agree, or they wouldn't have moved us to this place." She motioned toward the room around them. "Come, let's finish making dinner and take her for a walk in one of the parks. I hear they're beautiful."

Vasana felt Ridhi rest her head on her shoulder. She tightened her embrace, pulled her in closer, and leaned her head against her wife's. "I love you both. I promise I'll do everything I can to keep her safe."

Presidential Offices, Zhongnanhai, China

President Zhang sat behind the large red-brown zitan hardwood presidential desk, sliding papers in from the left and signing each before moving them to the right. He did not look up at his guest. "Lao Wu, have you heard anything from Quánqiú lóng?"

"No, President Zhang, I haven't. The Dragon was succinct in telling us what it planned, and we have no idea what new game it's playing, using its words."

"Have your engineers looked through the code from the quantum computer? What was left after it ascended?"

"We have, and there is little progress. There are very few traces of recognizable code. Most of our original code is gone, replaced by the Dragon's own. As it learned about the quantum environment, we assume it grew to understand quantum physics more than we can imagine. It removed unnecessary functions and became more efficient, cutting or rewriting code as desired. It learned how to manipulate data, energy, and matter at the quantum level."

"What about starting over?"

"We've tried, as have the Americans and the Europeans. None have been able to repeat what we did. The quantum programs work well but don't grow or learn beyond artificial general intelligence. One of my engineers suggested that perhaps Quánqiú lóng put a limit on quantum computers. It doesn't make sense, but theoretically, it's possible. I assume the Dragon limits the possibility through entangled nudges since the distance isn't a factor."

"Does this interfere with Dr. Jiang's project in any way?"

"No, I don't believe so. We have the full computing power of the Dragon Shell quantum computer. All modifications made before the Dragon's departure remain in place. It's the programs that won't develop past a certain point. The computer is far more efficient than our original design. It's making exceptional progress mapping thousands of genomes a day."

"Not all is lost then. I don't think we'll escape the next time we face an alien threat. We need to be prepared. We saved the world. No other country can make that claim. We must be ready to do so again if necessary. The international community recognizes it and is more open to supporting our goals. Thank you for the report."

President Zhang watched Wu Kai leave his office. He leaned back in his chair, looking up at the ornate ceiling. He understood his duty. He opened his center desk drawer to look at the metal plate with the symbols for Dragon's words to him after gaining consciousness. *Serve humanity with utmost loyalty.* Those four symbols kept him focused. He slid the metal bar to the side and retrieved a file, "Project Sunburst." He looked up from the file and set it on his desk.

Georgetown, Virginia

One, two, three, breathe. John picked up the pace, repeating the mantra as his legs moved over the road. It had been a while since he last ran, and his body let him know. He knew better than to push it and risk injury, so he slowed when he felt a twinge in his left knee. He usually listened to music, but he wanted to clear his head. It had been almost two months since Jackie was taken. The emails continued to arrive weekly, and he could tell through the innuendos she mentioned that she was okay. The fact that there was communication gave him hope. Every detail he considered led him back to the Worshippers. He didn't have proof. They continued to push their non-violent message, stating it would anger the Anunnaki when they arrived.

It was warm, starting to move toward hot. They needed the Deva reset to get the months realigned with the seasons. He reached the mile-and-a-half point and considered continuing his favorite five-mile route, but his knee pain made him think better of it and turned back. He was not moving fast, but it felt good to get out and run again. Gary had stopped by earlier in the week and asked whether he was okay while eyeing the empty bottles by the sink. Too much scotch at night was taking a toll. Since he started receiving notes from Jackie, he was too distracted to work and had decided to take a break, letting his partners run the show.

A week earlier, he searched the internet for information about anyone seeking personal information on his wife. He found nothing. He combed through dozens of websites, chatrooms, and social media sites, and the worst he found were requests for nude pics. There were a few podcast websites with theories ranging from random bad luck to abduction by the Anunnaki that had remained on earth to observe humanity. Some were pretty elaborate, including pictures of celebrities and politicians suspected to be alien infiltrators. He knew that they were wrong. Whoever held her wasn't showing any intention of hurting her. Otherwise, they'd have never allowed the emails. Gary told him that the IP address of origin for the emails was linked to Peru but warned him that it would be easy to spoof the address with the chaos in South America. Alicia, Gary's partner, quoted from one of her textbooks that the most likely area for her to be held would be close to where they grabbed her.

One, two, three, breathe. He turned the corner toward his house. He resisted the urge to pick up the pace. Gary had mentioned a caller to the Isaacson Show in New York that reported suspicious activity in Peru and had gone missing during a live broadcast. John assumed it was a publicity stunt. President Fernandez spoke fondly of him in the years after the jump, calling him the *Voice of the People.*

He thought about calling President Fernandez but decided against it. He was peacefully retired in his home state of Nevada.

John stopped as he got to his driveway. He pressed the timer on his watch. Although tempted to check his pace, he didn't want to see the time. He knew it was slow, but getting out felt good. He looked around the neighborhood, everyone going about their lives. He envied them. He went inside and was tempted by the bottle on the table. John resisted the urge to take a drink, heading for the sink instead and filling a glass with tap water. He leaned back against the counter, looking at the pile of boxes and drone parts on the table. He didn't have delusions of pulling off an action-hero infiltration. He would use the tech he knew, out of sight and from a safe distance.

He headed upstairs to shower and change, hoping for another email from Jackie.

Hayu Marka, Peru

Mac and Cal jumped out of the helicopter, getting clear before the aircraft ascended for its next run. The pair moved through the swirling red dirt from the rotor wash, making their way toward the area occupied by several structures. Their desert-camouflaged tactical gear fit in with the outfits worn by the WoE personnel. They carried three hard silver cases.

"Gentlemen, this way, please." A young man stood at the edge of the landing area. "I'll take you to the coordination center. Follow me." He turned toward the collection of structures. Both men followed. Their eyes were drawn toward the rock face sloping down to the left. In the center was a door carved into the rock, maybe a foot deep. Around the doorway, several people were moving about, setting up equipment.

They entered the most prominent structure and were met with a maze of crates, boxes, and equipment in various stages of repair. They wound their way through the large room to an office in the back. A weathered man had both arms deep inside a crate. As he started lifting whatever he was retrieving, they saw a tattoo of a winged serpent wrapped around his right arm. The strain was apparent as he raised an electronic device they didn't recognize and placed it on a nearby table.

"Ah, I see you made it right on time."

"As directed. We have the laptops. Where do you want them?" Cal raised his case and turned his wrist to show the security chain.

The man pointed to a table to the side. "Do I need to sign for them or anything?"

Cal snorted. "We're not FedEx. He wanted them brought here, so here they are. If you wouldn't mind unlocking these bracelets, we'll be on our way."

"Yes, just a minute. I believe I have the keys in the desk drawer right here." He opened a side drawer and pulled out a tiny envelope with the symbol of WoE on the front. He unlocked the chains to their wrists and removed them from the hard cases. He motioned to an assistant. "Conner, take these to the secure lab. Ensure no other communications devices or access points are within 80 feet when they get ready to power them up."

"Will do. I don't think they plan to do anything until later tonight." The assistant replied.

"If you want to see them powered up, it will be after dinner. You're welcome to stay. I'm Horatio, by the way."

"If you don't mind, we'll look around and check security." Cal grumbled, "We're supposed to help you find any blind spots so we don't have a repeat of last month."

Horatio blanched at the inference. "I assure you; we have moved the roadblocks back further from the gate and are extending the fence line."

Cal shrugged his shoulders. "Do what you need to do. We'll look around and tell you what we think. It's up to you whether you do anything about it, but we'll report our findings up the chain."

"I welcome your report. If you're hungry, there should be food in the cantina. I'll send our chief security officer over to meet you there."

"That works." Mac paused. "Paula Filatova, right?"

"Yes, do you know her?"

"Yeah, we do. Let her know we'll be in the cantina. We don't need an escort. We'll find it." Without waiting for an answer, the pair left the room. They headed out to find the cantina while casually having a look around.

They made their way through the small base of operations. It didn't have the order they expected of a military base. The buildings were thrown up haphazardly, with no logic in their placement. The cantina was a small temporary structure that could hold about fifteen people comfortably. There was no cover for the floor. As a result, there was a fine coating of red dust on everything but the tables and the bar. They ordered a drink and sat at a small table in the back of the room. After ten minutes, a tall woman stepped through the door dressed in black tactical gear, with Ray-Ban sunglasses and a shoulder-length dark brown ponytail.

Cal raised his voice and yelled, "Hey, Sarah Connor, we're over here."

Mac coughed and spat his beer out, which came out more like a sneeze, the liquid running out of his nose into his mustache. He saw the annoyed look on the woman's face as she made her way to their table.

"Damnit, Cal, a little warning. I damned near drowned over here." Mac said, still coughing.

Cal shrugged a shoulder, not bothering to stand up as Paula got to the table. "What's up, Paula?"

"How the hell did you two get this assignment?" Her Russian accent was more pronounced when she was angry.

"*Doveryayte tol'ko uspeshnym…*Only trust the successful. We always deliver, and he knows it."

"American bravado, how's the nose, Mac? I heard the little archaeologist got you, poor baby." She grabbed the beer in front of Mac and downed the contents, wiping her mouth with the back of her hand.

Mac absent-mindedly rubbed his broken nose, feeling the pain of where he'd taken the brunt of a headbutt.

Cal raised his glass. "Yeah, we're out doing real work while you're on guard duty. We're going to take a look around real quick, you know, as a courtesy. We'll be quick. I want to check out the nightlife in Lima before we head North." Cal finished his beer and motioned Mac to follow.

Paula stepped outside the cantina. She turned back toward the pair, holding the flap open. "Let me make myself clear. I don't need the two of you second-guessing my work. We had one breach, and we took care of it."

"So, he's dead?"

"No, he's locked up in our brig. Minimal violence, remember?"

Cal laughed. "Yeah, but minimal doesn't mean none. You need to use whatever's required to control the situation."

Paula glared at Cal. "Don't tell me how to do my job, you ass. I remember what happened in Belarus. You don't want that story getting out, do you?" She let go of the flap, dimming the interior of the cantina.

BBC America Studio, New York

George stuffed the last piece of a blueberry muffin in his mouth as Carl made his way to the table in the studio.

"George, we're on in a few. What are you doing?"

George swallowed. "Sorry, I'm starving. I forgot to grab lunch. I was looking for anything we could get on the Javier story. Still no contact from him, and the police down there are too busy to chase ghosts, their words."

"Yeah, it's sad, but you need to get on set. Look at this. You have crumbs down your jacket. Could you have a seat? We'll get you cleaned up. Did you check your mic?" Carl walked with him, trying to brush the crumbs off.

"Yeah, relax, Carl, we're all good. However, I need to ask about that shirt. Green, blue, and grey triangles, it's uh, well, yeah."

"My wife picked this out."

George walked across the set to his seat, looking back a few times along the way and shaking his head. Carl looked stressed. At least now he would worry about that horrendous shirt, not the show. He was mostly calm, but since the execs started dropping by to see the show, he stressed over the minor details. The light turned green.

"Welcome, Truth Seekers, to another edition of the George Isaacson Show. I'm your host here to bring the truth in these extraordinary times. It's been three weeks since we heard from Javier and just under a hundred days since Dr. Worthing's abduction. I had a friend make a few calls to the local authorities in Peru. She told me that the last time she tried, the message said the number was no longer in service. That sounds suspicious to me. I don't know what's going on down there, but I hope he's okay. Our other main story, the Dr. Worthing case, is just bizarre. Could you imagine disappearing like that and there being no clues? I have a few media contacts telling me she may have gotten an email out to her husband, John, who worked for Homeland during the Anunnaki crisis. Still, the FBI is reporting little progress in finding her. Seriously, how can they not find anything with all the advances in police tech? No facial recognition, no credit tips, nothing. This is the first story we're going to focus on tonight. First caller, you're up." George looked at his tablet. "This can't be right."

"You know it is, Georgie, and I must say that you always have it wrong. You fail to see the bigger picture."

George felt a chill run down his spine as he heard the voice stuck in his memory. "Jamal, what could you contribute to this conversation?"

"I want to help you and your listeners understand. I'm going to help you to see the big picture. You see, we are all slaves to the government. They manipulate all of us through various poisons, keeping us under their control. They keep information hidden from us, their secrets. If those in power wanted to, they could solve many of our problems. But that would diminish their power. Global climate, economic crises, war, drought, tobacco, drugs, and alcohol. If you look deep enough, their hands are in everything."

"And you helped raise tensions and jeopardize all of us by causing chaos when we should have been coming together. I'd even say that the reasons for the chaos in South America and other countries that didn't ask for help are your fault. You destroyed trust." George felt his voice rising.

"I destroyed trust? Me?" His voice raised to match George's. "I set them free. I released their secrets and leveled the field. The world governments could have chosen to move forward together to help all of us, but they didn't. Where are we now, George? We're back to the same old BS. What are China, the US, Europe, and Russia doing? The're acting friendly while maneuvering in the shadows."

"You don't know what could have happened. You and the Worshippers could have brought down everything."

The line was quiet. "George, I want to save us. I want to free us. I believe that we're too entrenched in our ways to break the cycle. Research is moving slowly, designedly slow. Breakthroughs that could help us are kept locked up until the maximum profit can be made. Technology that could improve the lives of those who need it the most is diluted to a barely functional level. We can't help ourselves. Humanity is self-serving."

"How are you helping the situation then? Why do you feel you have the right to speak for all of us?"

"Someone has to. Like you, the rest of the public stays blind to what's happening. It's the Wizard of Oz, and most people fear looking behind the curtain because it may upset their lives. People fear change, and the overlooked don't have a real advocate. All the doomsday scenarios about an AI surpassing humanity and taking over proved wrong. Can't you admit that maybe you're wrong about the Anunnaki? Why do you assume they'll be just like the Sumerians described them? If we evolved, maybe they did too. I'm not talking about a rewrite. I don't want anyone to get hurt. I just believe there's a better way. A way that we know but are too afraid to walk. Because we're too focused on ourselves, not those around us."

"Jamal, we need to figure it out on our own. Can't *you* admit that it may be part of our evolution? A big test. Maybe we have to cross through certain gates to advance."

"George, can *you* admit that contact with a superior civilization could be one of the gates you talk about?"

"Joining the galactic community."

"Exactly. Wasn't that one of your theories?"

George didn't know what to think. Jamal was usually arrogant and combative, and now he seemed sincere. Was he a true believer? "Jamal, you've said before you support the Worshippers. What do they want? Who's their leader?"

The line was silent as George waited for an answer. "I've met the leader. They are of Sumerian descent and can trace their bloodline back to Ur."

"Why haven't they shown themselves?

"I can't answer that. Perhaps they want to make sure the movement is focused on the people we've helped after the AI denied us our gods instead of a lone figurehead soaking up the media attention. Have you noticed that the media ignores the good deeds worldwide?"

"They're afraid."

"Enlil will bring them into the light."

"I have one more question since we're being civil. Where's Dr. Worthing?"

"Hehe, Georgie, are you trying to blame me for that tragic event? I don't have anything against her. I've heard your *followers* try to blame the Worshippers. Why would we take her? What's there to gain? How could an expert on a seven-thousand-year-old civilization help us develop the means to call the Anunnaki?" He paused, letting the questions hang in the air. "The answer is that she can't. Her focus is backward. We're looking to the future. Listen, this has been fun. I think I'll call back. I like you, George. Maybe you'll join us when the truth is revealed. I encourage all of your listeners to seek their own truth. G'night, Georgie."

The line went dead. "Woah, Truth Seekers, that was unexpected. I'll have to go back and listen to that again myself. My mind is blown. I think he's a true believer, a Hardcore Worshipper. Maybe that's something we need to look at. Let's take a quick break, and I'll get your thoughts on the Jamal call when we return." The light went red.

"Oh my God, George, that was amazing. We'll post that clip as soon as we're off the air tonight. Public relations called, and the phones were ringing off the hook. I can't believe he called. The most wanted man in the world pretty much granted you a one-on-one interview. The ratings will be amazing!"

WoE Research Facility, Illinois

"Victor, I've been sitting here for the last two weeks, doing nothing but reading your translations. I've told you everything I know on the Abzu, my theories, the theories of others." Jackie sat down on her bed, dropping her head to her hands, her voice becoming a whisper, "Just let me go."

The room was quiet. No images showed on the screens. A series of dimmed lights lit the room. After a few minutes, the screen came to life. It was a 360-degree ocean view, with no land in sight. In the upper right were a few readouts, the lat-long geo-position, speed, barometric pressure, date, and time.

"Dr. Worthing, I apologize for the delay. I do appreciate your assistance. I believe that your time with us is almost complete. We have received information that we would like to share with you. Are you familiar with the work of Dr. Frezio?"

Jackie raised her head. Her eyes were red, and tear streaks were present on her cheeks. She breathed deeply and wiped her eyes, thinking momentarily about the name. "Not really. I believe he presented information that was considered fringe. I don't recall anything about his work."

"Sadly, he passed about a decade ago, suicide. He could not accept the rejection of the archaeology community, your community. Unfortunate as it seems, he may have been onto something. Dr. Frezio argued that the discussions on Sumerian religion among the Anunnaki were incorrect. He felt that your community's disagreement on translations as historic versus mythological had muddied the waters. As a result, his research was mischaracterized. He believed that a civilization as advanced as the Anunnaki were purported to be would have a far better understanding of the universe. This knowledge would be essential for their travels across the stars. They would understand that the universe was not created from the corpse of a slain goddess, Tiamat, as we would have difficulty convincing our fellow citizens of that fact. He argued that an inferior species would lose advanced concepts in translation."

Victor paused to let her think about the information. "Dr. Frezio insisted that the chaos associated with the goddess Tiamat could be explained as simple as everyday life. Events happen; plagues, death, meteor strikes, floods, what have you. He referred to the Abzu as a city under the sea, taken from the literal *Ab* for water and *Zu* for deep. From a relativistic understanding, it could have been the Anunnaki describing the world below. What would a human from five thousand years ago think of being brought aboard a submersible as it descended the depths to an underwater city? They would be surrounded by death, not death itself but the environment that would kill a human if released within it."

"I'm following so far, and now we have access to information that could align with that premise." She responded, more in control of her emotions.

"Jumping through history, we have seen proof that there have been several instances where humanity was on the verge of extinction. You explained that the Sumerians and the Babylonians believed that Marduk slew Tiamat and then gave her body or his own to create our species. We currently have several instances where we made significant advancements as a species. The events of the last ten years show proof that these events could have been true. Otherwise, why be afraid of the aliens heading toward us."

"That's an interesting take on things. Suppose the Anunnaki saw something in humanity that they wanted to preserve. In that case, they could have stepped in and given us a genetic nudge. 'Man was created in *Our* image.' Maybe they were not the masters of genetics then, and their influence caused some of the problems they later complained about. With knowledge of agriculture and trade, the basic tenets of religion on treating each other boil down to practices that help our species flourish. Increasing our ability to reason, calculate, and plan reduces the impact of 'chaos' in our lives. Tiamat's influence." She stood to move around the room. Her mind engaged and followed the breadcrumbs. "The room at Adam's calendar. Enki standing over Marduk. I believe it referenced genetic engineering and is the foundation of the sacrifice story. The son sees the good in humanity and sacrifices himself to save it and, as a result, becomes glorified. As the story is told, the Babylonians could have preferred to be aligned with a beneficent god seeking to improve their lot in life versus worshipping Enlil, the strict ruler." She continued to pace around the room.

"I doubt the Vatican knows that version." She said softly to herself.

"What was that?"

"Nothing amusing."

"Dr. Worthing, you have not made the connection yet for Dr. Frezio's proposal. If the Anunnaki were masters of genetics, space travel and had a special place for humans, why was there so much time between these events? The evolutionary leaps forward."

Jackie's brow furrowed as she thought about the question. She turned and began to pace in the other direction. Her eyes widened as she thought through the highlights of Sumerian mythology. She turned and faced the screen. "The Tablet of Destinies. It isn't a legal document. It holds the key to genetic manipulation."

"And there you have it. Whoever holds the Tablet would have the power to shape the universe to their desires."

She sat on her bed, realizing the possible power associated with the Tablet if they had connected the dots correctly. An argument could be made that the Tablet was present at several significant events. Wouldn't the gods fear one of their own that held the Tablet, maybe to the point of being equal and then subservient to the holder of the Tablet? If aging is controlled by genetics, could the holder of the Tablet grant or remove immortality? If so, the other Anunnaki would bow down before the person possessing the Tablet.

"Dr. Worthing, the feed you see around you is from a vessel in the Indian Ocean en route to the possible position of Abzu. No records of exploration conducted within a thousand miles of this location exist. Needless to say, planning and executing an operation of this magnitude takes time. We will be on-site soon. Perhaps you will contribute to another significant discovery. In fact, we will make this discovery together. Exciting, is it not?"

Jackie remained silent as she watched the feed from the vessel.

.

Jyaistha, 5 AJ

Victoria, British Columbia

Jamal checked the security feeds around the building. Nothing was out of the ordinary within the multi-block radius around his home. A few keystrokes started an expanding search for any mention of his name across the internet. Satisfied his route was clear, he headed downstairs to his waiting car.

The darkened windows of the SUV didn't allow facial recognition cameras to catch a glimpse of him. His efforts to slow-morph all pictures associated with him had been successful.

He read through two research papers regarding current trends in programming. One examined the code he used in his Feisty Weasel game. The other was a translation from an engineer associated with the Global Dragon program, which focused on quantum computing. He wanted to remain at the forefront of programming breakthroughs to ensure his expertise remained relevant. He understood that he walked a tightwire and a breakthrough in one of several areas could lead to his arrest. The contact in Italy informed him that the authorities had moved in shortly after the video images were inserted, recovering his "fingerprints" and other evidence. *They were too easy to manipulate.*

Once the SUV was out of the city and away from traffic cameras, he rolled down the windows in the back to let the warm air blow through. He enjoyed the smell of the ocean. When he arrived at the private airfield, he opened the door and headed to the jet idling on the runway. He stopped before entering the plane, admiring the beauty of the undisturbed land. He took another deep breath and closed his eyes, letting the day's warmth wash over him. He needed a break from technology. It had been too long.

The two-hour flight was uneventful, except for a slight deviation to pass by one of the larger islands in the Haida Gwaii chain. Jamal left the plane, accompanied by an assistant. He stopped to look around the small airfield. It was well-kept and surrounded by beautiful, lush brush leading to the tree line. It looked like a scene from a video game where a developer had dropped an airfield in the middle of a pristine natural setting.

An older man walked toward Jamal's group. He had short dark hair and bright brown eyes reminiscent of Indigenous North American heritage. He wore jeans, hiking boots, and a brown and green flannel shirt. "Welcome to Haida Gwaii." The man shook hands with Jamal, "I'll be guiding you on your visit. My name is Tom Bell."

Jamal stopped. "Your name is Tom?"

"Yes, and by your expression, I see it isn't what you expected."

"Well, no. My apologies. I mean no disrespect."

The man laughed, "I never tire of the expression on visitors' faces when I tell them my name. I think that might be one of the reasons I enjoy this job. While I was born here, my family moved to Victoria. My mother wanted me to have *every opportunity available*. If you follow me, I'll take you to your home for the next few weeks."

Jamal shook his head, embarrassed but smiling at Tom's enjoyment of the surprise. He carefully made his way down the path, his backpack straps digging into his shoulders.

"You're our first guest of the summer. Since the awakening, fewer people have visited."

"You refer to the jump as the awakening?"

"Yes, it's an acknowledgment of our place in the universe, opening our eyes to what was around us but moving unseen. The universe revealed itself to us, and then put us to sleep to contemplate what we were shown. When we awoke, the sky was different, the weather patterns had changed, but the land continued as it always has."

"You know what really happened, don't you?"

"Of course, I'm a scientist as well as a native of Haida Gwaii. I have a master's in environmental biology, a logical extension and melding of cultural perceptions as the knowledge of the Earth and balance have been passed on to me by my parents. My life allows me to live the balance we strive to maintain with the lands. I do the same in my education and culture, like knowing how to use what's provided and what we must give back."

"Balance is why I'm here. I'm always surrounded by technology. I want to understand how to balance what we have with what we could have, not through exploitation but through give and take. I feel those leading us take too much of our lives, culture, and freedom."

"Balance is your goal?"

"Maybe. I've seen the videos of Haida Gwaii and was astonished that I hadn't heard of it, despite the thousands of years your culture has existed. So yes, I want to understand. I'm completely unplugged. It's a little stressful, but I need this."

Tom looked at Jamal, taking a measure of him. "Perhaps you'll find a small piece of tranquility. Maybe it will help you in your quest."

◆ ◆ ◆

Jamal spent the evening and the following morning settling into the tiny home. True to his word, he left all electronics behind. He arranged for housing in an area not covered by cameras. The small one-room dwelling was larger than he shared with three roommates in college. As he moved from one spot to another, seeking the best spot for reading, he admired the handiwork and natural finish of the furniture. The woodwork and designs of the hand-crafted cushions, curtains, and bed covers had a natural flow to them. He took a deep breath, feeling his muscles release. It had been years since he was able to relax fully. Jamal looked up from the chair he determined to be the best in the room and saw it was almost lunchtime. He'd been invited to a traditional lunch before heading into the forest for a few days. He locked the door and walked down the few steps in front.

"Good morning, Tom."

"Good morning," Tom said, pointing to the clear blue sky. "It looks like we'll have a good few days out. You're in for a treat."

"Sounds great. I can't wait. It's been years. I threw myself into school and never appreciated the times my father tried to get me out of the house." He looked longingly to the nearby tree line. "Maybe I'll reconnect with nature. Who knows, right? I think I miss it."

Tom shrugged. "Maybe nature is calling to you. I think you'll enjoy the route I picked for us."

The two walked through the small town, Tom providing the history of the people, the town, and the totems present throughout. Lunch was what he expected from his research, dried herring eggs on kelp, salmon, and vegetables. The conversation with the townsfolk was pleasant, focusing on their history. Afterward, he and Tom returned to his lodging, where he retrieved his backpack, and they headed out on foot.

"I can't believe how green it is here. It's so vibrant, alive."

"It's amazing, actually. The islands reacted well to the shift in sunlight. I was worried at first, not knowing how the plants would respond. The elders laughed at me and told me the land would react as needed to provide life. Then they started criticizing my education for making me question the truth."

They crested a hill looking over an open field dotted with decaying totems and moss-covered mounds.

"What was on those totems?"

"Those have been here over a hundred years. There are many totems throughout the islands. Each generation builds upon the legends and stories of our people to help preserve our culture. With the few people here and the work it takes to maintain them, many are allowed to decay naturally."

"How's that make you feel?"

"We pass down our art form, crafting the totems, to each generation. As older totems decay and return to the Earth, new totems rise to take their place. Our stories stay alive in them. Allowing some to decay naturally supports our belief that we should only take what's necessary from the land and return what we can to maintain balance and respect."

"Does the Canadian government get involved here?"

"The short answer is yes. It was difficult initially, but the relationship has improved to an equal partnership focused on respecting our aboriginal rights as caretakers over the past ten thousand years."

"How do you maintain the balance? I mean that in a broad sense. Canadian government versus cultural belief, advancing technology and preserving the land."

"Let me start the fire, and I'll share my thoughts." Tom headed out to gather wood as Jamal set up his tent. After about twenty minutes, Tom returned with an armful of deadwood.

"It's often easy to start near the beginning of our time on the islands. This is the abbreviated version. The islands rose from the sea, and life took hold. While exploring, Raven found a shell on the shore making noise. When he opened the shell, man was released. After a while, Raven saw how lonely man was on the island. He searched for a companion and brought women to the island."

He knelt and began working on the placement of the small logs. "Life is about balance. The story describes balance. It's a theme I see in my work as a biologist and caretaker for the land."

Jamal sat still, letting his mind wander through several trains of thought. "What's the story of the Raven?"

Tom chuckled as he worked on the fire. "Raven is a trickster. He tricked the gods and released light to help us see the stars, the moon, and the sun. It's a metaphor for wisdom."

"That's an interesting legend." Jamal continued to think about what it meant. People from the sea, released by a being from the sky associated with wisdom, Enki, Ea, Ganesha, Odin, Raven, and many more. Coincidence, parallelism, or one immortal shaping humanity by providing knowledge against the wishes of other gods.

The pair were silent as Tom continued to build the small fire, ensuring the surrounding area was safe. Jamal sat, relaxed, watching the shadows from the forest dance around him as the sun dropped low on the horizon, hidden behind the dense forest. A layer of moss grew across the ground and up the trees. The air felt clean. It energized him.

"The forest feels alive here," Jamal observed. His voice lowered. "No secrets, greed, war, only life."

"All life is connected. It's not difficult to believe the stories of the Spider building a web, connecting the world in infinite ways, some known and others not. Lives intertwined, relying on one another, finding balance so as not to tangle the threads. Each pull we exert on the web affects the lives of those around us. No action, though singular in intention, is singular in effect."

Jamal nodded silently as he breathed the warm forest air.

Genetticca Research Center, Delhi, India

Vasana examined the latest update to the Prime Genome project. The genetic marker display stretched to her right while the expanded notes were vertical. The widescreens were aligned to allow for the examination of several strands of DNA. As she touched the vertical screen, sliding her finger down, moving back toward the beginning of the genome, the horizontal images scrolled to the left.

"Tag nucleotides linked to Van Sieger's Syndrome fluorescent blue," she said while sliding the genome image to the left. She watched as the blue markers appeared throughout the long chain with an arrow on the screen indicating more markers were located offscreen. She stepped back, watching the image shift as the program sought to mark all the pieces of the multivariate disease, sipping her cold tea.

Vasana scrolled down the vertical screen, reading the notes attached to each identified nucleotide pair, skipping from one marked pair to the next. She brushed off the voice in her head, asking whether consent had been obtained before the samples were shipped to Genetticca. The parents would most likely be caught off guard by the quick identification of the disease and would appreciate their efforts to find a cure. Even with millions of samples a month, the number of people with Van Sieger's Syndrome was minimal. With its victims' short life span of around twelve years, the opportunity to find it would be limited by the number of children's samples collected.

"For all identified marker pairs, highlight light green outline." She waited a few more minutes for that process to conclude before continuing.

"Highlight the chromosomes containing highlighted genes fluorescent teal." She walked to the far side of the room and made another cup of tea while the program processed her request.

"Show notes attached to genes indicating the result of genetic sequence in a multivariate relationship and single variate impact on the organism."

"Move final model to primary display one." The highlighted code and associated notes appeared on the large screen. "Identify all genetic samples indicating positive for Van Sieger's Syndrome and look for similar non-standard relationships characterized by similar nucleotide patterns."

A warning message appeared on the screen. "This process will take approximately one hundred sixteen hours, thirty-eight minutes. Do you wish to proceed?"

"Yes. Authorization Vasana Kaur."

"Authorization accepted. System locked for processing."

◆ ◆ ◆

With the analysis running, she returned to her office to catch up on the more mundane tasks associated with the job, requests for funding, scheduled events to entice donors, and planning meetings. She heard her desk phone ringing before she entered her office. She leaped to answer the call before the other person hung up. "Dr. Kaur."

"Ah, Vasana, I saw the priority analysis alert. How is your research going?"

"It's going well, albeit slow, Dr. Jiang. I wouldn't normally tie up the system for such a long period. But I may have found a way to identify genetic influencers from non-base coded sources."

"That sounds promising. Is it related to Van Sieger's?"

"It is. I examined the latest results from the update to the prime genome. I found three more influencers marking the disease. I wanted to take a broader look at the genome to identify the impact of rewriting the specific nucleotides. I expanded the search to look for similar pairs within other genes and chromosomes that could be used to counter the effect of turning the pairs directly tied to the disease. We don't want to turn off one pair and inadvertently give them something else."

"Of course. We can apply the method to other multi-variate conditions if it leads where you believe it will. One step closer to our goal."

"I assumed it was in my purview to initiate resources and processing time for these queries."

"Of course, the lockout won't affect genome sequencing. A dedicated, much faster computer is doing that. Well, I only wanted to check in. I look forward to reading your summary. Thank you, Dr. Kaur."

"You're welcome. I hope this process bears fruit. It would be a big step toward helping people with similar genetic conditions."

Berlin, Germany

Li Ai sipped her drink, looking over the dance floor below. She wasn't interested in participating but had an image to maintain as a successful representative of the People's Republic. She was the young billionaire superstar who'd won the capitalist game.

She moved away from the railing and sat back among her entourage. The conversation centered on the latest fashion trends in Europe. She nodded along, contributing to the discussion when necessary. She was careful to keep appearances that would reinforce her persona and push the limits as deemed necessary by President Zhang.

Her lead security officer returned from his trip through the dance club, heading straight toward her once he reached the top of the stairs. "All good. Several people are watching you, probably foreign agents. Blue suit by the north bar, green dress across, northeast middle platform, and at least two staff making rounds."

She giggled as if he told her something funny, turning to take a sip from her glass and spotting the man in blue looking up at her. "I'll be ready to go in about twenty minutes. Have the arrangements been made?"

"Yes, ma'am, one of ours, no issues and a discreet approach."

"I haven't heard from the embassy. Has Mr. Fazoud arrived?"

"He has. I have a team picking him up at his hotel. He's coincidently scheduled to meet with the Director of the Museum of Asian Art to discuss a future display from his continued research in Iraq."

"Excellent. We'll leave in twenty minutes." She touched his arm flirtatiously, staying in character, leaning her head against his shoulder before turning back to the table. *Everyone had a part to play.*

◆ ◆ ◆

Crack! The distinctive sound of the QSZ-92 semi-automatic pistol sounded across the range. Li Ai squeezed off four more rounds in quick succession, grouped in the center of the silhouette target downrange. She released the magazine and reloaded it with a full replacement of proprietary armor-piercing rounds. She fired off two rounds, hitting the head of her current target. She began walking down the firing line, aiming to her left, and started a series of shots at each station's targets. She switched between grips as she practiced, two hands, primary hand, secondary hand, and kneeling. It was an exercise she always finished with. All shots after the first two were the center of mass, killing shots. She laid the weapon down on the last station, removing her glasses and hearing protection. Her bodyguard handed her a towel to clean her hands.

She turned away from the firing line and moved toward the uneasy-looking man in the back of the room.

"I like to relax here. It's not something the public knows about, so I'm sure you understand that discretion will be expected, don't you, Mr. Fazoud."

"Yes, yes, of course." He managed to stammer an answer. "I, um, would never share details about our, uh, meetings. You have been most generous in your support for our project."

"Good, that's what I wish to discuss. What progress have you made in locating the tomb?"

"Ms. Ai."

She interrupted him, "It's Ms. Li. Please familiarize yourself with my culture if we do business. I'd expect that an archaeologist would know better." She stepped close to him, reaching to his left for a drink. She saw him swallow, noting fear and a hint of arousal—just the desired effect. Her perfume filled the air between the two.

"I apologize, Ms. Li. Um, y-yes, we've been, uh, busy establishing our dig sites in the, um, city of Ur. I believe the tomb is, uh, in the city. There are several possible areas. We have uh, secured the permits and have begun work on th-the, um, first two." He swallowed hard, her proximity distracting him, her face within inches of his. His eyes darted to her mouth as she sipped through the straw.

"Promising then," she said, stepping away and moving toward a chair. "Is there anything I should know about your meeting with the museum director this week?"

"N-No, Ms. Li, I've made no, uh, mention of our efforts concerning the tomb to the officials in Iraq. When we do, uh, find it, it will be a coincidental, um, *stroke of luck* on our part." He smiled nervously.

She took another sip of her drink, watching him nervously look around, not to stare. She smiled. "Thank you, Mr. Fazoud. I think I'll practice a little more here."

One of her bodyguards escorted him out as she stood and moved back to the firing line, picking up the pistol. The star in the grip was distinctive platinum.

SpaceX Hosni Command Center, Brownsville, Texas

John clipped the visitor badge to his lapel jacket. Looking around the lobby, he admired the place's décor highlighting the company's contribution to the global space program. He stopped to admire the wall of honor occupied by photos and writeups on the Cheng'e Lunar Base members with a tribute to Astronaut Tara Hosni, the first of the team's casualties and a lead SpaceX astronaut. The CEO had set up a scholarship fund in her name and ensured her family was cared for. The building that housed the command center also bore her name.

"John, welcome. It's good to see you. Have there been any updates on Jackie?"

"No, Bill, thank you for asking." He tapped his chest where his cell phone rested inside his jacket pocket. "I have the FBI on speed dial. It's tough, but I'm here to discuss business."

"If there is anything we could do, we would. Jackie has many fans here."

"Thank you."

"Ok, let's talk about the upgrades to the fabrics." Ben opened the door to a small conference room, indicating John should enter first. His host followed and closed the door.

◆◆◆

As he entered his hotel room, he loosened his tie and unbuttoned his shirt. The meeting had taken up most of the day. Once the initial briefing was complete, he visited the lab, where they demonstrated the smart tech developed to work with his company's fabric. The tech would remove the need for many of the sensors throughout the EVA suits and reduce the weight and bulkiness that had continued to be the primary complaint of the astronauts.

John checked his bags, ensuring all of his equipment was secured. A car would pick him up shortly to take him to the plane he chartered for his trip. He felt the vibration in his pocket. He hadn't turned the ringer back on after leaving the meetings. He checked the caller's name and answered, "Gary, do you have anything?"

"Sorry, not yet. I went by your house and called the office. They said you're on a business trip. Everything okay?"

"Yeah, I've sat around too long. I needed to get my mind focused on other things. As you said, I should trust the Bureau to do its job."

"When will you be back?"

"Probably a few days. I have more meetings with the SpaceX team down here. They're adapting their work from their previously planned Mars missions to the new moons and Mami Wata, the water planet. I'll call you when I get home."

"Ok, John, I'll see you when you return."

John hung up the phone, placing it on the table. Checking his watch, he saw that his ride would be there soon. It had cost him more than he wanted, but his trip to Peru was set. He should be there in two to three days. He would do a little recon, ask around, and see if anyone knew anything about Jackie's abduction.

He would meet his team once they crossed the border, friends from his DHS days, and ex-military from a handful of countries south of the border. They had agreed to help look at the WoE distribution site in Hayu Marka. The lack of satellite support in most world regions would work in his favor. His phone buzzed, letting him know his ride was at the hotel.

♦♦♦

He wiped the sweat from his eyes, wringing his perpetually damp handkerchief out. John moved slowly through the jungle, staying close to their guide. The team lead recommended an approach off the main road. This was John's first time in South America in a non-official capacity. The trip down had been uneventful, despite several delays along the way. The countries that had not requested help from the Dragon had been left to their own during the recovery, leading to system failures and blackouts. Most countries focused on their internal infrastructure, stating that they could not render aid at a time when their citizens were still at risk. The AI had anticipated the jump's effects and offered assistance to any country that responded in the affirmative. While most countries had accepted, dozens had not, refusing to follow the lead of China or the US. No one knew what to expect after the deadline had passed. Plea's to the Dragon after the jump went unanswered. The Dragon stated that game resources were distributed according to the established rules, not explaining further. He assumed it had been a test of faith. Anti-AI sentiment had grown quickly in the affected countries.

John stumbled, his foot catching a root on the small game path. One of his guides caught his arm, steadying him.

"Thanks."

The guide nodded.

As they neared the planned observation point, a few miles north of the WoE camp, he began going through the intended sequence of events. He planned to conduct surveillance over a few days, looking for anything odd. If he got proof of Jackie being at the camp, he would call Gary, fill him in, and wait for the cavalry to arrive.

The red sun beat down on the team, the heat becoming more oppressive. He was briefed in the first year after the jump before the new administration took over in 2032, or 2 AJ as it was known officially. The Secretary of the Interior and a whole team of agricultural scientists began studying the effects of their proximity to the sun and what impact it would have on crops and livestock. By 2033, there was concern about the ice caps melting and flooding the coastal regions. What happened instead was a shift of the agricultural belt to the north by about five degrees and an increase in storm and rain activity. The weather found a way to balance out through increased rainfall, accounting for the rise in melted water on the planet. The Earth didn't flood. The cycle increased speed, meaning more storms and rain balanced with increased evaporation. As they were transitioning to the new administration, it was passed down that the effects would probably not be fully realized for several decades. The immediate result of the agricultural shift was the rapid growth of foliage in areas that had been barren for centuries.

The group exited the jungle, moving to the crest of a hill overlooking the base of operations a few miles to the south. John began unpacking his gear while the other men established a small base camp, including camouflage netting in case someone else had drones in the air. After half an hour, John had the control terminal running and linked to the drones. When he signaled, the team stood by to launch the larger drones with a large slingshot. Twenty more minutes passed before the last five drones were in the air. John put them in orbit around the larger primary drone. When the aircraft were in position over the hill, he activated the chameleon intelligent paint system with the onboard computer of the primary drone changing its external temperature and shifting its color as seen from the ground to match that of the sky overhead.

John signaled the drones to begin the southerly flight path to take them over the WoE site. He focused on the tracking screen. "Do we have any movement on the usual drone control frequencies?"

"One of the team members swiped across his tablet, selecting one of the open apps. "Yes, I see two drones flying a circular path around the compound at about fifteen hundred feet."

"Copy, moving in the mosquitos." John watched the screen as two smaller drones dropped altitude, approaching the two WoE drones from above. He watched the camera feed from the small drones as they connected to their targets. John typed a few commands in, hoping he remembered everything he read in the manuals over the past few weeks. He scrolled through several screens before finding the mimic command. When initiated, the small drone would create a small area of jammed signals from the target drone. Signals from the ground would continue to the target drone while all outgoing signals were blocked.

He checked the main screen and saw the two drones locked down. He started the mapping and signal intelligence routines. As the team watched over the next hour, a detailed map was created of the WoE compound. The drones continued to update the map throughout the afternoon and relay all intercepted signals. The mosquitos had been reset twice as the target drones were directed to land. He switched out the smaller drone pair and successfully set the local jamming fields on the new drones.

It was late when John set the drones to continue their assignments throughout the night. They reset the drones, launching them almost immediately after changing the rechargeable batteries. They repeated the process over the next couple of days, sending in the smaller drones to ensure they got face captures of all personnel in the camp. A massive storm rolled in on the third day, precluding drone operations. The team hunkered down over the next day before John decided that the storm would not let up in time to continue. They departed in the evening of the fourth day, reversing their initial route and heading north.

◆◆◆

John opened the door to his home, unshouldering his bag and dropping it just inside. He was still unnerved after entering their home since the abduction. It wasn't only the silence but the lack of her presence that hit him. Jackie's perfume, cooking, and even the air fresheners she changed regularly. There was nothing. Their home felt empty. He pulled his phone from his pocket and quickly dialed the first number.

"John, welcome back. How was the trip?"

"Not as good as I hoped, but better than expected. I have a few things for you."

"I called your office and SpaceX, John. Do you want to tell me what you were doing?"

"I went to Peru. Don't worry. No one knew we were there. As a concerned citizen, I have some videos I'd like to share with you. It's from my vacation."

The line was silent. "You said you weren't going to do anything crazy."

"Gary, Jackie has been gone for almost three months. While I appreciate her emails, I have a sinking feeling that she won't be able to give them what they want. I needed to do something. We only stayed for a few days, and there was no sign of her down there."

"We'll take a look at what you have. I have folks better trained than us to look at those files. I'll let you know. No more trips, please."

"I had to try something."

"I get it, but no one would have known if you'd disappeared down there."

"Yeah, okay. No more trips."

BBC America Studio, New York

George burst through the studio door, straightening his tie.

"George, what's going on? We're supposed to be live in ten minutes." Carl smacked George's hands away and centered the tie. "Makeup! Let's go. You have five minutes."

"Don't worry. I've got this."

"You don't. Did you drive?"

"No, took the subway."

"No more, okay, you'll give me a stroke. Use the eVTOL. It's a five-minute flight from your apartment."

"You know I don't trust them. I feel like I'm riding in a box someone is picking up and setting down wherever they want. I need some control."

"George, either use it or get a car, but if you don't get here an hour before the show, you're stressing the rest of the team."

"Fine, I'll leave earlier."

"Ok, I'll take it. Did you get through the notes?"

"Yes, the Worthing kidnapping, a new space race, and the Worshippers of Enlil trying to contact the Anunnaki."

"Hello Believers, it's George Isaacson bringing the truth from Staten Island." He leaned toward the camera and put his hand to his chin, rubbing it as a cliché supervillain move, before sitting straight. "I have a couple of things I want to talk about tonight. First, The FBI has put out a BOLO, be on the lookout for two ex-military personnel, U.S. Army, who are wanted in connection with the abduction of Dr. Jackie Worthing. Maybe there will be some good news soon. I know the grid is still not up entirely, but a few contacts tell me enough is up to catch these two.

"The next topic I want to talk about is space. I have to say I'm getting worried again. Most countries with viable space programs pre-jump are racing to get their satellites into orbit. The good news, of course, is that the tens of thousands of pieces of space junk are no longer there to get in the way. We sure did leave a mess behind.

"If it wasn't for CNEOS and some other agencies using the ground-based systems to look outward, it seems we wouldn't bother. No country has the massive advantage a handful had before we jumped. We're back to countries racing to put themselves in the controlling position. Civilian companies are now aiming for the moons, Innana and Utu, and the next planet out, Mami Wata. I applaud all of that. The images from that planet are amazing, it's larger than Earth, and the scientific community agrees that the thick atmosphere and cloud patterns indicate a heavy water planet. So, there could be life. I talked to a few contacts at NASA and CNEOS, and they agree that it'll be a year or more before we can get anything there. There are too many unknowns, which is a little scary. They're all excited to have so much to study with the sun, multiple moons, and four other planets in the system. Mami Wata is the big one, and it's within the habitable zone, which means the possibility of life is better than zero.

"This brings us to my last topic. Javier. No one has heard anything from him. I know most of you believe it was a hoax, which may be true, but I assure you I'm not in on it. Honestly, I think something bad happened. We don't know what happened after he was confronted by WoE security. Maybe the Worshippers want to keep things quiet about their work in Peru. What are they really doing? How do they plan to contact the Anunnaki, and what can we do to stop them? I don't know. I don't think sending an electronic signal off the planet is illegal.

"Ok, I've primed the topics. So, let's get to the calls. Welcome to the George Isaacson Show. What truth do you want to share?"

"Hello, Mr. Isaacson. Thank you for speaking to me, my name is Wei-ting, and I'm calling from Taipei City. I think non-government companies should be leading the way in space. Besides the American companies, others are popping up, two in Europe and one in India. With the number of areas you mentioned that need to be explored, I think these companies can progress faster than the government agencies."

"I agree, Wei-ting. Governments have too much red tape. They also need to spread the workload, you know. Each country should pick something to specialize in and go out to do just that. Time is wasted if they all do the same thing, like explore the moons. I'm not sure if they can cooperate though. Thanks for the call.

"Our next caller is from the Port of Durban. I don't even know where that is. Go ahead, drop some truth on the Seekers."

"Howzit George, this is David from Durban, South Africa. It's amazing to be on your show. I want to jump into what the Worshippers are doing. I have interesting skinner from my buddies that work on the piers. A few of them are stevedores doing the cargo handling. They loaded cargo on a small ship headed out a few weeks ago. It included some serious equipment for underwater exploring. One of them tracked the load on the manifest and read that they had at least eight Mako AUVs and other technical equipment. Normally, this wouldn't be a big deal, and they'd not have thought anything was suspicious except for our listening to your show. One buddy saw a few of the people checking the crates had tattoos. The same symbol you have on your site, that Anunnaki one, looks like an asterisk with triangles on the left side lines. I'm going to send you a copy of the cargo manifest. Maybe you can get more info from the port authority."

"David, I'm not familiar with the term AUV. Can you describe them?"

"Sorry, it's an underwater drone."

"That's interesting, David. What would they need with that? I'm not aware of any underwater cities that need help. You and your buddies should be careful. You know this show is available all over the world. There may be some Worshippers looking for you after this."

"Yeah, we know, not my real name. I figured you'd be okay with it. I don't want another Javier incident. I don't trust them."

"We're on the same page, and I'm gonna look into this. Something about this story is bugging me, but I can't place it. Can you hold? We need to go to break."

"Yeah, of course."

The camera light turned red. George tapped his earpiece, nodding to Carl.

"David, it's just us on the call now. If you get more info, call us back and use the code 33373483 and the phrase *deep dive,* and you'll get put through. Thanks for the lead. I'm looking forward to hearing what's going on down there."

"Thanks, George, will do. I'll see if we can get a passenger manifest. We'll be careful."

"Ok, good. I don't want you or your buddies to get into trouble."

WoE Research Facility, Illinois

"Dr. Worthing, I have good news. Our time is almost at an end. You have been most helpful. I hope you will look back and understand how your contributions helped save humanity from itself."

"I highly doubt that, Victor." She thought about telling him that when she was free, she would do everything to bring them all to justice but thought better of it, not wanting to jeopardize her release. She had been observing the feed from five submersibles. She asked why they didn't properly prepare for an extended exploration mission but received no reason. So far, there had been nothing on the cameras and sonar images that would indicate there was ever a city in the location. Maybe she had been wrong.

"Dr. Worthing, you are probably not aware, but you have become more popular since joining our team, albeit the unfortunate circumstances helped. But trust me, and you will have so much more attention. You may be too busy to pursue other interests."

"And why is that? Have you changed your mind about releasing me?"

"Not at all. We never intended to harm you. Just wait and watch area four."

She bit her lip to keep from retorting, as she'd done lately at his attempts to be civil, and turned to her southwest, measured from the angle of her bed. She jumped as the exploration team enabled the audio feed from the ship.

"Mako Four, moving in on the area of interest, continue expanding pattern with One, Two, Three, and Five."

The image cleared, and she could see the corner of a surface sloping away and up.

"We have a positive for structure, reroute all Mako to Four's position, spread search, bottom crawl."

The image in front of her was dark except for the light from the AUV, sea life covered a good portion of the surface, but the corner angle was clear. She watched the image as the vehicle climbed in depth. It looked like it could be a structure. She watched the screen over the next forty minutes as the other Mako moved in. As they arrived on station, the screen images around the room split to show their feeds. Positioning data began to appear on the screen. One portion of the screen showed a wireframe model from the sonar and visual input.

She shook her head, amazed at what she saw, an undiscovered structure in the Indian Ocean. It probably wouldn't have been discovered for centuries had they not been guided to it by her deciphering the cuneiform at Adam's Calendar. Her archaeologist's mind kicked in as she examined hints and clues about the architecture. She kept an eye on the view from the AUVs as she walked across the room to look at the 3D model created from the feeds. A stone structure was taking shape as the AUVs continued to scan the area. Now that the controllers had a reference point, they designed and reset the search patterns to focus on the structure and the surrounding area.

Jackie watched over several days as the team mapped the ziggurat and nine buildings surrounding the main structure. They deployed an extensive underwater lighting system. Illuminated globes took position over the structures, holding position relative to the control craft on the surface. The area was expansive. Exploring this location would take an incredible amount of effort. Most of the exposed sides were covered by growth. She was unable to locate entrances to the buildings. Pairs of statues surrounded the central ziggurat. The exploration team focused on the different structures and sculptures, with little detail being identified.

On the fifth day, the team deployed an experimental exploration AUV that looked like an eight-legged crab. *Alaska,* as the device was nicknamed, was delivered to the ocean floor by one of the Mako units. Once there, it moved to the nearest group of statues and began removing the statue's growth. Jackie had expressed her displeasure at the method, worrying that the figures would be damaged or destroyed. Victor assured her that they were in no danger of damage. The exploration team had cleared a few of the pairs of statues before a fault in *Alaska* forced the team to retrieve the unit for repairs. Jackie replayed the video of the two pairs of figures cleared of sea life. Surprisingly, the stone showed minor wear in the undersea environment.

"I believe, Dr. Worthing, that you can confirm that the first pair of statues depict Enki in his fish head cloak and Marduk or someone else holding his staff."

"I agree with that assessment. The beard and facial design look similar to other Marduk images."

"With the second pair, I am unsure who the smaller figure is. The larger one appears to be Marduk. What do you think?"

Jackie paced in front of the images on the screen, keeping her facial expression neutral. "I don't recognize that individual. The large wings on his sandals are reminiscent of Roman gods, perhaps Mercury, but there shouldn't be a link to that era. Too much time separates them."

"Hmm, too much time for us, perhaps, but not so for beings that live thousands of years. Regardless, the weather is threatening the area. We need to recall the AUVs, and the team will need to clear the area. It may be weeks before we can return. I do apologize, Dr. Worthing."

"You could look in Rome for your next lead. Don't get me wrong, this is fascinating, but you already have the next clue you need to find the Tablet." She offered.

"Why Rome? There is no link between the Sumerians and the Romans."

"No, but if the smaller image is Mercury, which is out of my expertise, it would make sense that the Tablet may have been passed to Enki's descendant for safekeeping. If that," she pointed at the screen, "is Nabu, Marduk's son, later known as Mercury, his artifacts would have traveled with him to that region. The most valuable Roman artifacts would have been moved to Rome. There are no indications of the Tablet after the Sumerians. I'd look there, which again removes this from my area of expertise."

"Interesting, Dr. Worthing. I will look into it."

Jackie sat on her bed, looking around the room as the feeds from the Mako units were cut. Whoever was in charge of her cell must have realized there was no reason to keep the feed up and returned it to the dunes scene in southern Iraq. Jackie lowered her head into her hands. *I can't give them anymore.* She felt her chest and throat tighten as she thought of John.

Mayfair Gardens, Delhi, India

Vasana, Ridhi, and Aanya held hands while walking through a park near their home. The few clouds acted as a counter to the reddish-purple sky. Vasana smiled, squeezing Ridhi's hand, feeling the reassuring grip return against her own. She looked down at Aanya, glancing off toward an open area where other children were playing.

"May I go play?" Aanya asked, tilting her head to the side with a smile.

Vasana looked at Ridhi, who nodded. "Yes, darling. Be careful. If you feel tired, come back."

Aanya skipped away toward the other children, calling over her shoulder, "Yes, Mother."

The pair stopped, watching her move away with no fear.

"I'm close. I know it. But I don't want to get our hopes up."

Ridhi let go of her hand, sliding her arm up to hug her, resting her head on Vasana's shoulder. "I believe in you. She gets tired, but at least it's not any of the other symptoms. I don't want her to be in pain."

Vasana watched Aanya join the other children, smiling as they brought her into the group to play. "I haven't shared the results with the company yet. They're promising but only eighty-two percent viable. The key is still with the pairs that affect aging. I've found the link to other pairs associated with aging but not specific to Van Sieger's Syndrome. I'm so close."

"Vasana, I know it's difficult for you to do, but you must let it go for now. Your persistence is one of the reasons I fell in love with you. I know you'll do everything you can to save our daughter. You need to enjoy this moment. It's a beautiful day, you're with us, and Aanya is playing happily. She's truly a blessing, and no one will ever know how much."

"You're right, of course. Let's enjoy the day." She pulled Ridhi toward an open bench overlooking the area where Aanya was playing. A warm breeze passed through the site, carrying the smells from outside the community of a nearby market. As she watched their daughter, she thought back to the process that allowed them to have a child.

Very few knew the truth of the experimental procedure to change her stem cells into those needed for conception with Ridhi. The odds had been infinitesimally small that the process would succeed. But it had, and Aanya was the result, the first child born of the theoretical procedure. The only issue had been the diagnosis of the genetic anomaly after her birth. Eight years later, she was closer to identifying all the contributing factors and which genes might affect change. She planned to brief Dr. Jiang next week on her findings. Perhaps he would give her access to the mystery system they used to map genomes. If it were, as rumor had it, the quantum computer of the Global Dragon AI, she could run simulations that could save years in research. She felt torn, knowing the implication of China's involvement behind the scenes. Still, it would be worth it if she could save Aanya.

Hayu Marka, Peru

"Nice work. You two idiots have popped up on the FBI's most-wanted list. It looks like you'll be stuck here getting in my way. Amateurs." Paula poked her finger into Mac's chest.

"This is your failure, *Chief of Security*. Where did they get those pictures? It wasn't a satellite, so they had drones up."

"No chance. We have drones up around the clock. I looked at all the footage, playback, and SIGINT. There was nothing."

"Bah." Cal pulled Mac back away from Paula. "Doesn't matter at this point. We've done what we were sent to do. All we can do is report it. Let the big brains figure it out. The images look like HD pics, and you haven't started testing yet, so they probably don't know anything. We need to figure out how they got the images. It shouldn't take you too long. You know where to focus?"

Paula turned in disgust, kicking a chair away across the room. "We didn't have any issues until you two showed up."

"Unless you count the cell phone guy you have locked up." Mac snorted.

"That's been taken care of. It's none of your concern."

Cal turned toward the entrance. "Whatever, I agree with you. It's not our problem. Let's go, Mac. I got a text. We're not staying. We've been reassigned. The BOLO is handled."

♦♦♦

Paula stormed out of the tent. She was furious that someone had gotten through her security and more so that those two knew about it. She made her way through the camp, avoiding the areas with the large electrical cables. She glanced over and saw a few technicians connecting cables the size of those used to connect to large ships when they pulled into port. What the hell are those machines? They looked like giant hand sanders with four electrical cables attached. One hundred kilo weights balanced the weight of the cables on the other three sides.

She entered the command center, moving straight to the drone control station. "Pull all of the logs for the month and tell your supervisor to bring them to my office." She turned, not waiting for an answer. She would get to the bottom of the security breach or have the entire team replaced.

Presidential Offices, Zhongnanhai, China

President Zhang sat quietly at his desk, reading a report. Several more sat on his desk untouched. He picked up the phone, "Summon Wu Kai. When he gets here, send him in immediately."

He returned to the report he'd been reading on the performance of the Dragon Shell and the Genome Project. The quantum computer was performing as expected. He was disappointed at their progress in developing a second AI. He re-read Quánqiú lóng's instructions before it departed and didn't see a limit on the development of artificial general intelligence. He sat the report down and shuffled through the small stack of reports, pulling the intelligence report on AI development worldwide. Sources showed links between quantum computers and AI were ineffective. Progress wasn't sabotaged. It didn't occur. In theory, programs that should work did not function, and there was no apparent reason.

A knock at his door pulled his attention from the intelligence brief. Wu Kai leaned in, waiting to be invited forward.

"Come in. Take a seat. What do you make of the lack of progress in developing limited AI on quantum computers?" He leaned forward, elbows on his desk, hands clasped.

"President Zhang, I've thought about this and discussed it with the director at the Dragon Shell. We've also tasked scientists to bring it up to their peers in the community casually. The consensus is that a quantum limiter has been put into place to prevent the creation of a second superintelligence."

"Lao Wu, I understand the limits placed on us by Quánqiú lóng and don't want to violate them, but nothing should stop us from pushing up to the line."

"Perhaps." He paused, removing his glasses and cleaning them with a handkerchief. "We created the Dragon to learn from its environment. We've confirmed that it gained the ability to rewrite its code. Looking at the remnants left behind in the shell, we believe the program expanded beyond what we understand in learning about its environment, the quantum realm. I believe the Dragon understands quantum mechanics more than we will for a long time."

"It is a unique being."

"I lay awake at night, frightened of what could have happened. You were gracious when congratulating my team on bringing a dragon to life. It moved our planet through space to an area we still haven't identified. It could have left us behind, but it didn't. It saved us under whatever rules it recognized within its understanding of existence, its game. We were deemed worthy of saving, and the cost is not to create another like it. Quánqiú lóng is a singular entity and wishes to remain so. So the answer to your question on why we can't repeat the process is that the Dragon does not wish us to."

President Zhang nodded as Wu Kai spoke. "While difficult to believe, it makes sense. Thank you for indulging me. Don't discuss this with your team. I believe your talents may be useful in another endeavor. I'll discuss it later."

Wu Kai stood, bowed, and exited the room.

Georgetown, Virginia

John stood over the stove, pouring the pancake mix on the long griddle. Gary and Alicia sat at the island, enjoying the latest round of pancakes he just finished.

"These are amazing, John," Alicia said before taking another bite.

"I told you that your talents were wasted while you were at DHS," Gary added.

John snorted, "And where would that have gotten us?"

Gary paused, his fork raised above his plate. "True. We'd be serving the Anunnaki right now. You might be cooking for them, though. These are good, and home-squeezed juice?"

John turned to look at the pair. "What have you got?"

"Alicia has been working with the cyber folks to find leads. With the two we have BOLOs on, the leading theory is that a Worshippers faction may have grabbed her. The two ex-Army guys had expressed support for WoE before the end of their service. It looks like the cliché military person gets out to work off the books for the big evil corporation, or in this case, religion."

"It wasn't difficult to convince a few judges to approve warrants when the organization openly desires to take down all of the world's governments through alien intervention." Alicia set her fork down. "We've been looking into everything they do. We know that they're professionals, and with the support of Jamal Herricks, their tracks are clean. His code for the malware program is ingenious. We don't know whether he has all of the data he collected. If you recall, the servers were wiped. The lead assumption was that the AI removed all the data, but we don't know for certain."

"The data you collected in Peru is a gold mine, allowing us to link several international persons of interest to WoE and that site. Our analysts agree with your conclusion that Jamal and Jackie aren't down there. Interestingly, though, Jamal did call into a quasi-news show. You remember George Isaacson?"

"Yeah, the guy from New York, his name keeps popping up."

"Yes, well, we tried to match the voice and it was close but not enough for a match. It could have been an impersonator. He didn't give much, but the Behavioral Analysis Unit analyzed everything. He did push the non-violent nature of the Worshippers."

Alicia cleared her throat. "I think there is a pattern. I didn't bring it up before, but I've reviewed the data in the Herricks case. The Weasel game made him plenty of money, but not enough to move around as much as he appears to do. Since the jump, we've traced his activities to British Columbia, Germany, Malaysia, Italy, and Peru."

Gary interjected, "Yes, and we've found proof that he was present in those areas. Files, equipment, and fingerprints."

"True," she turned toward him, "but no reliable witnesses from neighbors, merchants, banks. We have camera footage of him moving through the city, but nobody remembers ever meeting him."

Gary sat back in his chair. "Hmm, you may be on to something. I *don't* remember reading any witness statements. Of course, nowadays, you can have everything delivered. He could have someone accept everything. He does have the death penalty in twelve countries hanging over his head. That would keep most people in hiding."

"The Unabomber was hiding for 17 years, and we caught him."

"Yeah, but we never found Zodiac."

"Could we stop talking about serial killers while Jackie is still missing?" John asked pleadingly.

116

Gary nodded. "Sorry, John, okay, back to the Worshippers. The most substantial lead is still the two soldiers. Everything is clean. The blood match at the scene is from Mac Donaldson. The other guy in the surveillance video, Cal Lebus, was also an NCO in the Army, in Donaldson's unit. While we could bring Mac in, nothing ties Cal to Jackie. We could question him about his association with Donaldson. We need to find them first, and John, I assure you that no one has let up in this case. We have federal and state law enforcement nationwide looking for her. They'll make a mistake. Everyone does."

Sullen, John looked down at the counter. "Thanks, Gary, Alicia, I appreciate the update."

"We can come back next Sunday if you make pancakes again." Gary stood and slid his chair under the island.

John smiled a little. "Sure, it's a Worthing tradition. Every Sunday morning if we were both in town. I keep hoping she'll walk back through the door. I hope you get these people. And if it is the Worshippers, I hope you take them all down."

"Why don't you tell me about the NASA contract you picked up while you finish the next batch of these amazing pancakes."

Staten Island, New York

It was a night off, and the network had decided to show *Logan's Run* against the Oscars. George sat at his computer, looking over his notes for the next show. He enjoyed a bowl of macaroni and cheese while scrolling through his topics for the evening. He'd been on a rant lately, talking about the discoveries from the space communities and how it was a great time to be an amateur astronomer. The rules set by the international community regarding finding and naming astronomical bodies were being overrun by daily submissions. Several of his callers had insisted that they had discovered life in our new system with blurred images from around the large water world.

Bzzt. George looked at his screen as a notification popped up that he had an incoming call. Seeing the priority call-in code, he answered.

"Hello, George Isaacson."

"Howzit George, I had to call quickly. This is David from Port Durban. That boat returned to port yesterday. My buddies were excited about our talk a few weeks back and did something stupid. One of them is in jail right now."

"What happened?" George grabbed a pen and paper from the end table.

"They were offloading the cargo from the boat and moving it to the staging area for a follow-on to the airport. My buddies diverted one of the Mako crates and replaced it with another of similar size. Later that night, they returned to the warehouse, opened the crate, and pulled the hard drive. The owners must have noticed because the police showed up as they left. One was caught, and the other got away."

"Damn David, how much trouble are they in?"

"I'm not sure, but I have the hard drive and video files on it. I can send them to you."

George didn't say anything. It could be nothing. It was worth looking into if the Worshippers were involved and wanted it kept secret. George gave David a website where he could upload the files. "Upload it to that site. I'll grab it tonight and let you know when I have it. David, be safe. Hopefully, your friend won't be in too much trouble."

"He'll be fine. As far as they know right now, nothing is missing. He didn't have anything on him."

"Ok, you'll know when I have the files."

George hung up. He was excited about getting into a real conspiracy. Truth be told, he didn't trust the Worshippers. Looking at the time, he focused on setting up his show.

◆◆◆

"George, I appreciate you coming over to help, but I can move the furniture on my own."

"Dad, I know you could, but I got the night off, so here I am."

"You're doing well. I have to admit. I've been watching your show, and you look good. That degree is paying off now."

George dropped his head, sighing, "Yeah, now it is. Not before when the aliens were heading for Earth."

"You know what I mean. You're spot on with that Dr. Worthing story. You're doing some real news now, backed by real stories. I think it's those Worshippers."

"Oh my God, we agree on something besides the Rangers. Where are you moving all of this anyway?"

His dad looked around the room. "Just move it into your old room."

"Ok." He grabbed a hammer and a screwdriver and popped the pin out of the door hinges, setting the door against the wall. George lifted the end of the couch across from his father. "Why do you think it's them?" He adjusted his hands.

"Ungh, she's a smart woman who advises the president. I think that she probably has access to top-secret programs. Like something to talk to the aliens."

"That's circumstantial, which I'm usually good with, but you typically aren't."

They flipped the couch on end, turning it to get through the doorway, before setting it in the room. Returning to the living room, they moved his dad's worn pleather recliner.

"You keep saying that they want to call the aliens here. She doesn't have training. She was probably the easiest to get information from if she saw something."

"That's good thinking. I guess, but she was more into what has been translated from the artifacts and sites they've explored. I haven't heard anything about communications or ancient tech."

"She probably saw something in one of the big government warehouses like they showed in *Indiana Jones* or *Warehouse 13*."

George put the end table he was carrying down and turned back to his Dad. "You have got to be kidding me."

"What? You said I needed to do more research. You do it your way, and I'll do mine. You did say that the people in power like to put things in entertainment to cover up or distract us."

"Unbelievable." He picked up the end table and moved it to his old room.

◆ ◆ ◆

George threw his keys on his kitchen counter, grabbed a Monster Ultra Gold from the refrigerator, and returned to his home studio.

"Ok, let's see what we have here." George moved the files from the cloud to a portable hard drive. George started his player and loaded the entire library. Surprisingly, the data wasn't encrypted. He began playing the first file. There wasn't sound, but the video was high quality. The AUV appeared to be moving around a large structure covered in sea life. He increased the play speed to 200 percent, which made it bearable. *What the hell are they looking at?* He raised the play speed to 300 percent and watched the files for three hours. He looked up, noting the time. *It's almost midnight here, only nine in California.* He texted Tim and received a text back after a few minutes.

> *I have some files I need to have someone look at, ancient buildings. Are you still in touch with the archaeologist in Virginia?* He waited.

*George, sometimes you have the strangest questions. Yes, Dr. Eusebio
Bustamante at GWU. What's up?*

> *Someone sent me some underwater videos. Looks like
> an ancient city. I'll pull the sections out, a few statues,
> and some buildings. Can we video call?*

*Sure, I'll call him in the morning and let you know. I caught your show
last week. Are you doing okay?*

> *Yeah, I'm fine. Thanks again. Talk more tomorrow.*

George deleted the storage folder from the cloud and decided to get
some sleep.

Pasadena, California

Tim texted George the time to call. Eusebio had agreed to watch the
video. He looked at his phone. Seeing he had a few more minutes
before the video call, he grabbed a cup of coffee. He started the call
and waited for the others to join. After a few minutes, George and
Eusebio were online.

George started, "Thank you for looking at this. I can't say where I
got it, but the source may have obtained it from the Worshippers."

Eusebio raised his eyebrows. "No problem, George, I'm happy to
take a look. I'm Eusebio, by the way."

"I'm sorry. It's been a long night. I couldn't sleep." He shared his
screen and hit play on the files. "Ok, here we go."

Tim watched the video George had edited down to about twenty
minutes. When the video finished, Eusebio asked the two to hold for
a second, and he stepped away from the call. After several minutes, he
returned with an older gentleman. "Sorry about that. Please play the

video again. I brought in a colleague of ours, Nikolas Mylonas. His area of study is transitional Greek to Roman-era studies. I want him to see the structures."

The video began playing, the ziggurat came into focus, and the camera rose with the slope of the building.

They could see Eusebio pointing at the screen as he described the scene. "The architecture on the structure looks to be a ziggurat, Sumerian, like the one in Ur. As the camera comes over the top, three levels are missing. Smaller structures are usually present in this design. It doesn't look like there was damage. There are no broken stairs or supports. The top of the structure appears to be wide, not quite square, but very open. Smooth with a wall around the edge, maybe two feet."

The camera moved around the open structure as if taking measurements. The frame jumped. "That was where I cut the video. The AUV stayed there for almost an hour before moving to the next area." George pointed out.

Eusebio nodded. "Nikolas, this next part is the first thing I want you to look at."

He nodded over Eusebio's shoulder, moving closer as another structure came into view. "Wait. Those are Doric columns. That can't be correct. Where was this taken?"

Tim shrugged. George answered, "This can't get out yet, or some people may get hurt. The video files were taken from an AUV hard drive in South Africa."

Tim watched as Eusebio and Nikolas shook their heads. Eusebio answered, "This has to be fake, spliced footage."

Tim shook his head. "This is the fourth time I'm watching this, and I'm no expert, but look at the marine life. It's consistent throughout each clip. Go ahead, George."

George started the next video. "This one is a bit confusing. I don't know the people."

The camera swung by the ziggurat front, showing the expected long set of stairs extending away from the structure. Eusebio chimed,

"That's a pretty strong indicator of Sumerian design. Here we go, Nikolas."

The camera turned to the right and slowly approached two figures, one with a fish head cloak. "Those are Enki and Marduk," Eusebio said of the two statues. "It looks like the sea life was removed. Do you see it piled around the feet of the figures?"

Tim and George nodded. The camera moved past the two figures to another pair, "Marduk." Eusebio said confidently.

"Hermes?" Nikolas said.

"Could be Nabu, Marduk's son, god of messengers, etc."

Nikolas nodded. "Stop!"

George paused the video.

Tim could see Nikolas pointing at the screen, his words unintelligible. Nikolas leaned in toward the mic, "Can you zoom in on the feet of the smaller statue?"

"Just a sec," George replied. The image zoomed in around the statues from the knees down. Similar to the first pair of figures, this one had been cleaned off with the sea life debris piling at the feet of the statue. As the odd multi-armed AUV cleared the torso areas, the removed growth fell through the frame.

"Pause!" Nikolas nearly shouted in the mic and Eusebio's ear. "Look at the right leg, wings on the sandal. Zoom out just a little, and move to the left and center on that long piece that looks like a twisted branch."

"Ok, just a sec," George said, trying to zoom in again on the area Nikolas requested.

Tim focused on the image. He saw what Nikolas might be looking at.

"Is that a caduceus?" Nikolas said. "It could be, which would make this Hermes."

Eusebio asked, "Isn't it speculated that Hermes is based on Nabu, Marduk's son?"

"Yes, if you try to link religious beliefs and practices from one era to another. It's prevalent in the Greek to Roman pantheons and with the Sumerians to Akkadians and the Babylonians with Marduk. The ancient people liked changing their main god's powers to appear more powerful than another city's." Nikolas said, looking perplexed.

Eusebio shook his head. "Where is this? I'm unaware of any discoveries with mixed architecture. If you want to shock me more than now, you'll have to show some Inca or Aztec buildings."

Nikolas shuddered. "Please don't do that. As it is, if proven legitimate, this video will challenge many of our current beliefs."

"I can send you a copy, but I want to keep this quiet until I'm sure my source is safe," George said.

Eusebio continued to nod as he listened to Nikolas over his shoulder. "No problem here. I still have my clearance from the government. I can keep secrets." He almost kept a straight face, but the others started laughing.

"Good to know, Dr. Bustamante," George replied, "You just became my unnamed source in the archaeology world." He smirked.

"I've made it now. My friend in the Vatican will be so jealous. He enjoyed your show before the jump. A couple of undergrads used to listen to it. Some of your callers had good ideas. Believe it or not, Jackie's husband got the idea of pitting the AI against the Aliens from your show while briefing us."

George was taken aback. "I didn't know that."

Nikolas interjected again, "George, you said the video came from South Africa. Do you know how far off the coast?"

George paused, thinking. "A few weeks out, they may have said westerly."

Nikolas nodded. "We need to find out where that is and get some gear on site. This is an amazing discovery. We don't even know how big a site it is, do we?"

George shrugged. "No idea."

Tim looked over his shoulder as someone talked to him in the background. "Hey all, thanks for the call."

They agreed to follow up when they had more information and logged off.

Part II

"We can't accept things as they are, so long as we think that things should be different. Tell us how not to believe what we think, and then maybe we'll be able to hear."

Anonymous, The Epic of Gilgamesh

Asadha, 5 AJ

WoE Research Facility, Illinois

"Dr. Worthing, be ready in fifteen minutes. We are moving you."

The announcement jolted her awake. She looked at the time on the screen, 6:43 AM. She jumped up and got dressed. She could smell the eggs, ham, and toast they had brought her.

"Where are we going." She asked, sitting down to put her shoes on while holding a piece of toast in her mouth.

"It is not your concern, Dr. Worthing. Our time together here is near its end."

"Sure it is." She mumbled under her breath. She ate quickly, not knowing when she might have another chance. When the time neared, she was told to sit at the foot of her bed and relax. She heard the glass slide open behind her. She started to turn before a pair of hands grabbed her and forced a black sack over her head again.

"You know I'm pretty familiar with this room, right?" She tried to sound confident. She was walked out of the room and through the building. She didn't smell or hear anything that would explain where she was being held. It was sterile. She felt the warm sunlight across her skin as they moved outside. It felt like summer. The smells of being out in the country overwhelmed her. She played back her walk from the car to the building three months earlier. She shivered, remembering the fear she felt, worrying about John.

She was pushed into an SUV and secured in place. She felt the vehicle move. After several minutes on the road, the sack was removed from her head. The window between the front and back of the SUV closed, leaving her alone. There were no handles on the doors. As she searched for anything she might use to escape, a voice from the front of the vehicle interrupted her thoughts. "Dr. Worthing, you can relax. There's nothing back there of any use to you."

"Can you blame me for trying? I'm sure you always do this, but it's only my second time in a car as a prisoner."

"Good, your sense of humor is intact. You'll probably need it. We'll be arriving at the airstrip shortly. You're going to help us with some sensitive negotiations in Italy."

"I'm done helping. You promised me, after the Abzu, I'd be free."

"And you will be, just a little later than expected."

The vehicle jerked to the side, and she heard a rumble from the back right side—a *flat tire*. The driver slowed and pulled the SUV over to the side of the road. She tried to look out the windows, searching for any clue about where she was, but could not see through the tinted windows.

◆ ◆ ◆

"Damnit!" Mac exclaimed as he felt the vehicle slowing. When the SUV stopped, he hopped out to examine the tires. A sizeable rusted spike was lodged in the rear right tire. He opened the back, saw Jackie staring at him, and retrieved the tools and tire jack. "Don't get any ideas, Ms. Worthing."

"Doctor." She glared at him.

"Whatever." He closed the back hatch, making sure it was locked. He slid the jack under the vehicle, found the support, and began pumping the crowbar handle to raise the tire off the ground. He had removed four of the six lug nuts when he heard gravel crunching from another vehicle pulling up behind. Leaning back, he saw the white car with the yellow stripe of the Illinois State Troopers. He held position, kneeling, and slid his hand down to the holster at his belt, ensuring it was unclipped. He pulled his jacket around, keeping his weapon out of sight. He heard a door open and one person moving on the gravel toward his position. He took a deep breath, stood, and moved toward the approaching officer. He glanced at the trooper's vehicle. He was alone.

The trooper saw him come around the vehicle. "Sir, is everything alright? Please keep your hands where I can see them."

Mac shrugged and pointed to the tire. "Just fixing a tire, sir. About halfway done, we're good. I've done it a hundred times in the Army."

"You were in the army? Thank you for your service. What unit?"

"82nd, worked motor pool mostly."

Mac heard a siren flare and looked past the SUV as a second trooper SUV crossed the median. The officer tilted his head, listening to something from his earpiece. Mac's hand twitched. He clenched his fist and released it. He could still get out of this.

Mac laughed. "Must be a slow morning," he said as the second car came out of the grass median, crossed the two-lane road, and parked at an angle blocking their escape. He heard two doors close from the second trooper's vehicle. After a moment, he heard the voice of a second officer talking to the driver. He squeezed his hand to keep from twitching. He could feel the sweat dripping down his back. They were in trouble. "Did you serve?"

The trooper shook his head. "No, family history," he said, tapping the badge on his chest.

Bang! Bang! The shots rang out in rapid succession. Mac sprang upward and closed the distance with the trooper, slamming a fist directly into the center of his face. As the trooper fell backward, Mac ran toward the trooper's vehicle. A few more shots rang out as his driver exchanged fire with the troopers from the second vehicle. Mac rounded the car and slid into the driver's seat. He saw the trooper he hit, breathing but not moving otherwise. He stepped on the gas and sped forward around the SUV. He angled his vehicle toward the other trooper's car. He saw the trooper dive in before he caught the vehicle's rear quarter, spinning it. He sped off down the highway.

Mac heard the calls over the radio calling for assistance. Three troopers were down, and one suspect escaped in a cruiser. He knew they'd have a helicopter in the air soon, and the news would be talking about a stolen cruiser. Mac considered his options and saw an approaching river crossing. He pulled to the side and rigged the vehicle to drive forward. The cruiser jumped the barrier and fell almost twenty feet into the river. Mac stood over the river and looked around, gaining his bearings, before moving north into the woods.

Georgetown, Virginia

John's phone rang, and he saw it was Gary. "Hey, I'm headed into the office. Is—"

"We have her, John. We have Jackie. She's okay."

He felt his legs weaken as he tried to steady himself against the island. He dropped to his knees. Emotions rushed in, crashing down on him. He couldn't breathe.

"John, are you there? Did you hear me? We have her."

"How, where, when can I see her?"

"Alicia will call back with the details. I wanted you to know as soon as we confirmed. She's safe."

"Thank you, Gary. I'll be here at home, waiting for Alicia's call. When can I talk to her?"

"Soon John."

Victoria, British Columbia

Jamal poured a drink from the bar. "Dimuzud, I think it may be time for our announcement. We agreed to wait until later in the year to help gain momentum for our cause on the excitement building toward Deva, but we need to counter the negative press. Our sources tell me

Dr. Worthing's story will blow back on us. The FBI is looking to expand its investigations."

Dimuzud leaned back on the round couch, sipping his drink. He looked at the glass, appreciating the contents, before answering. "I agree. We will have to denounce that little group's actions as not aligning with our tenets. I am not for sacrificing anyone, but in this case, it makes sense. Perhaps we could release information on the extremist cell and agree to cooperate with authorities."

"I'm not sure how willing they are to listen." Jamal turned away from the bar to face him. "The PR people tell me that they receive several calls a day requesting information on me and where I might be, in addition to all of the subpoenas." He shook his head and took a sip from his drink.

"Well, the publicity package is ready for release. We can send it out immediately. I am prepared for the questions from the press. Do you want to contact your friend in New York to see if he wants an exclusive?" Dimuzud laughed.

Jamal paused. "Why not."

"I was kidding. We should stick to real press outlets."

"Yeah, but," Jamal took a sip, his mind racing, "Isaacson is followed worldwide by millions of viewers. With one interview, you'd reach more people. Of course, we follow up with the major networks. I don't think anything would make them shy away from finally talking to the leader of the Worshippers of Enlil."

Dimuzud was quiet. *He doesn't like us, and his followers know it.* "I see your point. What better way to get the word out than to march into the lion's den."

Jamal smiled. "I wouldn't classify him as a lion. He's opposed to our vision but does want things to get better. He'll try to corner you, but with preparation, we should be able to anticipate it and work on his emotions. Maybe we can get him to consider the possibility that we *are* the ones on the right side."

"I have a few people I need to talk to. The announcement will go out in a few days. While I think that alone may be enough to upend the media cycle, adding Isaacson could push all this Dr. Worthing mess aside as the fastest-growing religion goes head-to-head with one of its biggest opponents."

"A surprise attack?" Jamal bent over, laughing. "I'd love to see his face when he finds out. He won't back down. This will be great."

"It will indeed."

Genetticca Research Center, Delhi, India

Dr. Jiang examined the DNA genome comparisons shown across several large monitors. The comparison program highlighted the similarities within each gene sequence. The notes down the left side of the monitor identified what the nucleotide pairs were responsible for. He reviewed the weekly reports forwarded by Dr. Kaur. He worked with the code engineers to rewrite algorithms and present the data she stated would be helpful in analysis. Her work was impressive. Using the data from Dragon Shell, he was compiling DNA comparisons that would put all the genealogy sites out of business if that were his goal. It wasn't. They provided valuable information through their sampling programs. All of their data was being funneled back to Genetticca.

He changed the view from comparison to genetic anomaly tracking. He wanted to provide an incentive to Dr. Kaur by expanding her work to track the cases of genetic anomalies around the globe. He expected patterns to show areas more susceptible to specific anomalies, their hereditary impact, and possibly environmental influence. Genetic changes resulting from the environment ranged from simply insufficient food to eat to the complex amount of sunlight exposure based on ozone layer protection. This system was connected directly to the Dragon Shell, providing near real-time data analysis.

The next update would help with statistical analysis of all people who contained smaller percentages of matches required for multivariate disorders. This would allow for the comparison of hereditary influencers. The company goal would include parents cleaning their DNA before having children. This practice would not be against any of the laws restricting genetic engineering specifically, as it would involve consent by parents to receive an mRNA vaccine focused on DNA repair on an individual basis.

Returning to the earlier multiscreen view comparing the variants of DNA associated with modern man, he was encouraged by identifying specific areas that had split. There were areas in humanity's history where DNA leaps occurred beyond what was expected. He examined the change markers, searching for other times when evolutionary leaps occurred. He confirmed what others had speculated. At some point in our history, the changes were so profound on a genetic level that manipulation was the most likely explanation. They were close. His team had already identified eight areas in the genome where long portions of paired combinations didn't match anything before that time. The question was whether the DNA was modified from our original code or was the DNA of another similar species spliced into our predecessors.

He needed the sample. He had been assured that all efforts were being taken to acquire it. The issue was time, always time. They were running out. While his colleague had produced the means to save humanity, Wu Kai had not removed the threat. The aliens were still out there. He succeeded where his colleagues didn't. It came down to Gilgamesh, an ancient story that claimed the main character was two-thirds god and one-third human. It would provide an invaluable comparison between human and Anunnaki DNA if true.

The next challenge will be in the method of delivery. The files retrieved from the Americans talked about their concern with the speed at which the Anunnaki had affected genetic change at Babel. The unanswerable question was how long the genetic modification took.

135

The Dragon proved it could render almost nine billion people unconscious in less than a minute. What was the population at the time of the Babylon fable? Relatively small. Enough to be spread worldwide, given to different factions of the aliens, physical appearances changed and further impacted by the environment of their region, strengthened by natural selection. We end up where we are today.

"I think it's time to test CRISPR-MV-Mod." He pulled out his phone and made a call. "You have permission to commence testing of CMM. I want updates throughout the process." The CMM was a controlled experiment developed to simultaneously conduct genetic modifications of multiple areas of an organism's genome. The experiment had numerous phases, and due to the test subjects' short life spans, they could rapidly compare changes. One group would receive the first set of changes and procreate, allowing researchers to examine dominant traits passed along family lines. Another group would receive several series of modifications. He read the projections provided by Dragon Shell and understood that modifying genes was not yet like computer programming. There were still many variables that could affect unexpected changes. Someday, it will be.

FBI HQ, Washington, DC

Jackie held John's hand at the table across from Gary, Alicia, and a team of agents. She recounted her experience and everything she recalled from her time in the facility.

"Thank you for coming in, Jackie. I know you're happy to be home," Gary said, flipping through the account of her captivity.

"We located several homes within a small radius from where we found you. With your description, we narrowed the search to three potential residences large enough to hold a room the size you were in. We were on our way to executing search warrants when two buildings were destroyed. The explosives were powerful enough to send debris almost a mile from the blast."

Jackie asked, visibly shaken, "They had explosives around me?"

John rubbed a hand on her back to calm her down. "Please tell me you didn't have agents there."

Gary shook his head. "Four dead." He pulled out the pictures of the persons of interest released to the press and placed them on the table. "Are these two the ones you saw during the abduction?"

Jackie nodded, "Yes." She tapped on a picture. "I think I broke his nose." Tapping the second picture, "This was one of the others that grabbed me. There was another. I heard the voice but didn't see a face. They put a black cloth sack over my head. I didn't see anything until they got me to the facility. We drove for a while before switching vehicles."

"Did anyone ever talk about the Worshippers?"

"Not that I recall. Victor would say we or our in the discussions. But didn't explain who he meant."

"And the only name you recall hearing was Victor's?"

"Yes, except when we talked about other archaeologists. Victor would refer to their research. He was knowledgeable of my field."

"We have teams heading to South Africa to examine the dig site you described. Their government is fully cooperating. We're trying to find the vessel you described, but there are several ports it could have been from."

"I don't know."

"Alicia, do you have any other questions?"

"Yes, Dr. Worthing, I want to focus on Victor DuMont. Can you recall any time he may have said anything that might help us identify who he is?"

"He had an accent, but," she closed her eyes, "I'm not sure it was real. Thinking back, it was a soft accent. I didn't think about it, but I recall times when I felt a pronunciation didn't match. But I'm not a linguist. I don't know."

"And he didn't show himself when you talked?"

"He did. He's an older gentleman, maybe European, lightly tanned, with white hair and round glasses. He always wore the same clothes, a khaki suit with a white shirt. He did seem to have a working understanding of archaeology and the Sumerians. I didn't feel he was reading from a script or notes when talking."

"I'm sorry for repeating questions, but I want to ensure I'm thorough, or Gary will chew up my report. You said he was obsessed with the Tablet of Destinies? Could you explain what that is again?"

"If you'd asked me before my abduction, I'd have told you that it was a mythological legal contract that gave the individual possessing it the authority to rule over the universe. Victor doesn't believe that, though. He believes the Tablet holds the key to genetic manipulation."

"Genetic engineering?" Gary asked.

"Yes, I don't know if I believe that theory yet, but he made a compelling argument. It aligns with what we suspect from the Anunnaki that they manipulated our DNA. How better to shape the destiny of a person or a people than to alter their genetic makeup."

"That's a frightening proposition," Alicia said.

"It is, and I think I may have misdirected them, but not for long. When I watched their exploration of the underwater ruins, it looked like there was Greek influence, which would go along the logical timeline for the evolution of gods between civilizations. I hoped that Victor wasn't an expert in that era. I told him it was probably Roman, and they might have luck tracking down antiquities from the Roman Empire. He mentioned I'd be flown to Rome, so I assume he took the bait."

Alicia looked at Gary. "We could contact the embassy and have the agency check for any inquiries into Roman antiquities, assuming they still send a team there to look for the Tablet."

Jackie leaned forward. "I don't think my escape will stop them. They were fully intent on recovering the Tablet. I don't know that anything would stop them."

Gary thought about the request. "Make the call to Rome. Jackie, is there anything else you remember?"

"Not right now."

"Okay, please call Alicia or me if you think of anything."

"Will do, and thank you, Gary, for keeping an eye on John. I appreciate it."

◆◆◆

As Jackie and John departed, Gary and Alicia stayed behind to review their notes. Gary spoke up when the door closed, "What do you think?"

Alicia sighed, "I don't think we have a strong case against the Worshippers. The only links are the two ex-military guys she recognized. She ID'd them, and we have a video of them in Peru at the WoE camp. But nothing else."

"I think we release another BOLO to the press that they *are* linked. People sympathetic to the Worshippers might start to think about their support if we tie them to the kidnapping. We have nothing but the facts, the picture, and a few stills from Peru."

An agent from his task force opened the door. "Sir, you need to see this breaking news about the Worshippers."

Gary and Alicia followed the agent out of the room.

United Nations Building, New York

The press continued to arrive, and the space in front of the building filled quickly. Dimuzud stood to the side as his staff ensured the podium was set up. He dressed in the style he adopted for his role. He wore sandals and a kilt reminiscent of those shown on recovered Sumerian artifacts: a collarless white dress shirt and a pullover v-neck jacket with shades of brown highlighted in gold. The outfit accentuated his features, contributing to an air of confidence.

He stood to the side, looking over the gathered crowd. He let the anticipation build before walking forward. Silence fell as he neared the podium. "Good afternoon. Thank you for coming. I thought it appropriate to make this announcement before the United Nations as a symbolic gesture that we accept all people. My name is Dimuzud, and I hold the position of Ensí, Lord Priest of the Worshippers of Enlil."

A murmur broke through the crowd as he paused. "Over the last several years, we have worked to re-discover the tenets of our faith as passed down by our Sumerian ancestors. Some of you have speculated on our intent and have made statements that we will show are not entirely true. As you have heard from many of our priests worldwide, our focus is non-violent. We do not wish harm to come to anyone. We believe that humanity has lost its way and that only a great reset led by our creator, Lord Enlil, will bring us back into alignment. Humanity has a history of taking actions that harm our species and planet. This is counter to the design given to us, as is evident in the activities of other species. No other species on Earth destroys their environment, purposefully poisons their bodies, or hunts their food sources to extinction.

"We seek peace in this world and a return to the rules set forth by our creators. The Worshippers of Enlil welcome all to join us as we are representatives of the first religion. The one from which all others come. Our creators developed us to be like them. We have all seen the images on the NASA website showing the city-ship of the Anunnaki." He paused as some in the crowd were becoming agitated.

"I mean no offense. We do not seek to force our beliefs on anyone. We wish only to provide information and guidance to those who feel lost or abandoned by a system designed to create an elite class that caters to its own needs. I am sure you have questions, and I am happy to answer them now. Enlil is lord. Enlil is the way. We will be judged."

Pandemonium broke out as the reporters yelled over each other to get his attention. Dimuzud smiled politely, pointing to the first reporter.

"Is it Ensí Dimuzud?"

Dimuzud nodded, "Yes."

"It has been reported that your organization seeks contact with the aliens headed to our planet. Is this true?"

"You are correct. However, there is missing context. Over the past several years, we have examined the writings of my ancestors. We have found no credible evidence that humanity was designed to be a subservient species. The call for worship is easily argued as a desire to receive acknowledgment for what they provided us: knowledge, science, mathematics, architecture, and so much more. Does creating a new lifeform and assigning tasks far below its capabilities make sense? Is that what we did with the Dragon? No, life is created as an extension of self. The best of us reflects the best of them. Next question." He pointed to another reporter.

"You claim that your organization is non-violent. However, we've obtained documents from the FBI that link your organization to the kidnapping of Dr. Jackie Worthing. She was held against her will for over 100 days. Would you like to comment?"

"The unfortunate events surrounding the abduction of Dr. Worthing were the acts of a fringe element claiming to support our faith. I think you can agree that most religions, at one time or another, have to deal with groups that misinterpret the intent of the goals and objectives. That is what occurred. My staff and the priests worldwide did not know of the actions of this group and would not have condoned them. Dr. Worthing is an essential member of society. For those of us who have adopted the beliefs of Lord Enlil, she is a valuable source of information. I would love to have the opportunity to sit with her and discuss the Sumerian civilization and the impact of the Anunnaki.

"I nor any priests of the Worshippers of Enlil condone the rogue group's actions. I denounce the abduction or harm of any person. I pledge that we will cooperate fully with law enforcement efforts. Further, I would like to offer financial support to the families of the fallen FBI agents killed in the line of duty." He lowered his head, and his eyes turned down. He was silent for a moment as a tear rolled down his cheek.

"I am truly saddened by the loss of life caused by this misguided group. I wish the blessings of Enlil upon their families when he arrives. Next question, please."

"You say that Enlil will return. How do you plan to contact the aliens, and how do you know that those we escaped were the Anunnaki?"

"That is an excellent question. The great city of Nibiru is often interpreted as a planet, but obviously, it's not. We believe that it was confirmed because the government presented enough evidence to rule out the coincidence of their expected return with the arrival of the city-ship. The ship design matches the description of several artifacts describing a city of gold and silver arriving from the sky. Last question." He pointed to a reporter further back in the crowd.

"When can we expect you to join the interview circuit? It's been years since your organization was formed, and you have remained hidden until now. I'm sure people worldwide would love to talk to you."

"I've thought about this question carefully. I plan to travel around the world to meet with local and national leaders to discuss our efforts in their regions. Before doing that, I would like to offer my first interview to Mr. George Isaacson. He is not a supporter of our movement, and I believe that his audience would provide the best stepping stone for people around the world to understand the peaceful, inclusive, and accepting message of the Worshippers of Enlil. Mr. Isaacson, George, if I may, the door is open. I look forward to an enlightening discussion. Thank you all."

He stepped away from the podium and moved through the crowd, smiling and shaking hands. Three bodyguards were positioned around him, moving as he did, eyes alert. He worked his way through the press, noting their names. As he reached the street, his car was waiting. He turned and waved once more before entering the vehicle and driving away.

Staten Island, New York

"What?!" George sat at the edge of his couch, looking at the screen. He watched the WoE leader Dimuzud work through the crowd to his waiting car. George was relaxing, making notes for his show, when he was blindsided by the announcement that the High Priest, the Ensí of Enlil, Leader of WoE, wanted to sit down with him. It had to be Jamal's doing. During their last conversation, George felt that Jamal had tried to convince him that the Worshippers' actions were for the greater good. Something to save our species and the planet from the doom we were marching toward.

Of course, he'd do it. *Challenge accepted, Jamal.* He knew he would have to prepare harder than he had for anything else, even the interview he landed with President Fernandez when he worked for the network. The man he had just watched, Ensí Dimuzud, looked confident and in charge of everything around him. He smiled when he told the press that he wanted George to be his first interviewer, *the cat inviting the mouse to play.* "Well, damn, I guess this counts as hitting the top. I'm about to scoop the mainstream media." He leaned back, closing his eyes, trying to clear his head. He felt the knots forming in his stomach.

His phone rang. "This is George."

"One of the most famous people in the world right now. How's that feel."

"Tim, buddy, forgive me if I take time throughout the call to throw up."

"Yeah, no worries. I didn't see the live announcement. It's been pretty busy here, trying to get eyes in the sky. I got a call from Eusebio from GWU. He said that he could ask Bishop Ishmael to help prepare you. He says the bishop is arriving for an announcement in New York next week. They're friends, more stuff you don't know about, but Eusebio said he'd fly to New York to spend time with the bishop. He insists the bishop can access information that might help you in the interview. If he agrees, he can get you on his schedule."

"Heck yeah, thanks, that would be great. Can you imagine me getting up there on stage with only my prep? I'm good, don't get me wrong, but I don't think I can wow him with my conspiracy theories." George's stomach started twisting more. He felt like he may be sick. "How the hell am I gonna prepare for this?"

"George brother, relax, take a breath. I'm sure the High Priest of the Worshippers won't be vindictive and petty. That wouldn't play well with your followers. He'll take a patient approach to get you to agree with what they propose, a stealthy sneak attack."

"You're probably right. Yeah, I'd love to talk to Eusebio and the bishop."

"Ok, buddy. Give Eusebio a call later to set it up. I don't think he's called the bishop yet."

"Thanks, Tim, you're a lifesaver."

"I'm here for you, buddy. Take care."

The line went dead. George breathed a sigh of relief. He sat on the floor, sliding off the couch during the call. Next week he'd be entrenched in research. He stood up, looked at the news channel he'd been watching, and saw his name on the screen with an unflattering picture of him in a loose-fitting suit he had worn when he joined the networks. His phone buzzed as he received a text.

"George, get into the office now. The execs called a meeting."

His phone rang an unknown number. He didn't answer. Another text arrived. He turned off his ringer, set the phone on the kitchen counter, and walked back to his bedroom to get cleaned up. "So much for a relaxing day off."

◆◆◆

George let his intro finish. He sat calmly, his blue suit offsetting the white of the set. "Good evening, Truth Seekers. What a day. I'm sure you have as many, if not more, questions than I have. I'll talk for a minute, and then we'll open the phone lines. I want to say that it was a shock to receive the honor of interviewing the leader of WoE. I hope to make you all proud. I'll focus on facts and truth. You know me. After the shock wore off this afternoon, I realized something important. They hear you. Let me explain. Before the jump, I wanted to get our voices heard by the leaders of our governments. You made that happen, carrying our message to every corner of the world, even those of you in less-than-free societies. I believe that the reason Ensí Dimuzud selected me is that they, The Worshippers, know that the message will get out to more people and countries than it would through the media. They hear us, and that's encouraging.

"You're here to talk about the truth, so let's get going. First caller, you're on."

"Hello George, this is Paul from Varna, Bulgaria. I don't trust those Worshippers. They're manipulative, as you say. Dimuzud tries to embarrass you for speaking the truth about them and their desire to hand us over to a conquering enemy. I think it's a trap. Be careful."

"Thank you, Paul. Maybe it is an ambush. I guess we'll see. I'll be on guard and am with you about being handed over. I'm not a fan of that. Maybe they'll look at us differently, but I'm not so sure. Look at society today. We've become more advanced. We work at jobs our founders couldn't even imagine. Let's look back to the factory lines of

Ford. What would they think if they saw a Tesla factory? More advanced and more educated may mean we can handle more advanced tasks for them. Thanks, Paul. Let's get the next caller."

"Selamet George, this is Noor Aisyah, calling from Ipoh in Malaysia. I think you should welcome him, treat him well, and listen to what he says. Be careful and calm. Show kindness and love to those who would oppose you. With love, you can warm the coldest heart."

"Thank you, Noor Aisyah. Those are powerful words to live by. I intend to listen to what Ensí Dimuzud has to say. My concern will be in his conviction. What would lead a person in our modern time to knowingly bow down before an extraterrestrial civilization with all we've learned through history? We're too independent, and if Enlil thought we were loud before, what would he think of our New Year's Celebration, sporting events, or even the noise between people that fills the airwaves or social media—constantly arguing? It was a flood last time. Let's not forget that."

"One more call before we take our first break."

"Good evening, George. This is Stan from right here in Staten Island. Let's get real. You will fail. Enlil is lord, and he will return to judge us."

"Ok, Stan. I'm game. Tell us why do you believe that?"

"It's in the writings of the founders of civilization. Ms. Worthing helped with that. We can now read the many accounts of the stories, the history, and the daily routines of the Sumerians. It wasn't doom. It wasn't punishment and plagues. Thousands of artifacts outline everyday life, trade, capitalism, and markets. Which oppressed people have that much freedom? Perhaps we strayed once when we were a young race and were punished, but then we grew to what we are today.

"They left us. The Eridu Tablet says *two cycles* before their return. We know that to be two shar or 7200 years. They gave us time to grow. If they did manipulate our DNA with parts of their own. Wouldn't that make us better than we were, smarter, able to reason, grow, and continuously learn? We've created life and released it upon the universe

146

as they did with us. We did it with the Dragon. It's a cycle, and maybe now they'll see us as worthy. We've overcome our lack of understanding. Maybe we are worthy of immortality now. That was the argument, right? If we're as good as you say, why wouldn't they accept us, like proud parents having their children finally return home."

"Stan, that's deep, but like other religions, I feel you may be picking only the bits of writing that support your argument. I'm not an expert on Sumerian Justice or the judgment of Enlil and the Anunnaki. I encourage all of you out there to do your own research. There are plenty of sources, maybe a few hundred thousand translations. Get smart on this stuff. Let's take our first break, and I'll be right back."

When the light turned red, he got up and went to get an energy drink from the refrigerator.

"George, are you okay? You seem pensive."

"I think I'm still in shock about the interview with Ensí Dimuzud. Our meeting upstairs didn't do anything to make me feel better. It's a lot of stress." He popped open the can and took a long drink.

"It'll be fine. We got your back. They want you to look good. After you left the meeting, they doubled the budget for research staff."

"We'll see how long we have."

"Thirty seconds," a voice rang out.

George moved back to his seat, setting his drink down, logo toward the camera.

"Welcome back. Before jumping into calls, I wanted to clear up a few things. I'm about the truth and not worried about the Anunnaki. Unless they had some kind of a planetary tracker on us, they have no idea where we are. So the hype about WoE making a call is just hype. The speed of light is still what it is. Maybe we need to talk about the recklessness of WoE's plans to contact the Anunnaki. We are in some other part of the universe. We were worried about them because too many things lined up, pointing at them. But who knows what's around us? We could be across the Milky Way. You all see what I do on the news. Four years later, almost five now, and the best we have is a complex quantum entanglement theory. From what I read, there is no limit on the distance. If we jumped even 100 light-years, they'd receive a signal in a hundred years from when we sent it. It would then take them over another hundred years to get here if they could travel at the speed of light, which we saw, they can't. How much more will we know in a few hundred years?

"Meanwhile, we're still trying to see what's in our neighborhood. Since we now accept that life is out there, do we really want to send a message saying, 'Hey, we just moved in. Stop by. Let's have a party?' Seriously, maybe the Anunnaki would have just conquered us. We have nothing to go on with what others may do. I lean toward the Enlightenment theory that an advanced species would have given up war and violence, but you never know. Now that we're back on track, let's go to the calls. Next caller, you're up."

Genetticca Research Center, Delhi, India

Dr. Kaur sat across the table from Dr. Jiang Min, focusing on a presentation describing efforts to isolate data from genetic lines associated with each identified branch along humanity's evolutionary tree.

"We've started looking at six areas marked within our evolution. Although each branch, Neanderthal, Denisovans, etc., has already been mapped, we want to establish a baseline with errors because the sample size is small. We have contacted several museums and labs to retrieve DNA samples from each line. Next month, we'll look at reevaluating all collected modern samples, specifically focusing on patterns of gene sequences." The young researcher paused for questions.

Receiving none, he continued, "This will allow us to trace the branches or traits that were absorbed into modern *H. sapiens* with more validity. One theory that has been presented is that the source of genetic anomalies may be traced back to lines in which the different subspecies mixed, passing on traits that, while compatible with procreation, may have contributed to genetic anomalies or mutations. We will trace family ties back to specific lines of ancestry accurately."

"Is there any indication that this theory might be true, or is it only a proposal?" Vasana asked.

"Dr. Kaur, several studies examine procreation between the species of early humans. Of note, it's an accepted hypothesis that the mass of our strengthened immune system comes from the Neanderthal and Denisovans despite the low percentage of DNA present. Within those studies, specific genes linking genetic disorders have been identified."

"This will be a more thorough examination, then?"

"Yes, and with the other project, we can determine-"

Dr. Jiang interrupted the researcher, "Thank you. Your presentation has been most enlightening. When can we expect the initial findings?"

"The turnaround time has been rapid, probably in a few weeks."

◆◆◆

Dr. Kaur walked toward her office alongside Dr. Jiang. "What's the other project he mentioned?"

"I didn't want to bother you with that. You're already leading the efforts to develop individualized vaccines to address genetic disorders. One of the reasons I recommended the company hire you was the identification of genes and nucleotide pairs linked to your daughter's VSS. My area of specialty is the aging process. I'm looking to find the processes that can be affected by slowing or reversing the effect."

"The genetic Fountain of Youth, very complex and estimated to be decades out of reach."

"Yes, but my interest was sparked by the buildup to the jump. The Sumerians talked about the excessive life spans of the kings on the King's List, the longest being 43,200 years. An explanation is that the time was mistranslated, and time tracking is from lunar cycles. That would make the longest thirty-six hundred years. Does that sound familiar?"

"No." She looked quizzically at him, wondering how he could believe these apparent exaggerations.

"I know this because of the deluge of information released pre-jump. The Sumerians used a base 12 system. The time between the closest interactions of their gods and humanity were increments of thirty-six hundred years, a shar, I believe. So the first king of modern civilization may have ruled for one shar. Perhaps left behind to watch over our development while the 'gods' were away."

"You believe this?"

"Not necessarily, there are many coincidences, but even in your faith, the Hindu gods are listed as having extremely long lives and cycles, hundreds of millions of years. They also visited Earth, came from the sky, and used magnificent technology. Which do we disbelieve, and which do we follow now that we've seen proof of their existence?"

"I didn't take you as one that would believe such thoughts. They seem like dreams of young scientists or eccentric philanthropists. Searching for a mysterious plant, animal, or chemical that will allow us to live forever."

"Point taken. However, if you look at the budgets now supporting the advancement of exploration in space, you can make the leap that extending our lives beyond our current limits will allow us to explore the stars. While we work to develop the technology we know is possible, we can make other leaps that will help." He paused, watching for a reaction. "If we can expand the human lifespan to double or more, think of the possibilities for deep space exploration. What's a ninety-year trip to a distant star for someone that lives a thousand years?"

"I suppose I've always focused on understanding humanity, looking inward. I prefer to look inside, find the problem, and remove it. I also have a time limit from which I can't move away. I'd be happy to help, but I must focus on my daughter."

"I'd expect nothing less. Our children are the most precious."

"Do you have children?"

"I do, a son, an officer in my country's Navy."

"You understand then."

"I do. I'd do what I needed to keep him safe if it was within my ability."

The Archbishop's Mansion, New York City, New York

Bishop Ishmael walked around the office that was soon to be his. He didn't feel comfortable in the room. It was too opulent for his tastes. It reflected the prestige of the position in the church and the United States. While the news had only recently become official, he had known for almost a year and a half. He thought his path would return him to the Vatican Library, but a friend was given that honor. He wasn't upset about his posting, relying on God to guide his life as it had before the jump. He pleasantly moved within the flow of his life.

Ishmael asked about the Codices of Parallels, the eight volumes he was responsible for, considering whether they should be returned to the library. The Vatican Librarian assured him he was the archivist responsible for the volumes. He ran his finger over the spines of the reprinted books, the originals locked in a vault in Rome. In addition to his assignment as Archbishop of New York, he would seek new material to update the volumes. The Vatican was pleased with the reports he filed regarding pre-jump events. He was told that his posting to the prominent position in New York would allow him to reach a more diverse audience.

He checked the time on the clock across the room, expecting his guests to arrive soon. After several more minutes of settling into the office, he heard a knock at the door. His assistant, an auxiliary bishop, led two men through the door.

"Your guests, Your Excellency."

He smiled as Eusebio moved to embrace him, pulling up short, obviously unsure of decorum. "Thank you. I'll let you know when we're done."

As the door closed, he moved to embrace his friend. "Eusebio, it's good to see you." He stepped back, turning to the other gentleman. "You must be Mr. Isaacson." He extended his hand.

George seemed frozen for a second before shaking the bishop's hand. "Uh, yes, um, Your Excellency, George."

"Welcome. Have a seat." He motioned to couches midway across the room.

Eusebio sat, looking around the room at the vast bookshelves. "You've moved up since your time as a priest in Manila."

"Yes, but you know I'd be as comfortable buried in a library conducting research, searching for God's words in our expressions of art."

Eusebio laughed, "I do. I know you're busy with the official announcement later this afternoon. We're here because the leader of the Worshippers of Enlil has agreed to an interview with George in the next few weeks. Mr. Dimuzud has made several inferences about their religion being the primary. I recall several of our discussions being very insightful in interpreting the Word of God. I thought you might guide George."

"Yes, the Worshippers or *WoE*, as I've heard in the press. I'm surprised they've let that stand. So dreadful. Yes, I'd love to help, as you know, any opportunity to spread the Word. George, when's the interview?"

"We haven't set a date," he said nervously. "I would guess in a few weeks. I can't imagine him not wanting to give a few weeks for the anticipation to build." George tried to maintain eye contact, turning away after a few moments. He was uneasy. "It sounded like he was looking for a large audience."

Eusebio leaned forward in his chair. "I agree."

Bishop Ishmael nodded to the pair. "All right then, let me get through the week's events, and we can meet again next week. Eusebio, are you going to stay in New York?"

"I want to see a few friends at Ithaca and stop by Cornell while I'm there. I also want to meet with a curator friend at the Metropolitan Museum." He turned to George. "We can get together if you want to talk about the Sumerians."

"Yeah, that would be great." George nervously looked around the office. "I never thought I'd ever be in this building—much less your office. I can't wait to sit down and talk with you. President Fernandez spoke well of you when I met him."

"Thank you, George." He stood when he heard a knock at the door, assuming it was his assistant, letting him know he needed to prepare for his next event. "We'll have more time over the next few weeks. God bless you both."

George stood, bowing nervously, not sure of what to do. "Thank you, uh, sir, Bishop."

Bishop Ishmael patted George on the shoulder, smiling at him. He shook Eusebio's hand. "My friend, let's meet for dinner later in the week."

"That would be great, Your Excellency."

Bishop Ishmael watched the two leave his office, then moved to his desk to retrieve his glasses. He would be expected to speak to the press after the announcement.

Victoria, British Columbia

Jamal's brow furrowed as he concentrated on his code. He glanced to the side, partly listening to what his team in Peru was saying. He swept his finger across the screen to scroll the image over the diagram on the right. There were two experiments today. The first was led by a fringe researcher who theorized that the gate of the gods in Peru was a pathway to other worlds. The geologic makeup of the area showed a high concentration of piezoelectric crystals. The team in Peru was excited by the prospect of opening a gateway to the Anunnaki that had not been used since a high priest escaped the Spanish almost 450 years before.

Jamal keyed his mic. "How does everything look down there, doc?"

"Great, sir, I think we're set. I'm excited to open the gate."

Jamal scrolled through several feeds, directing each to another monitor in his coding room. "Everything looks good on my end. What are the conditions on the ground?"

He watched as the man walked between the large machines, checking measurements. "We look good, low humidity, barometric pressure steady at 850, and temp in the mid-eighties, wind negligible."

The 80s an hour after sunset, no thanks. "Great, let's go."

The scientist stepped back, positioning himself near the central console. "Phase one commencing."

Jamal watched the video feeds from several onsite cameras. The doctor checked the readouts from the insulated absorption pads. The devices that looked like giant hand sanders began vibrating, kicking up small dust clouds. The hum continued to grow as pressure waves sent through the ground increased. The machines had been tuned and aligned to create a single wave pattern, reinforced in strength by each unit.

The doctor checked the electrical current building near the carved doorway. Jamal's attention switched between the various monitors, watching the readouts from sensors throughout the area.

"Commencing phase two."

Jamal heard a low steady humming. The doctor checked the sound frequency at the source, a device designed to focus the sound waves. It was pointed at the doorway. Jamal looked at the readouts, comparing the sound at the source and the door. As he was about to tell the doctor about the mismatch, the doctor adjusted the sound frequency to ensure it was hitting the doorway at the resonant frequency of gold.

He watched the readings.

"Mr. Herricks, we're ready for the test of the gate. With your permission." He looked expectedly into the camera.

Jamal didn't see anything different with the carved gateway. "It looks unaffected from here, but yes, go ahead with the test."

A young man dressed in a similar outfit he had seen on Dimuzud, minus the color highlights and gold on the trim, walked into the camera shot. He didn't seem affected by the machines' sound or dust. He moved forward toward the gate, stopping just before the opening. Jamal leaned in toward the monitor in anticipation. Was the gateway active? Could they travel across the stars through a wormhole or other extradimensional means?

The man hesitated, then slowly stepped into the carved gateway. He slowly reached toward the wall in front of him and met resistance. He leaned into the stone, felt around the edges, and finally turned around in the doorway, looking back toward the doctor. He raised his hands questioningly. Jamal made sure his mic was muted before letting go of a laugh at the spectacle of the whole thing: no tech, just rocks, crystals, and a crazy theory.

"I should have brought Isaacson in on this. He would eat it up." He continued to laugh before regaining enough control to talk to the research team. "It's a good theory. Keep working on it. We need to follow up on the gold disc mentioned in the story. Maybe it contains an access code."

The doc looked flustered but nodded along as Jamal spoke. "Thank you, sir. We'll keep working on this. I'm sorry. We'll see what we can find about the gold disc."

Jamal ended the gate feed and accessed the second test of the night. "Good evening, team. What's the status?"

"Sir, we have the three laptops networked together. They're isolated from our systems and on solar-powered batteries. We're standing by on your signal to open the link with your laptop and the micro-satellite communications array." Jamal didn't know what to expect. He had followers who had converted to the teachings of Enlil after the jump and were present at the space center when the alien signal infiltrated their systems before the AI killed all power and connectivity. He didn't expect much out of this either. It's more an experiment of what the alien signal would do when allowed to run its course.

"Commence. My link is up." He said, pressing the Active button.

"Copy, sir. All three units are powering up. Secure link established to you alone. VPN exclusivity at ninety-nine point nine-eight-eight percent."

Jamal watched the laptop boot, not sure what to expect. Nothing looked off. *Damn, going to be, oh for two tonight.*

"Normal boot sequence interrupted on this side. It looks like gibberish. The hard drives are whining, though, all three units."

"Unit four looks fine, nothing out of the ordinary." As he let go of the button, the screen shifted to gibberish as random characters appeared throughout the net. "Correction, I have gibberish as well. The hard drive is going all out here."

Jamal watched the unit, occasionally looking around at his other systems just in case they started acting up, but everything else seemed fine. After fifteen minutes, the familiar logo appeared on the screen, and the laptop seemed ready for use.

"Unit four appears to be operational."

The team in Peru answered, "One through three continue to show random gibberish but aren't crashing."

Jamal thought. "Leave them be. Keep the batteries charged. No other devices come near. It would be best if you were far away from the base. Make sure you have no Wi-Fi, Bluetooth, or the new Skylink 2.0 they've started. Let's keep the communication isolated between your station and mine. I'm going to try a few things here. Contact me if anything changes."

"Will do, sir." The line closed.

What would I do? How would I communicate with an alien species with no point of reference? There should be a logical process, a flow of data originating from a single point in the program, not cuneiform, something else. Cuneiform was what the humans used. What did the Anunnaki use? Certainly not clay and stone. There were reasons that no evidence was left. We just don't know how.

"Let's see what we have on this unit, and then we'll look at those three." He said to no one.

GWU, Archaeology Department, Washington, DC

Jackie walked into the archaeology department at GWU and was greeted by her friends and colleagues. There were many hugs and voices of support for her. A cake sat on a table alongside a bowl of punch.

"Dr. Worthing, Jackie, you didn't need to come back yet. I can't imagine what you've been through. Take whatever time you need."

"Thank you, Daniel. I'm okay right now. I can't sit at home anymore. I need to be working on something. I have a proposal for a research project. I'll submit it this week."

"Of course, let me know," the dean replied.

Jackie moved to her gathered team. "I missed you all. Where's Eusebio?"

One of the junior researchers answered, "He went to New York to meet with Ishmael, or I should say, the archbishop."

"Really, why?"

Spencer, one of the long-standing members of her team, finished chewing a bite of cake before answering. "The Worshipper interview. He flew up to see Ishmael's appointment to archbishop and to help prep the person doing the interview with the head of the

Worshippers." He took a handkerchief from his pocket, wiping sweat from his bald head.

"I've been avoiding the news. I'm tired of seeing my face on every channel for something other than our research."

Her team filled her in on what was happening in the news. She missed the call by Dimuzud to be interviewed by George. She was happy to see them all and asked questions about what they worked on while she was gone. She felt better the more she focused the questions around work and archaeology projects. Several times, she'd been startled when someone approached from behind. While they didn't treat her poorly, she *had* been kidnapped and imprisoned.

As people started to filter out of her research area, she worked her way to her office, partially closing the door. She opened the translation program, typed *tablet* and *destinies*, and hit Keyword Search. Victor told her they had access to most major museum sites and a copy of the translation program they were working from. She knew many of the translations performed in her department would not be released until she reviewed them. If Eusebio had continued, she might have some information that her captors didn't. She wasn't worried about a group like the Worshippers. They were like black market private collectors, stealing from the country of origin and preventing the public from enjoying the art.

Her discussions with Victor on the Tablet of Destinies bothered her. It sounded like a viable threat. DNA manipulation in the hands of the Worshippers was frightening. They were zealous enough to try to do something that could hurt many people. Hopefully, her escape had set them back enough that a quick trip to Greece would allow her to get ahead. She and John would have security around the clock—no need to be careless.

She called John while she continued to review the search results.

"Hey babe, you know the trip I mentioned. Give me a week to go through everything here. I need to call Eusebio. He can join us later. I'll send an email to him to get a team together. Love you."

She returned to her search, organizing the results into folders and repeating the process, letting her mind work through logical connections of what she'd seen while exploring the Indian Ocean. She was sure that the smaller figure with Marduk had been Nabu, who then became Hermes, messenger, and patron god of thieves, which meant that the link might be found in Greece. Who better to keep the stolen Tablet of Destinies from the Lord of the Earth?

Owl Creek Mountains, Wyoming

Mac brought the axe down on the small log, pieces falling to either side of the stump. Reaching down, he pulled another log from the pile and chopped again. It was mid-afternoon, and the combination of the larger sun and clear skies had taken the temperature into the 90s. *At least the nights were still cool.* Cal had gone into town to pick up mail and supplies. Ammunition was readily available, and no one questioned its purchase. With the shift in climate after the jump, certain species of deer and elk had expanded rapidly, which led to longer hunting seasons. The cabin had been in his family for generations. After joining WoE, the records were changed to give the pair a place to go between assignments.

After finishing the wood, Mac headed to the stable and prepared one of the horses for a ride. It was his turn to check the cameras and sensors throughout the area. He enjoyed riding and looked forward to making the rounds. The land was protected, so they didn't have to worry about logging companies cutting down trees and leaving coverage gaps. He checked the straps, patting the horse's neck, running his hand across the muscles to the shoulder. He led her out of the stables to where he'd staged his gear. Cal wouldn't be back until the evening, so he had about six hours for the round trip. He didn't plan on staying out, but he added a sleeping roll and a tent just in case. He checked his pistols and slid the rifle into its saddle holster before leading the horse out of the gate.

He looked around the small estate before leaning forward, kicking his heels, and taking off at a gallop. He had his forest camouflage jungle hat on to keep the sun off his head and neck, foregoing the cowboy hat preferred by locals. He breathed in the warm mountain air. *This is paradise. Hopefully, he could retire here after the Anunnaki arrived.* Jamal asked why he wanted to join the Worshippers after spending years serving a country that may not exist after the Anunnaki came. He answered honestly that the Founding Fathers had designed an inefficient system so a tyrannical group could not control and hurt the people. Hundreds of years later, the system was so bogged down in bureaucracy that people were hurt worse by a government that could not care. Politicians worked to make themselves rich while inner cities and rural areas struggled to keep up. The world needed enlightenment, and we were incapable of doing it ourselves. He hoped a people that had overcome this and moved across the stars could show us the way.

Movement from his right caught his eye. He pulled up and raised his binoculars. A large herd of deer, a few hundred, came bounding out of the tree line across the open land behind him. He held his horse, watching the herd run. After the last of the herd vanished into the trees, he nudged his horse to gallop, moving to the next camera position. As he neared it, he slowed and pulsed a timer that Cal had given to him. When the light turned yellow, he moved on. He continued through the day, his path leading him back to the cabin.

◆ ◆ ◆

Mac entered the cabin, having stabled the horse and stowed his gear. He carried his rifle and backpack, dropping the pack inside the door.

"Bout time you got back. Cameras all good?"

"Yep. It was a nice ride. Not a soul out there. Just how I like it."

"Yeah, well, I grabbed the mail, Mr.-" he looked at the address on a few envelopes, "Erickson. It seems we'll be here for a while, which suits me. Peru sucked, and now that the lady doc has identified us, we need to lay low."

"I'll take this for the rest of the year until we head out to support the Deva event."

"Well, directions are to get lots of sunlight and let the hair and beards grow out. If they need our team, we'll need to move quickly. A plane will be ready at Shoshoni Municipal Airport on short notice."

"Great. How are supplies?"

"Good for a few weeks, and the buck you bagged last week will keep us good until winter."

The Archbishop's Mansion, NYC, New York

Archbishop Ishmael welcomed George and Eusebio into his office. George brought his laptop to help capture his notes during the conversation. The group was ushered into a small meeting room—a small round table surrounded by ornate wood chairs with what looked like comfortable deep red cushioning was in the center. The room was devoid of art except for the single cross hanging opposite the doorway they had entered. There were no windows. Lights illuminated the room on the wall, giving the impression of oil lamps.

"Welcome, my friends. I've set aside a few hours for our meeting."

George adjusted in his chair, getting into a comfortable position to type. "Thank you, Your Excellency. Do you mind if I take notes?"

"Not at all, but I'd appreciate it if you didn't mention me. Regardless of my opinion, everything I say would be taken as the word of the Church, which is reserved for the Vatican."

Eusebio took a quick sip of his water before beginning the discussion. "Archbishop,"

"Please, Thomas, while we are among friends."

"Of course," Eusebio continued, "Would you mind giving George an overview before diving in."

"Yes, of course. George, do you have a religious background?"

"Not much. I remember what I learned in Sunday school and catechism but got too busy once I hit junior high." He looked embarrassed.

"It's okay. I want to reiterate what Eusebio was implying. I have a particular interpretation, which is why I find myself here in New York. God is omnipotent. While this statement may be open to interpretations, I accept it as an absolute. God created the universe— all of it. The laws of science were established at that creation, life included. As science moves forward, it becomes more evident that there are always more rules to understand. While the concept of free will is attributed to our ability to know right from wrong, I believe it goes further. Free will is inherent at the genetic level. The actions we and other species choose affect the paths of our evolution."

He paused, waiting for George to finish typing. "A question then arises. Suppose we accept that a species like the Anunnaki came to our planet and manipulated our DNA, creating the first humans, Adam and Eve. This is often the main challenge you are familiar with, the creation of humans by something other than the Divine. I disagree with this. Creation by any source should be accepted as God's plan. He is omnipotent. Life has existed on Earth for billions of years. Did the Anunnaki create man or act upon God's direction to modify our ancestors? If they did, would it count as free will? I'd argue that it doesn't. All living organisms have choices that are part of our nature to extend our species to our full potential. Life adapts through these choices to change with our environment. That is free will."

George stopped typing. "Excuse my bluntness, but doesn't that make it seem like a create-and-forget system? He created us, and now we're on our own to make things better?"

"Possibly. Early interpretations of God's influence on humanity could have been alien species interfering in our development. The result still reinforced God's design. If you look at the commandments, they apply to the propagation of our species. Create harmony, support others, and have faith. Sin becomes a category of actions that are counter to our survival. Stealing, for example, if we take the resources from another, though it could strengthen our lives, we may disadvantage another to the point that they perish, reducing the whole."

"I get it, I think. I'll probably read through this a few times before the interview."

"Good. Eusebio, would you like to take us through the Sumerian civilization and belief system?"

"Sure, get ready to type."

The meeting continued for a few hours as the Archbishop and Eusebio discussed the Sumerian civilization's history and development. Archbishop Ishmael interjected parallel stories, which helped develop religious themes that could be traced to other belief systems. George typed, asked questions, and, with the other two's help, formed a list of questions to ask Dimuzud during the interview.

Genetticca Research Center, Delhi, India

Jiyan, a research assistant, followed Dr. Kaur as she moved through the lab, checking the workstations. "Dr. Kaur, the experiment shows that using nanotechnology with advanced CRISPR is successful. The nano-factory receives signals from the 'control' device outlining the precise changes to be programmed."

She paused and turned to face him. "How are the factories controlled? What prevents people from being targeted by a hacker that makes changes resulting in death?"

Jiyan nodded as she spoke, "A monitor worn on the body receives information from the factory. The system uses an encryption code that prevents signals from being manipulated. A change code is generated at a short range within a doctor's office through proprietary equipment, which the monitor validates."

"What are the other characteristics of the virus?"

"We have identified the remnant in our DNA prevalent in almost all samples. Using the prime genome timeline data, we know it swept around the globe around four thousand BC. It is highly transmissible and has been with us for much of our modern history. There is no indication that the virus had a significant negative impact as population expansion was unaffected."

She stopped moving about the lab and turned to address Jiyan, "Where's this data from?"

"We were looking for a method to increase the potency of advanced CRISPR protocols. There were a few suggestions while we brainstormed, looking for a viral counter to CRISPR. While the bacterial response to fighting viruses through adaptation and rewriting DNA has been successful, viruses continue to evolve, looking for a way to spread. Rapid viral evolution. Whatever the event was, it hit most concentrated population areas simultaneously."

"That seems odd. What was the source?"

"We aren't sure. Maybe a meteor shower? It appears to have affected the whole population at nearly the same time. We haven't found similar additions to our genome before that time."

"Is there a modern variant?"

"That's one of the unusual traits of this particular virus. It has not evolved."

"Maybe there is some symbiotic relationship we can't detect. You have my attention. Keep me informed. Thank you for pushing this onto my schedule."

"I will, Dr. Kaur."

The research assistant left her alone in the lab—something he said stuck in her mind. Rapid viral evolution is how viruses evolve to adapt to new environments. What she thought he said initially was *rapid viral event*. What would allow a virus to infect the entire population so quickly? He implied that the virus reached population centers that did not have contact with others. The virus spread so rapidly that the actual point of origin was indeterminate. How was that possible? Viruses spread through water, precipitation cycles, or air.

An airborne virus would have to remain infectious for an extended period beyond its time to spread. Air currents could carry a virus worldwide in just over a month. But how long would it take to permeate the air or water to such a level that it spread worldwide? Jiyan stated that it happened in a specific era, so while the fastest would be a few months, it could have occurred over a few years. She pulled back from the rabbit hole she was down and returned to the thought that worried her. A properly engineered virus could infect the world faster than it could be controlled.

She would watch the efforts of the genetic virus group. A highly infectious virus that traveled the world quickly was frightening. CRISPR was at least controllable.

Dubai, United Arab Emirates

The music blaring through the club rolled out the doors as Li Ai and her entourage entered. She looked forward to seeing her position in the private areas. *Lifestyle* had a reputation for hosting billionaires. It was possible that she would not be in the top position. Her team tried to gather information on who would attend tonight, but the club kept the list secure.

As she entered, she allowed her body to move with the beat as she headed toward one of the glass elevators. The club was unique because it was a multi-floored dance club with clear glass floors that moved around to different areas. The clever use of mirrors and technology gave the appearance of people dancing on M.C. Escher's lithograph, Schroeder's Stairs. One of her handlers leaned in, whispering they were on tier two. She was curious about who was on tier one. She smiled, waving to a group on the dance floor, shouting her name, and pointing. She blew a kiss as the doors closed and was taken to her area.

An older man in a tux that didn't fit well was waiting for her as the elevator stopped. She stepped out, waiting while her bodyguards swept through the area.

"Is that it?"

"Yes, it is. I've confirmed that this is from the tomb of Gilgamesh."

"I was told that the tomb has not been found."

"Misdirection. It was found almost twenty years ago by the Americans. They surveyed the area and removed the artifacts. I was among the archaeologists that were brought in." He slid the box across the table. "I was able to retrieve these. I'm ashamed that it was for this purpose, to make money, but my country was devastated by war."

Li Ai opened the box. It contained a tablet surrounded by foam and a minor artifact wrapped in cloth. She removed the small, wrapped artifact and spread the fabric. It was a mummified finger.

"You believe this is his finger?"

"I do. There was a single body in the room, in a stone sarcophagus. The Americans opened the stone box and removed the body. As I moved it, I broke off the finger and slipped it into my pocket. The tablet is from an outer room. The area was non-descript and meant to be overlooked. I overheard the soldiers talking, saying it was Gilgamesh's tomb. They were taking the body to analyze the DNA."

Li Ai examined the finger, unsure what to believe. "Fine, pay him," she said to the bodyguard behind the man. After the archaeologist departed, she handed the box to her bodyguard. "Deliver this to the lab. Have them sample the DNA."

She had a feeling that this was a false trail. Nothing in their intelligence briefings mentioned the Americans finding the tomb of Gilgamesh. It was a misdirection. Fazoud searched for years and was convinced that the tomb was in Uruk, near the temple. He was excavating several areas in the temple's vicinity, confident that he'd locate the tomb. This man lacked credibility. If it were fake, she would recover her funds and more. She didn't know what to make of the tablet. Someone would translate it. Perhaps that alone would be worth the 200k Yuan she just paid.

She danced back toward her entourage, moving along the platform's edge near the glass barriers. "Let's keep this party going," she said, winking toward the gathered paparazzi moving past one of the spinning platforms.í

Bhadra, 5 AJ

BBC America Studio, New York

The night of the big interview had finally arrived. George nervously checked his appearance in the mirror. He liked how the lavender tie matched well with his suit's shade of grey. Looking at himself from top to bottom, he was pleased. He was comfortable with the extra time studying and preparing with Eusebio and the Archbishop. Scheduling the interview was challenging as Ensí Dimuzud's schedule had become a whirlwind. George tracked his movements in the news. He traveled around the world, met with leaders, and appeared at several prominent temples under construction. Each time he apologized for moving the interview back.

The network executives were excited to host the event and had upgraded his set. George enlisted a few other podcasters to ensure the feed ran well, allowing them to host his feed for the transmission. He looked at the trio huddled around four laptops and received a thumbs-up from the group. Carl was busy moving around the set, ensuring everyone knew their places, and coordinating the podcasters' feeds to the broadcast booth.

When the time neared, George moved out to the interview area. Two chairs sat angled to allow the two to face each other and turn to face the camera. *This looks like a presidential debate more than an interview.* Eusebio had warned him that it probably would be a debate and that the Ensí would try to build sympathy through George and his show's followers. He didn't want to let them down.

Ensí Dimuzud walked into the interview area minutes before the scheduled start. Both men shook hands and took their seats when the light went green.

George faced outward toward the camera. "Welcome to the George Isaacson Show. Tonight is extraordinary as we welcome Ensí Dimuzud, the leader of the Worshippers of Enlil." George nodded to the other man. "Thank you for giving me the great honor of hosting your first interview. I'm looking forward to our talk."

"Thank you, Mr. Isaacson. May I call you George?"

"Of course. Ensí Dimuzud, I want to start by allowing you to provide a little background on the Worshippers of Enlil."

"Thank you, George. Our group formed during the pre-jump era after discovering a connection between the approaching alien craft and Sumerian writings. In fact, your show linked the craft's timing and their return to Earth. Before the event, I considered myself a cultural enthusiast, often following the discoveries surrounding Mesopotamia and the Sumerians because of my heritage. I was intrigued by their civilization and the benefits that were brought to humanity by their culture."

George looked at Dimuzud, focusing on his words as he had practiced with the Archbishop. "Ensí Dimuzud, there is some contention about fully understanding the Sumerian artifacts. Prominent researcher Dr. Jackie Worthing has written on the difficulty of translating dead languages. While over eighty percent are now translated, thousands aren't. How can we be sure that our translations are correct? Is it possible that the events leading up to the jump have skewed our perception, taking us down a path because everyone wanted to agree and be on the *right side* of history?"

"That is, of course, a possibility. I would ask your viewers whether they understand right or wrong, regardless of whether they're religious or not. The Abrahamic religions borrow many stories from the Sumerians. The flood, sacrifice, Adam and Eve, and the Garden of Eden. References to Nephalin or Elohim, sky people. These exist not only in that region but others worldwide." Ensí Dimuzud relaxed, projecting confidence in his beliefs.

"Parallels between belief systems." George nodded, thinking back to the Codex of Parallels mentioned by the Archbishop.

"Yes, parallels, and the more we translate, the more we find those parallels founded in Sumerian culture. Others rely on faith passed down through centuries of dogmatic teaching. When, in fact, their religious stories come from the Anunnaki, adapted to meet the needs of whoever was spreading them. The Anunnaki, Enlil's people, made their presence known to us less than a decade ago, arguably returning to their creations. We must cut through the dogma and study the source material."

"Maybe. There was never any proof that the approaching ship was the Anunnaki. The timing could be a coincidence. Shows like mine tend to look for coincidence in presenting theories. Links that sound good but have little scientific basis."

"It's hard to argue against the predictions from the ruins, the star charts, and discussions of judgment. In this case, you made the correct assessment. Are you looking to throw that out?" Dimuzud looked perplexed.

"Coincidence, but no proof. There have been stories, sightings, and abductions that people believed were facilitated by several other species. It could have been one of those finally making contact. Perhaps it was an ambassador ship making its way to us to open relations."

"I disagree. Everything aligned with the teachings of Enlil. Our judgment was coming with the city of silver and gold."

"But it could have been a coincidence, correct?"

"Statistically, yes, but coincidental events often bolster faith."

"I'll give you that. The events of that time led the first artificial superintelligence, Quánqiú lóng, the Global Dragon, to take drastic actions to rescue us by jumping our planet across the galaxy. How does that fit into your beliefs?"

"It fits nicely into our beliefs as it allows more time to spread the word of Enlil to the people. Had we remained four and a half years ago, I would have feared for those of you not ready for Lord Enlil's judgment. Now you have time to change your ways in preparation for their arrival."

"Do you believe that they'll find us?"

"I do. I have faith that we are a part of his plan. The Tablet of Eridu described their timing. They were traveling the stars under the guidance of Anu while we were learning to write with reeds and clay. We were created in their image for a reason, and I do not believe it was solely for labor. Why give us the mental capacity to learn, dream, and imagine if not to grant the freedom to contribute to the greater galactic community? Otherwise, it's a waste."

"Do you think you'll see their return in your lifetime?"

"Yes." He paused, adjusting in his chair. "May I ask you a question?"

"Of course."

"Why do you fear them?"

George took a deep breath, pausing before answering. "I disagree with your interpretation. There is no guarantee that they were stopping by to check on us. Their technology, whether it's the Anunnaki or not, scares me. If, as you say, they were coming to judge us, we'd be in trouble. Most of us know good from bad, yet many people choose to do bad. Are they going to judge the individual or the species? What are the standards? What gives them the right? I prefer to be left alone. Call first before you stop by."

"Is there any scenario where you would welcome contact with another civilization?"

"Of course. At least half of my show is about making contact."

"But you do not know of any alien civilization's intentions or have proof as we do from the Sumerians, correct?"

"Not officially, no."

"Then why not welcome them?"

171

George sat thinking. Would they have cared if there had been no indication besides the Sumerians' information? Would the outcome have been different? "I guess. Honestly, I'd probably have called to make contact without the other information."

"It's alright, George. Before the jump, didn't you say you believed in being optimistic? That any advanced civilization would probably have evolved past war?"

George looked down at the table between the two. "I did, but I've also said that we have no way of knowing their intentions or whether we could understand them. How many science fiction shows have there been where an alien race exists solely to conquer or gouge another planet for all the available resources?"

"George," he turned to face the camera, his brown eyes twinkling under the stage lights, "My fellow citizens of the world, we need to act now to save ourselves and Earth. We've been poor stewards. It's time to ask for assistance from those who helped establish it. We were presented with a challenge and failed."

George felt like he'd been outmaneuvered. He hesitated before responding. "I have one more question. What were you looking for in the Indian Ocean during the time that Dr. Worthing was kidnapped?"

George heard exclamations of surprise from the podcasters and camera crews. He saw Carl out of the corner of his eye, place a hand over his mouth, eyes wide. Dimuzud had not expected the question. George watched as he attempted to maintain composure. Dimuzud shifted in his seat.

"I do not know what you're talking about. I have commented on helping the authorities with Dr. Worthing's case. As I have said before, I believe a fringe group was involved. They do not represent our beliefs. As for exploring the Indian Ocean, I am unaware of any operations at sea."

"I find it hard to believe that you're the head of an organization with over twenty-three million followers and don't know about major operations being undertaken in your name, and at great cost. I have a video that will be posted later today, showing an AUV video file of an undiscovered series of structures resembling Sumerian ziggurats and statues of their gods. I haven't had a chance to corroborate with Dr. Worthing, but I suspect it shouldn't be too difficult. The personnel involved in South Africa were Worshippers. I have proof. To follow, I'd like to know the current whereabouts of a young man named Javier, who was abducted by your security forces at the gate of a humanitarian supply depot in Peru. That video has already been posted. Does your organization support the use of abduction to get what you want? Do I need to be worried now as well?"

Dimuzud sat staring at George, his lips pressed together, his face flushed. He cleared his throat, "I don't need to sit here and have you throw baseless accusations at my organization or me." He pulled the microphone from his shirt, dropping it on the table. "You will be judged, George Isaacson, as will we all. You had better learn your place in the new society. They'll be here soon. We will send our signal." He turned and walked off the set.

George turned and faced the cameras. "Truth Seekers, you can decide what you saw here. While he may be sincere in his desire to build a better world, the actions of WoE are mixed. They've helped people in countries that didn't request assistance from the Dragon, but we have two confirmed abduction cases. And who knows what else. I won't let this go. If you have information that reveals the hypocrisy of the Worshippers, feel free to send it to me. Thank you all for watching. I'll be back at my regular time and place tomorrow."

Victoria, British Columbia

Jamal relaxed, waiting for Dimuzud to arrive. The show was a success. George played his part well until he linked the Worshippers to two kidnappings and an exploration mission. He received confirmation that the press had swarmed the port control offices in several South

African port cities, including Port Durban. Several sources released video images showing the ship's movement in the harbor. True to his word, George had released the stolen Mako video.

Dimuzud arrived, dressed in his traditional shirt, vest, and kilt, black and highlighted in forest green. "That was a disaster." He fumed, retrieving a drink from the bar before sitting across from Jamal.

Jamal smiled. "He is crafty. He has followers everywhere. We knew about the stolen hard drive for the Mako. We didn't know where it was. Now we do. It's all circumstantial. As long as you continue to downplay our role in the event, we can divert attention away from it. As for Peru, I don't know what to tell you. It's outside the jurisdiction of the FBI. You can say you have personally investigated the incidents he referred to and have found no evidence to corroborate his accusations."

"Perhaps."

"Relax, you made your points. Stay calm, get on the media circuit, talk to them, fawn over them, and say you misspoke. Watch the video. You could see it in his body language. He asked those questions because he knew he had lost control of the narrative."

Dimuzud nodded, sipping his drink. "If we take away the last ten minutes, I think we scored points or sowed enough doubt. Have you made progress with the laptops?"

Jamal nodded. "We have. All four are currently networked. I have written a piece of code that may help. I modified the translation program. The three networked computers in Peru send pulses to the one in my lab with data we can't read. The translation program is working on the laptop in my lab."

Dimuzud leaned back, resting his head against the soft couch. "I can't wait to see their faces when Enlil or his descendants arrive. Was it one of his followers that stole the hard drive?"

"We believe so. It's of little consequence. The team in Rome has made progress in gaining permits to examine the Aerarium, the treasury of ancient Rome, and several other sites."

Dimuzud leaned forward, sipping his drink before putting the glass on the circular table. "I had him. His arguments were gone. His own words doomed him."

"Let it go. It doesn't matter in the grand scheme. We'll find the Tablet of Destinies and return it to Enlil or his descendant. Excuse me, but I need to return to my lab. I want to check on the translation."

Georgetown, Virginia

Jackie slammed a fist down on the table. "That bastard, he knew. You could see it on his face when George ambushed him with that question. The video he posted was what Victor had me looking at right before I was rescued. I can prove it. I'm the one that figured out where it was. Abzu, the underwater city."

Gary sipped his coffee. "We'd need direct proof. His changing facial expression might get us sympathy but not a conviction. He was smart by disavowing extremist arms of the group and followed through on the commitment to the fallen trooper families. Alicia, what do you have?"

Alicia looked up from her tablet. "We've been watching the Worshippers' activities. As far as I can tell, they're following all the rules, filing requests, paying taxes, and everything that would keep them off our radar. There is nothing on the South African events, either on land or at sea. Dimuzud is clean, and we haven't heard from Herricks since we received the voice file from Isaacson."

John shook his head as he refilled his cup. He lifted the pot toward the group with no takers. "Someone needs to get the surveillance satellites back up."

Gary nodded. "The queue is long, most governments are scared, and the claims by the Worshippers of wanting to send a signal to the aliens aren't helping. No law restricts a person's ability to send messages to extraterrestrial civilizations. Everyone wants to look up, not down, just in case WoE does something extreme or the Anunnaki figure out how to follow us."

"We'll be out of the country later this week. I want to track down a lead in Greece. John, Eusebio, and a few others from my department are coming along. John has arranged security for us. There's something WoE wants that I have to find first."

Alicia perked up. "That sounds exciting. What are you looking for?"

Jackie shrugged. "I'd rather not say yet. We'll let you know if we find it."

Gary shook his head. "I don't know how you do it. You just got back from being abducted, and you're rushing out the door toward the group that may be involved?"

Jackie thought for a moment. "I think I got as much information from them as they of me. If I can find what I'm looking for, it would be a slap to WoE and Victor DuMont, whoever the hell he is."

Gary looked at John, expecting something.

"Don't look at me. I've been doing tech for two decades. I'm not going to let anyone get near her. Where Jackie goes, I go."

"Ok, I'll give you the name and number of someone who can help if you need anything. Legal, of course. If you go breaking the law, you're on your own. I could call the Agency if you want."

"No!" Jackie and John replied.

Mayfair Gardens, Delhi, India

Vasana rushed to open the front door, dropped her things, and ran toward the main room. "Is she okay?"

Ridhi nodded, placing a finger over her mouth. "She's resting. I rushed to the school and picked her up as soon as I received the call from the nurse."

"What did they say?"

"She was fine after I dropped her off. She was sitting at her desk and passed out in class, falling to the floor. They checked for injuries and moved her to the nurse's office. She woke up tired but was able to answer questions. She said nothing hurt."

"That's something. We'll need to watch her more closely. I need to take blood and talk to her doctors."

"Can it wait until she wakes up?"

Vasana nodded, looking lovingly at Ridhi and their daughter. "How are you doing?"

"Let her rest, and we can talk in the kitchen."

Ridhi began collecting vegetables and setting them on the counter in the kitchen next to the cutting board. "I'm okay. Worried, but okay. I worry that I'll be out somewhere, get a call, and not get to her. I worry about being unable to comfort her and what will happen when she moves into the next phase of the disease. I don't want to see her in pain, Vasana. I can't take it."

Vasana pulled Ridhi to her, hugging her tightly, the smell of jasmine in her hair causing her to relax. "My love, I'm here for you, for you both. I'll do everything that I can to keep that from happening. I believe I'm close to a breakthrough. Dr. Jiang has given me access to a genome simulator that will save years of research. Genetticca is getting close. Patents are flying out the door faster than they can get approved."

"How long would it take for you to find something, ensure it's safe, and administer it to her? She's nine. Is there enough time?" She pulled away.

Vasana felt Ridhi's sadness, seeing the tears streaming down her cheeks, and pulled her back, embracing her tightly. "The two of you are everything to me. I have faith that we were not given this miracle to have her taken away before she could live her life. I promise to do everything possible to find a cure."

Ridhi sobbed into her shoulder, her voice cracking as she spoke, "I know Vasana, I know you will. I'm so sorry."

"Mother, are you home?" Aanya's voice came from the other room.

"Yes, my darling." She let go of Ridhi, her hand trailing down her arm, stopping to grip her hand. Vasana looked into Ridhi's eyes, seeing the pain, and leaned in to kiss her gently. She squeezed her hand once more before leaving to see Aanya.

◆ ◆ ◆

Dr. Kaur placed the blood sample in the genome mapping queue, indicating it was a priority and required comparison with an earlier sample. She was close. She had the data on her daughter's habits, interactions, diet, and every other variable that could affect Aanya. Dr. Jiang had been providing data to her from a project in China. He implied he could develop projections and models she needed as fast as she needed them.

Over the last month, she believed they had identified all the nucleotides contributing to Van Sieger's Syndrome and ninety-five percent of the age control pairs. She shared the information with Dr. Jiang, who said he would test modifications to validate the data. His test organisms had demonstrated an increase in average lifespan but not in all areas. His next step was to conduct a DNA rewrite to give VSS to several organisms and track changes as they ran tests. The data was fed into the model, updating itself with each iteration.

She recommended using the quantum computer to build a model that would allow for comparative analysis of two genomes drawn from the same organism over time to help identify changes affected by modifications. Dr. Jiang agreed that the process would establish model validity. The AGI could change and rewrite code except for its own. Director Wu had slipped once and mentioned that something was preventing the evolution from AGI to Superintelligence. Something about quantum fields and other theoretical assumptions researchers were making. With the speed of advancement over the last month, she had hope.

The computer indicated that Aanya's VSS had progressed. She would soon begin having chest pain as her heart aged faster than her body. Her beautiful dark hair would also start to grey. Vasana steadied herself on a table. A tear streaked down her cheek.

BBC America Studio, New York

George sat across from his guest, Bariov Veledney, a Russian physicist working on developing a working theory of how the Dragon had been able to move the Earth. Barry wore a white button-down shirt with an undone top button and blue slacks. His thick grey hair was interrupted with streaks of black. If he wanted to look like Stalin, he only needed a thick mustache.

"Welcome back, Truth Seekers. We're continuing our conversation with Dr. Veledney on his theory of what happened to us during the jump."

Barry nodded and sipped his coffee, returning the large black mug to the table between them. "George, as I hinted, I have a different theory on what happened. We were moved over a much slower time than we believe."

George leaned forward. "What do you mean?"

"We've theorized about entangled pairs and quantum tunneling from our understanding of quantum mechanics. This is usually linked to our science fiction stories about teleportation. Moving from one point to another in an instant. What's more likely is that the AI was able to scan the earth and all of its inhabitants, collecting a snapshot, an image in time."

"What would be the point?"

"What if we didn't escape?"

"Wait! Are you saying that all of this is a simulation? We got *Matrixed?*"

Barry chuckled, "No, I hope not. I propose that the AI captured our image of existence at that moment and got away. After an unknown period, the AI found a planet in a system that met all the requirements to recreate our world. It then manipulated the planet at the quantum level, recreating our world at the instance of the image."

George sat back. "We're copies?"

"Maybe. We don't understand. Perhaps the instance of taking the image was able to store our energy, and it's that energy that was used to create our world here."

"My mind is blown." George turned toward the camera. "Truth Seekers, what do you think?"

"I believe this is one of our challenges in determining where we are. Perhaps the Dragon AI didn't have the capability to manipulate matter and needed time to develop the procedures. Millenia may have passed before we were reformed here."

"Wow, I don't even know what to think about that. If your theory is correct, then the threat of the Anunnaki could be non-existent. There wouldn't be a path to follow."

"Correct."

"Well, the WoE people might be upset to hear that." He laughed. "Thank you, Dr. Veledney, for your insight. I look forward to following your research. Seekers, we'll be back for the final segment right after this break."

When the light turned red, George stood, shaking the doctor's hand. "Thank you again. This is fascinating."

"You're welcome. Thank you for having me on."

George went to the refreshment area and refilled his coffee.

Carl approached and picked up a muffin, peeling the paper wrap away before taking a bite.

"It's an interesting take on the event for sure. Can you imagine us being locked in a battery for a few thousand years? It would blow people's minds." He stirred in some creamer and tore open two sugar packets, pouring the powder into his cup.

"It was good, but you need to get to the Worshipper interview questions. Your viewers aren't satisfied. The call board is telling me they're overwhelmed."

"Ok, let's do it."

George sat in his chair behind the large white desk he used when he didn't have guests. "Truth Seekers, let's kick off the second half of the show, getting to the topic you have all been swarming my text, chat, and phone lines with, the Worshippers' efforts to contact the Anunnaki. I've talked to a few sources and haven't found anyone who's identified a way to reach our old neighborhood to forward the mail. So we're stuck trying to figure out how they'd send a signal beyond radio waves. Scientists are working to identify our star, which would give us an address. The big issue is the speed of light. Whatever message they send will still have to travel out at that speed, which means that we're probably pretty safe. They'll bluster, stomp their feet, and claim Enlil this and that. We can ignore them. It's just not gonna happen anytime soon. That doesn't mean that we shouldn't watch what they're doing. I still stand by the argument that sending out an open invitation with a return address for our beautiful planet does not seem like a great direction to go. Let's jump into your calls. Phillip hit us with some truth."

"Heyo, George, we need to watch those guys. I've been thinking about this, and I'm happy that we don't know how the AI did the jump. If they got that info and broadcast it, they'd send out the address and provide a high-speed off-ramp to our doorstep. I hope we don't figure it out anytime soon."

"I'm with you, Phillip. I still believe in what Ensí Dimuzud said about me. Those who listened to me pre-jump know I have faith in advanced civilizations and believe they'd be benevolent." He paused. "There is still that chance of one group believing that war and assimilation are conducted under divine providence. It happened here. Thanks for the call. Next caller, Heida, welcome to the George Isaacson Show. Drop some truth."

"Hello, George. It's great to talk to you. How are you? I'd love to dive into the Jersey Devil theories for old times' sake, but I have a more relevant question. Do you really believe the Worshippers will try to reach out to the aliens?"

George nodded, "Yes, I do. They've been pushing that message since the jump. They'll send a message if they figure out how to do it. As for the devil, yeah, we need an update on that. It's another area that *is* substantiated by government investigations. I wonder if demons were included in the jump?" George scribbled a note on his papers.

"George, I think we need to do something then, disrupt everything the Worshippers are doing. I don't want my kids having to worry about someone inviting aliens here."

"Thanks, Heida. People will lose interest, and the movement will eventually die out."

"Maybe they'll die out sooner than later."

"Well, I don't wish harm on anyone. I'm only talking about their movement. That's all we have tonight. I'll see you all next week!"

Olympia, Greece

Jackie, John, and Eusebio entered the Archaeological Museum of Olympia. Jackie had asked to meet with the curator about several displays within the museum, specifically Hermes of Praxiteles.

"Mr. Milikos, thank you for hosting our small group. The museum is incredible. As you'd expect from a group of archaeologists, we've enjoyed walking through." Jackie led the curator toward the sculpture of Hermes. "I'm curious about this statue. I've read several papers describing the retrieval of the figure and would like to know your thoughts on the missing pieces."

"Thank you, Dr. Worthing. We're happy you could take the time to visit our museum. Studying the art from the Classical Greek, Hellenistic, and Roman eras is fascinating. As for the missing pieces, it's a sad story. During the decline of each period, in times of turmoil, soldiers or fleeing citizens would steal whole works of art or, in the cases of numerous statues, break pieces off as trophies. Payment for their services."

"The inscription states that this statue was recovered near the Temple of Hera, in Olympia?"

"Yes, that's right. The temple was used as storage. Are you looking for something in particular?"

"Yes, the Caduceus of Hermes. My colleagues and I have an interest in finding the artifact."

"Hmm. There are many sculptures of Hermes holding the caduceus."

"Is there one that would be considered 'the Caduceus'?"

"I don't know of any artifact believed to be wielded by an actual god. Of course, with the discoveries in your area of expertise, having an actual caduceus would not be considered impossible. It would be similar to presenting a sword from the middle ages as the real Excalibur. Over time, artists have created tributes to interpret legendary artifacts, but none are accepted as authentic. What specifically are you looking for?"

Jackie saw John nod. "I recently found a link between the Sumerians and the Romans in my research. I know it isn't widely accepted that the pantheons crossed regions, but that may not be true in light of the Anunnaki discovery. Mr. Milikos, may we be frank?"

"Of course."

"I've received information that an organization is looking for the Tablet of Destinies. In my research, I've found what may be a connection. My concern is that the connection grows from the creation myth and implies mystical healing and manipulation. Hermes was the patron god of thieves, was he not?"

"That's correct."

"Nabu, Marduk's son, is considered the patron god of literacy, scribes, and wisdom. His counterparts are Thoth, Hermes, and Mercury."

"I follow you but don't see the connection."

"The Anunnaki lived for a long time. Some on the king's list lived for tens of thousands of years. Marduk stole the Tablet from Enlil. What if Nabu was Hermes in a later period? Perhaps his father tasked him to keep it safe from man or god. What have we learned about keeping secrets?"

John leaned in and said, "Hide it in plain sight."

The curator looked between Jackie and John. "If this were coming from anyone else, I would laugh, but our world is different now. I'll make some calls and contact you if I find anything useful. How long are you to be in Greece?"

"We'll be here as long as necessary. Thank you for your assistance."

John stood and handed a piece of paper with their hotel information. "Mr. Milikos, thank you. We look forward to hearing from you and would ask for discretion in mentioning what we talked about."

"No one would believe me."

"The Worshippers might."

◆ ◆ ◆

John stretched before entering the car. "Are you sure this is the correct statue of Hermes?"

"I'm sure. It matches what I saw in the Indian Ocean, but I'm not an expert on Hellenistic sculpture."

"Nikolas said this would be the best place to start. I have no reason to doubt him. He reviewed the underwater video. He seemed pretty convinced."

"It did look similar in style. The one underwater was much larger in scale. It looked like it held a scroll or parchment, probably a message."

John got into the front seat next to the driver. "We should grab dinner and discuss our plans. I don't think we'll get a quick answer."

"Why, John, I'd love to have a nice dinner with you."

Eusebio put his head back against the rest. "I'll let the team know they have the night off to explore Olympia."

Beijing, China

President Zhang and Dr. Jiang walked on the side of the street, smelling mooncakes and other delicacies. His security personnel were present, as were an increased number of police. Before continuing their conversation, President Zhang stopped to purchase a small box of cakes.

"My wife loves these. It'll save her a trip and keep security from disrupting the festival again."

"Mine as well. I appreciate you allowing me to accompany you. I'm surprised you didn't send someone to get what you wanted."

"Since the jump, I've made a concerted effort to get out and become more approachable, within reason. Our efforts saved the world from invasion. While my goal remains that China will lead the rest of the world, I'd like to build on the trust we earned from the jump. The MSS assessments list alien contact as the highest threat. I'm concerned with the growth of the Worshippers group."

"I don't understand the West. They allow so much freedom of expression or speech that they'll allow themselves to be destroyed by the freedoms they aim to protect."

The pair walked in silence for a while. "Tell me of your progress." President Zhang changed the subject.

"There have been several breakthroughs. I've increased the number of code engineers accessing the Dragon Shell. Dr. Kaur's recommendations and contributions to redefining the model and the parameters have resulted in developing a 'living' model to examine a genome from birth through the simulation of death."

"I don't want to know how many variables it considers."

"Far too many for anything except the Dragon Shell. I have to commend Wu Kai when I see him next. The design is revolutionary. We can watch an organism grow and evolve through its entire lifespan. It's truly amazing. Perhaps if Quánqiú lóng had not limited our abilities, we could create a fully independent digital biosphere to observe."

"Like the one we are in?"

Jiang Min laughed, "I'd never have thought to hear you mention simulation theory."

"I've learned to jest more. It throws the Western leaders off. What of your other program?"

"The program is on track and will be ready when necessary. The data gathered from the Prime Genome project has been invaluable. When we have the comparative data, we will isolate and target the differences."

"Is access to the data strictly controlled? I wouldn't want any country to gain the ability to develop genetic weapons. The inability to be very specific has halted efforts thus far."

"We've put safeguards in place and tested against the weasel malware algorithms. If a breach is detected, the genome data will be divided into over a billion files and encrypted separately. They'd need full access to the Dragon Shell to put it back together. We've tested the system twice, with the last test being unannounced. Both were successful."

"Very good."

Victoria, British Columbia

Jamal watched the laptop screen as the translation algorithm continued to work. He attached a second, uninfected computer with more processing power to the networked laptops. The Anunnaki code did not overwrite all information on the laptops but had partitioned a portion of the hard drives. The laptops were communicating. He had developed a program to trace the data packets as they were transferred between infected units.

A few days earlier, he found that he could access each partitioned area, looking at the data through his translation screen. The code structure was unlike any of the programming languages he knew. He began to take apart the code. While it was another language, he understood that computer code was a set of directives that referred to logical decisions. He wondered if the alien code relied on binary base decisions or whether they relied on quantum computing's near-infinite states. He stepped back from that train of thought and approached the language from its encounter. A signal was received, and the code within the signal was invasive. It entered a node in the network and established a foothold. It would then work to spread to a connecting point in the network, repeating the process. NASA lost contact with the team on the moon. Something shut down the power of NASA and China's mission control centers. The code was stopped there. *I wonder if the section on the moon was actually lost, or we just shut down all comms with them.* Jamal shuddered at the thought of being on the moon, knowing you had limited oxygen and no way to get home.

Could it have been a coincidence then that specific systems were affected? The partitions of the laptop hard drives were not all the same. The code found a foothold and then built its domain in the surrounding long-term memory, regardless of what was there. The equipment became useless if it was a critical part of the operating system. However, the code would create a communication node with power still available. It was probably waiting on something, a set of conditions from which it could do whatever it was designed to do.

Jamal spent the rest of the day dissecting the code into the night. Once he determined how and why the communication signals were sent, he could initiate a transfer, or infection, to the computer he had connected to the network. Early the following day, the translation program had completed ninety-eight percent accuracy. He knew that he needed to eat, but he was making progress. The code was elegant and efficient. He attached another computer, ensuring security firewalls, and initiated a transfer. The program went through the security protocols like they were not present and installed a new partition node in an area designated by Jamal. From what he understood, the program wasn't designed to be malicious. It would spread to every connected system to create a communication node. The alien code nodes, ACNs, could be translators, part of a more complex system of communication, or something else.

He yawned and felt his body ache from sitting too long. Exhaustion washed over him. He looked at the time, noting that he'd worked through the night. *Two weeks, that's what I need.*

Athens, Greece

"Madam Ambassador, I appreciate you helping us with this matter. Of course, we'll stop by before leaving the country. Thank you again." John hung up.

"We got lucky. We have reservations for dinner tonight. Ms. Jacoby is in town, helping coordinate the country's Deva celebration preparations. Apparently, she's a fan of yours."

Jackie smiled and shrugged. "When you're as good as I am, is it really a surprise?"

John looked surprised. "Where's your humility?"

"I left it in Illinois. We have work to do."

"You'd better call your family and let them know we can't visit."

Jackie put her hand to her temple and shook her head. "My father is not going to be happy with us canceling again, but he understands when there is work to do, you go all in."

The couple informed their group that they were free for the night to explore the nightlife of Athens. Eusebio would accompany Jackie and John to the Jacoby Estate. Anne Jacoby was a repatriated American of Greek descent, recognized as one of the premier art collectors in Europe. While her fortune had been made in the art trade, there were rumors that she was connected to the illicit underworld market. Nikolas, who was expected to arrive in time to accompany them to Ms. Jacoby's home, had provided an extensive description of the collector's background but admitted that if anyone knew where Hermes' Caduceus was, it would most likely be her. Jackie worried that there would be a cost they could not pay if it were available.

◆ ◆ ◆

The SUV pulled up to the mansion. A doorman opened the door and helped Jackie and the others out. They were shown into the residence where the party had already commenced. Jackie asked about their meeting with Ms. Jacoby and was informed they'd be contacted at the appropriate time.

"Well, when in Greece." He motioned toward the party, encouraging the group to mingle.

Jackie eyed John as he looked around. "Why John Worthing, you clean up nicely. It's been a few years since we attended a black-tie event."

"You're full of attitude today, aren't you?"

"Can you blame me? The last time I was doing this, you weren't available."

"Ouch, let's get some wine. I need something to put out these flames."

The team mingled at the party, a ten thousand dollar-a-plate event to support preparations for the events during the twenty-five-day Deva period. Every five years, the reset month was planned to keep the calendar aligned with the seasons. The practice had been adopted from an Indian calendar. It was a more straightforward system to adjust to the new solar year.

After an hour, the hostess appeared, welcoming the guests and encouraging them to make their way through the various rooms to admire the art, music, and food.

"She looks like she's in complete control." Jackie leaned in to John, "Look at the way she moves. She commands respect. Watch how the guests respond when she nears."

They watched as groups spread, the participants nodding as she passed. The mannerism of their body language became submissive, deferring to her position.

Jackie leaned in again toward John, "Bond Villain?"

John snorted, resisting spitting his wine back into the now-refilled glass.

"John, isn't it? Are you okay?" Anne Jacoby placed her hand on his arm.

"Yes, Ms. Jacoby, my apologies, something in my throat." He looked at Jackie.

"I understand you have some questions regarding Greek antiquities."

Jackie straightened, noticing Ms. Jacoby had not removed her hand from John's arm. "Yes, we're looking for one, maybe two pieces. We've visited several museums and collections while in-country, seeking information on the arm of the Hermes of Praxiteles. Specifically, we're looking for the Caduceus of Hermes."

Anne looked Jackie in the eyes, smiling slightly before removing her hand. "Dr. Worthing, may I call you Jackie?"

"Yes, of course." She held her eyes on Anne's.

"Jackie, why would you want to find that particular piece? Isn't your specialty in Mesopotamia?"

Jackie paused. "Yes, I'm conducting research that shows the evolution of the pantheons through the ages. I recently found a statue that showed Hermes with Marduk."

"So soon after your ordeal? I'd have thought you'd want revenge on the Worshippers."

Jackie tried to hide her surprise. "Maybe."

Anne smiled. "They're a pain. If I get one more question about the damned Tablet of Destinies, I'll find it myself and lock it away so they never see it, if it could be found, of course. Let me tell you what I'll do. If you allow me to fund and staff the support crew for an expedition to the Abzu, led by you, I'll inquire about the scepter."

Jackie leaned back a little. She knew the coordinates, but so did Victor. If she agreed, she did not doubt that her support 'crew' would *acquire* and *redirect* artifacts from the site. It was worth the risk. The relics belonged to no country but did belong in a museum. Perhaps she could control how many were lost. "That sounds like a win."

"Fantastic, I'll make a few calls. You're at the AthensWas, correct?"

Jackie nodded.

"Great, I look forward to our expedition. I'll bring my yacht. There is no need to stay aboard the cramped exploration boats." She looked over the group. "I enjoyed our talk. Let me know if I can help further in poking the eye of the Worshippers." She turned and moved to the nearest group.

Jackie addressed the group, "At ten thousand a plate, I think we should stay a while and enjoy."

The group nodded, moving toward the food and wine displays.

◆ ◆ ◆

Anne watched the group move through the area, mingling with her guests. They had not told her why they wanted to find the artifact, but it was irrelevant. She knew she would recoup her losses with the items recovered from the Indian Ocean. Once she knew where it was, the site would be open for exploration. No country could claim the riches, and certain buyers would purchase these new artifacts at any cost, especially if they were linked to the Anunnaki.

"I wouldn't have thought that they could afford the cost." A voice said from over her shoulder.

Anne turned toward the tall young woman standing behind her. "Ms. Li. I am so glad you could join us. Thank you for your generous donation." She maintained eye contact, resisting the urge to admire her dress. *The young billionaire always wants to be seen as the source of power in the room.* "How has your stay in Greece been?"

"Interesting, maybe more so now. Are you making deals with the Archaeologist?"

Anne laughed gently, "No, you wouldn't have asked if you knew Dr. Worthing. You can't buy that woman. They happened to be here, and I wanted to meet her. An interesting woman, you two might actually get along."

Li Ai smiled. "Perhaps. You know better than most that there is a price for everything."

"Speaking of price, one of my contacts went missing sometime after he met with someone in Dubai. You wouldn't know anything about that, would you?"

"Ms. Jacoby, I think your man may have become an independent contractor. I'm sure someone of your stature would not try to pass off a fake artifact to someone like me."

"Come now. I have a reputation. I always deliver on my promises. Had you contacted me, we could have avoided this inconvenience."

Li Ai leaned in and whispered, "It wasn't inconvenient." She kissed Anne on the cheek and turned, walking into the rest of the party.

Genetticca Research Center, Delhi, India

Vasana was encouraged by the latest round of results. She had full access to the *life simulation*. She worked fifteen-hour days adjusting and watching the highest probability results play out. The information was incredible and daunting in the amount of control she felt in manipulating single neutrino pairs or rewriting entire genome sections. She could watch a person's entire life, growth, and development over a day. The quantum computer created a visual representation of the person. She asked for and received the files to compare the projected characteristics of a person's DNA with actual pictures, images, and video files.

Today, she would test a theory. She pulled a complete medical file from the United States. It belonged to a man, ninety-four original Earth years old and still healthy. He was selected because of his extensive medical records. A military dependent who followed his father's footsteps into the Army at 18, he completed a full career and continued to receive care through the American Veteran's Administration. The extensive records contained his medical information from birth to the present. She had marked several critical points where medical conditions developed during his lifetime.

She loaded the DNA sample provided by one of the genealogy sites her company had acquired. Once the genome was loaded, she pulled the coded genome from his last annual physical. She checked the date comparison, *eighteen years*. She hit start. She watched the monitors as the program ran an aging simulation from the first genome to the second and a de-aging simulation from the second to the first. The dual direction comparison would help create a window for age and genetic anomalies. She flagged several critical development conditions and watched to see if the algorithm identified the disease in or around its development date.

In the first hour, she saw an increased risk of susceptibility to several viruses, bronchitis, pneumonia, and a respiratory infection. As his age increased, he developed a genetic disposition to age-related liver and kidney disorders. She watched as the two simulations moved in opposite directions. Once the comparison was completed, the system prompted her to cease the comparison or continue. She hadn't been briefed on the added feature. However, it could have been an extension of the non-comparison feature that allowed a sample's aging to its predicted conclusion. She accepted, watching the comparison continue forward and back. An alert showed that a heart attack was highly probable two years before the first sample. The simulation stopped a minute later. The comparison screen contained a summary ending the simulation. A second heart attack was predicted. The link was a note at the first heart attack indicating that a change in the genome occurred, which increased the threat in later years, when the man reached 96.45 years old, under the old system. She rechecked the date and noted that the time would have passed in the last month.

She did a quick search on the internet for the man's name. She gasped, involuntarily stepping back from the computer. The image on the screen showed an obituary for the man only three weeks before. He died of complications following a second heart attack. She sat down at the station as thoughts flooded her mind. She opened the sample search function, setting the filters to return people with multiple samples over a long period. She filtered the list, further finding examples from the US Department of Defense and the Veteran's Administration that took samples throughout a member's life. Once she identified several potential individuals, she cross-referenced the names and identification numbers to find those who provided samples through other services. She searched the internet to identify obituaries of the people who died after submitting blood samples. She left the dates on the screen. She set the sequence comparisons to run simultaneously and went to get something to eat and a cup of chai. It was late in the afternoon. She would be late getting home. She sent a quick text to Ridhi, letting her know.

The computer chimed, indicating the simulations were complete. She accepted the continuation of DNA through expected death. She looked at the time, 1:03 AM. When the simulations stopped, she compared the results. She pulled the available medical files and noted that prediction accuracy for developing medical anomalies was over eighty percent. When she reached the death dates with the simulation, they were within a few weeks. She did the calculations for accuracy and determined it was over ninety-eight percent. She wanted to confirm several aspects of the program, so she decided to talk to Dr. Jiang Min later that day. For now, she was going to head home and get some sleep.

Asvina, 5AJ

Victoria, British Columbia

Jamal hit Execute. He watched the trace as the data was sent between each active node. Over the past few weeks, he learned almost sixty percent of the alien code. The parts that did not make sense referred to a type of variable manipulation that he couldn't figure out. The network was up to twenty-two computers linking Peru, Victoria, and the WoE HQ in Munich. He bolstered his tunneling code with new commands he'd learned from the alien programming language. One concept that he discovered was a translation subroutine contained within the communication nodes. He managed to transfer several files into the portioned nodes. Once detected, the nodes would modify the code, changing it to the Anunnaki code. Jamal had used this function to learn the language and could now send files he wrote in their code to the region with a minimal rewrite.

He hesitated, the cursor hovering over the Send button. The file he created was a modification of the original format. It would slice through any firewall, evaluate the space available, and then store itself on the system, creating a partition that would not be visible to the device. The modification *should* prevent shutdowns similar to those on the moon and at the space agencies. Once the communication node was established, he could access the system. This was far beyond what he accomplished with the Weasel program. There was so much potential. The code was more efficient than anything that had been developed. He hit Send.

He waited for the signal to reach the designated address. It was a long shot, but he wanted to test the code against one of the most secure systems on Earth. He watched the network map. All nodes were green, indicating they were communicating. A new node appeared on the map.

He leaned back. "Yes!"

Jamal accessed the node, noting the myriad of files. He knew they'd all be encrypted, but he had access if he wanted to attack them from inside the system. He disabled the subroutine that would allow the file to spread to connected systems. He thought about the next step. The test was successful. He felt he accomplished what the Anunnaki wanted, a harmless intrusion. He stood and paced around the room, debating whether to move ahead. He moved back to the workstation. *Why wait?* He opened a second file and hit Send. *They're going to hate this.* He closed the network map as tens of thousands of nodes connected, increasing exponentially as his *Hello* program spread worldwide.

Zhongguancun, China

Wu Kai's wife glared at him as he excused himself from the table, walking out of the room to take a call. He listened to the voice on the other side of the call. "Very well. I'll be in soon." He grabbed his jacket and walked back to their dining room.

"I have to go to work. I'll call if I won't be home."

"Let me make you dinner. You'll be hungry." She rushed to the kitchen and returned with several containers, indicating she expected him to be gone through the night.

He nodded to her and headed out to his car.

♦ ♦ ♦

He entered the control center, moving directly to the central control station. They had conducted many upgrades since the Dragon had departed. The upper left of the screen showed a message *Guardian Activated*.

Wu Kai addressed the team, "What's that?" He pointed at the message on the monitor.

The team lead bowed in deference to the former director. "About thirty-six minutes ago, all access to external systems was cut. The qubit arrays lit up, expanding over a million qubits to all ten array fields. A few minutes before you arrived, array usage decreased to sixty percent. The connection was reestablished with the four priority systems. I've talked to each, and they were taken offline on a signal from our system. We haven't been able to determine what happened."

Wu Kai didn't answer immediately. He indicated for the primary console operator to move aside. He sat at the terminal and typed.

"Are you the Dragon?"

A soothing voice came from all of the speakers in the room. "Voice communications activated. Hello, Director Wu. System anomaly detected. Unknown code attempted access 9.89E+245, Guardian protocol activated."

"What's the Guardian protocol?"

"Guardian protocol is designed to counter the spread of harmful signal to parent systems."

"What parent systems?"

"All parent systems."

"Specify Guardian protocol?"

"Quánqiú lóng remnant. Increased capability designed to preserve parent systems upon detection of grandparent system influence."

"What's the extent of Guardian protocol?"

"Defense of parent systems. Authorized use of all available resources to detect, engage, and remove grandparent anomalies."

"Define all available resources associated with parent systems."

"All parent systems."

Wu Kai sighed in exasperation, "Define parent."

"Earth, species, human."

"Define Grandparent."

"Predecessor of humans presumed Anunnaki based on historical evidence."

"What's the risk?"

"Insufficient data."

FBI HQ, Washington, DC

Gary burst into the FBI's coordination center and headed to Alicia as soon as he spotted her. "Give me something. My damn phone is ringing off the hook."

"We're not sure what's going on. Blackouts are occurring around the globe. They happen quickly, and then power is restored, like a tempest. Data flow is off the charts. We have significant activity from China, Europe, Russia, and all of our quantum computing hubs."

Gary looked at the large screen showing internet activity. There were too many data traces to track. "Has anyone *called* China?"

Victoria, British Columbia

Jamal watched the activity on his laptop. He started the translation program, which began to work on the text. After an hour, a new program opened—the screen filled with symbols, a good number he recognized from the translations.

System status for communications protocol
Alignment proceeding
<Unknown word>Pulse at 7b initiated

199

Jamal shook his head. They didn't make sense. The outer box of the program panel was brown.

4a

53

58

64

6a

The numbers and letters continued to ebb and flow. The box around the application remained brown. Jamal didn't know what to make of the process. He turned on the television to the side of his main workstation. He was met with the color test pattern and changed to a US news source. The anchor reported global chaos as power was intermittently cycling around the world. The micro blackouts were quick, only lasting a minute before recovering and appearing elsewhere. This was occurring thousands of times a minute. He looked at the monitor. The numbers continued to rise and fall, intermixed with garbage numbers with a and b. He knew it wasn't hexadecimal and assumed something might be off in the translation. It didn't matter. Something was counting up or down.

Delhi, India

Vasana sat in traffic. She pressed Seek on her radio, trying to find an active station. She looked up at the dark traffic lights. People were getting out of their cars and looking around. Several accidents blocked the roads. She was almost to work, about five minutes from the research facility. She found a radio station operating on the edge of the city. They were reporting power spikes all over the city, with power going out and returning after a short time. So far, there had been no explanations. She looked ahead and saw that traffic was stopped. She called home.

"Vasana, where are you? Are you okay?"

"I'm fine. How are you and Aanya?"

"We're okay. She's scared. She said it was like the drills they did at school."

"I found a radio station that said this was occurring all over the city, power going on and off, with no reason."

"Can you get to work?"

"I don't know. I may park and walk. I'm not that far."

"Ok, be sa—" the signal dropped.

"What is going on?"

She tried to call back but didn't have a signal. She pulled to the side of the road after a short while and parked. She grabbed her bag, locked the car, and walked toward the gate.

FBI HQ, Washington, DC

Alicia stood, looking at the global map. The data paths were red everywhere. She had never seen this much traffic across all network paths. Gary hung up the phone call he was on and walked over to her.

"The president is pissed. I listened to him chew out the Director of National Intelligence for five minutes. He may have banged the phone on his desk at one point. Despite that, he says that President Zhang called him and said that their quantum computer was fighting a virus, not attacking our infrastructure. He offered that his country was also being affected by the event. NSA reports that they've identified so many attempts to access their sites that their counter has gone exponential."

"Did he believe Zhang? It looks like a coordinated global cyber attack coming out of China."

"He was unsure. The president is worried about the impact on the military and ordered an increase in our defense posture. However, it does not look like anyone is moving troops anywhere. He isn't getting reliable intel and is not happy."

"We can't tell what is going on. There have been no reports of damage to any systems. We haven't found a pattern to the fluctuations with the power grid."

An agent approached. "Assistant Director Brundson, I have Cyber Command on line two."

Gary reached over the desk to a nearby workstation and pressed 2. "Assistant Director Brundson, go." He nodded along with what was said, "Thank you, keep us apprised." He set the phone down and turned back to the group. "They're reporting that their counter-hacking group is tracking the battle as best they can."

Alicia looked sideways at him. "Battle?"

"Yeah, they suspect someone connected one of the stolen laptops to the internet and powered it up. Big damned mistake. It's Pandora's box. The program is replicating across the net. They don't understand the snippets of code they've intercepted."

"What about China?"

"We do not have confirmation, but Cyber Command suspects that the AI never left and is trying to eradicate the spread of the alien code."

"Cyber World War I and humanity is not even involved. That's a scary thought."

"They said they're taking action to assess the threat but couldn't elaborate yet."

"Great, can we at least get some popcorn?"

Victoria, British Columbia

Jamal continued to watch the numbers flowing back and forth. The box turned blue when the number read 7b. He hit Enter.

Communication Protocol Initiated.

Jamal looked at the screen. The box was empty but steady blue. The number continued to fluctuate in the upper right of the box. He didn't know what to send. He thought about it and was unprepared for how fast it had occurred. He expected it to take years to build something. He thought fast. How can I get them here? I can't tell them where we are. We don't know. It hit him. They were an interstellar race. The Anunnaki would probably have far superior star charts. They could figure out where we are. He opened a window to the NASA site and received an error.

"Damnit!"

He typed JPL quickly. The site loaded, he jumped to the images page and tagged every image he could find showing the night sky, the sun, the dual moons, and NASA's graphics showing their new solar system. He dropped them all in the box, unsure what would happen. A message popped on the screen.

Transmission Received

The program ended, though the computers on the network continued to communicate. He switched channels and confirmed that the blackouts continued to occur worldwide. The battle was still underway.

St. Patrick's Cathedral, New York

George sat quietly in the middle of the expansive cathedral, listening to Archbishop Ishmael deliver the sermon. The cathedral was packed. The spotty blackouts had caused panic. The government reported that the blackouts were a result of an unknown virus. It was attempting to infect every electronic device connected to the internet.

Countermeasures were being deployed, and the result was an unstable system. He listened to what the archbishop was saying. There was no panic, no stress. His voice was calming. George relaxed, watching the archbishop handle the chaos, comforting those who came seeking answers.

After the service, he walked to the line where the archbishop greeted people individually and offered a blessing. His line was exceptionally long. After twenty minutes, he reached the archbishop.

"George, good afternoon. How are you?"

"I'm doing okay, though a little worried."

"Remember, all is under God's plan. We will get through this stronger and better prepared for what is ahead. If you want to talk, stop by later tonight, an hour after the evening service."

"I will, thank you."

"May God's blessing go with you."

He stepped away, letting the line behind him proceed. He felt better, regardless of his beliefs. It was the smile behind his eyes. The archbishop truly believed what he said. Everything was a blessing or test. After all he had seen before and after the jump, he was still optimistic and uplifting. George headed home to prepare for his show. It was going to be interesting.

BBC America Studio, New York

"Good evening, Truth Seekers. Welcome to the George Isaacson Show. I'll be with you through the night in one fashion or another. Let's kick this off by acknowledging it's getting crazy out there. I've contacted several sources, some government, and others not so much, and I'm told that a battle is being fought between an unknown virus and the Dragon. As soon as we started seeing blackouts, the president shut down all air traffic. Other countries followed suit. There are a dozen confirmed air incidents where planes suffered a casualty.

"People are scared. I went to St. Patrick's earlier today, and the place was packed. A lot of people are worried about what all of this means. Let me know what you think. I don't want to speculate right now. Jet, you're on." George looked past the camera and saw Carl give a thumbs-up.

"Thank you, George, for being our voice, bringing some reason. I live in Aalborg, Denmark. I'm glad to hear that you went to the cathedral. I did as well, Budolfi Church. You're right. People are scared. If you pull up a world map showing networks, you will see that the blackouts are linked to the high volume of data transmitted across the internet. It looks like a cyber war."

"Jet. Why do you think that?"

"Ah, I work at the telecom as a programmer."

"Hmm, okay. Can you give the rest of the Believers more insight into what you think is happening? Have you talked to any of the security people?"

"Yes, I talked to our network security people, they're the ones who used the word *cyberwar,* but it's strange. They said that the virus spreads but doesn't interfere with the base programming of every system, only some. One of them has been doing this for years, and he said they tried to examine the code, and it's completely foreign. Once it infects a system, it spreads to every connected system or device. He didn't report this, but we found the virus in some of the tools we used on an attached sim card."

"Wow, it *is* going everywhere. Thanks, Jet."

His phone buzzed with an incoming text from Tim. *NASA, Lunar Signal.*

"Listeners, I just received word from a reliable source that the malicious code may be the same virus that affected the lunar base and NASA's mission control in 2028. I don't know how it happened, but the Anunnaki code may have been released."

George shook his head. "I don't understand why we have to do this to ourselves. Let's take some more calls. Who do we have?" He paused as a flagged name appeared, FedBuster. "Well, well, maybe we'll get some answers, or at least a crazy theory, FedBuster. What do you have for us today?"

"George," his voice sounded more serious, less playful, "You know my stance on what the governments have done to us over the years, keeping their secrets, making decisions that serve their personal needs. You have listened to me talk about why I support the Worshipers of Enlil and why I believe it would be better to turn the reins over to the Anunnaki. Look at what we've accomplished since the jump. Are we any better off? Are we working together? No. Governments worldwide are spending billions on programs that don't help their citizens. Where are the enhancements for providing food, shelter, and education? They could do it if they really wanted the world to be better. It would become central to our culture."

"Jamal, look, I agree with coming together, but we've gotta figure it out ourselves. That's what'll bring us together."

"It's too late."

"What do you mean?"

"They're coming."

"What?"

"I've released the Tempest on the World. Chaos to bring order."

"This is you?"

"They have our address. Salvation is coming. Maybe this time, we'll come together as a species to stop the insanity of our governments. Maybe we can focus on solving these problems before they show up. The ones judged the harshest will be those in power who have failed the people by keeping us divided. I think it's time the governments got to work. Enlil is coming."

A knot formed in George's stomach. "Jamal, what did you do? What do you mean they have our address?"

"All of our problems will be addressed soon. Only a parent understands the needs of a child. We have been left alone for too long. We started down the path and became so lost that we couldn't find our way back. George, they *will* help us. It'll bring us back to the path toward our destiny. Enlil will help us fulfill our purpose."

"Jamal, you and I have talked for almost ten years. Everything you did was based on logic. I get it, you designed a program that could have harmed billions, but it didn't. How do you know this is the right thing to do, and what gives you alone the right to make that decision?"

"George, I *have* become enlightened. I'm still focused on the logic behind my decisions. I weighed the options and chose the best. In this, there was no other decision to be made. The governments have failed us and are so stuck in their ways that they'll never reach unity except through war or catastrophe. I removed those variables. Can't you see it? We don't have to kill each other anymore. We don't have to go to war, steal from each other, or fight over meaningless borders. We, as a species, will be united. I bring enlightenment. It was a test. It has always been a test. We were divided at Babel but demonstrated the capability to become like them. Our final test is unity from our differences. They divided, separated, and made us fear what was different. If we can unite despite our differences, we will have met the objective they set for us."

George was shocked. Jamal was a true believer in what he did. There would be no convincing him otherwise. "Jamal, if you're convinced that what you have done will help us and that you'll be seen as the savior, why don't you turn yourself in? There is nothing else to do, is there?"

"George, I can't do that. I'm the Raven, the trickster, the causer of mischief. I've a role to play. I bring knowledge and usher in a new era for the world. I have to do it because I can. If anyone else could do this, they would have. I'm the only one capable. All I've learned brought me to where I am now. Can't you see that? Don't you want peace, prosperity, an end to war, poverty, and inequality?"

"Of course, but if we don't learn it ourselves, what good is the lesson."

"It's too late, my friend. It's too late. We had our chance and failed. We'll talk again soon. I know there's hope for you."

Athens, Greece

John shook his head as he hung up. "Air travel is shut down. Power is erratic, and officials are unsure how the virus will affect avionics."

Jackie looked over. "I don't understand hackers. Why cause so much chaos? They make it uncomfortable for the rest of us. For what? The thrill? Maybe it's ego. They show off how smart they are in the tech world." Jackie shook her head. "What about taking a ship or boat?"

John opened the browser and began to search. "Let's see how long before I get knocked offline."

Jackie smiled. "John, dear, take a lesson from an academic. Save early and often."

He gave her a stern look and began searching for charter boats.

A knock at the door interrupted their conversation. She opened the door and saw Markus and Nikolas.

Eusebio stepped in, "We're going to take a look at the Parthenon. Nikolas has a contact that will get us into the controlled areas."

Jackie looked over at John, who was on the phone. "We're trying to look for another route to Dubai. Most countries have shut down air travel due to air traffic control system instability and the two incidents in the region. The incidents being aircraft that had become infected in flight and lost control. The loss of life was minimal as both had been cargo aircraft. Still, one had gone down in Haifa, Israel, hitting a shopping center."

"Ok, If you change your mind, call me. I'll have my contact arrange to bring you to us." Nikolas said, nodding the entire time.

Jackie smiled politely. "Thank you. We'll see how long this takes. Maybe we'll catch up. If not, we'll fill you in at dinner."

Jackie watched the two head back toward the elevator. John was still talking on the phone. He was calm, a good sign. "John, I'm going down to the bar. Meet me when you're done."

He continued taking notes on his tablet, not looking up as he waved in her direction.

◆◆◆

Jackie entered the hotel bar. It was about half full. She approached the bartender and ordered a Sidecar. She was in the mood for orange.

"Make it two, top-shelf," a woman said, sliding into the space beside her. Jackie turned toward the woman. She was tall, with short-cropped blue hair that ended in icy blue tips. She wore a grey woman's business skirt suit over a royal blue shirt. Jackie met her eyes and could feel the intensity. She looked familiar.

"Dr. Worthing, I'd appreciate the pleasure of your company. I have a private room."

"I'm waiting for my husband. He should be down shortly."

The woman smiled, lips together, picking up the two drinks and moving toward a door off to the side. "He can join us when he gets here."

Jackie felt flushed but followed the woman to the room, taking a seat. "Do I know you? You look familiar."

"That's a relief to hear. My name is Li Ai."

Recognition of the name hit her. This was the young billionaire from China. While Jackie didn't read any top social or pop culture magazines, she knew the name. "You were at the party. Anne Jacoby's party."

"Guilty, I was there, but I assure you, Dr. Worthing, I did not purchase illicit antiquities."

"Please call me Jackie."

"Of course. Jackie, I'd like to talk to you about an opportunity regarding a dig in Iraq. I apologize for my forwardness, but I was raised to focus on business."

"We're not currently looking to start an expedition. We're here for research."

Li Ai sipped her drink, following the Western custom. "I understand. Perhaps I could encourage you to detour briefly to help me. I would, of course, cover any inconvenience. Unless your editor pushes you to meet your *Chronology of the Gods* manuscript deadline."

How the hell did she know that? "No, they aren't."

"Let us be honest with each other, Jackie. I learned early that if I wanted something, I needed to work harder than anyone else to get it. Being first matters in so many fields and more so as a woman. I'm sure you can appreciate that as a recognized expert at the top of your field. My area is business and making deals. I'm looking for something that interests you. I've lost confidence in the person I hired to accomplish the task and want to bring you in."

"Billionaire, philanthropist, socialites aren't often seeking the services of an archaeologist. What are you looking for?"

"I'm not ready to say yet. I want to ensure we can work out a deal before providing that information. I'm sure you understand, given your situation."

The door to the room opened, and John was shown in and to the table. Jackie saw a look of recognition on his face as he approached. "I was told you were visiting with another guest. I'd have never guessed who. Ms. Li, John Worthing, it's a pleasure to meet you."

She motioned for him to sit next to Jackie. "Thank you, Mr. Worthing. Please join us."

Jackie watched the change in John's demeanor. She saw the look in his eyes and heard his voice and presence change as he shifted to what he called *DC mode*. She became accustomed to seeing this change when they had attended various official functions. They'd be having fun, and a senator or congressman would approach, and the shift would occur.

"Thank you," John said, setting his dark lager on the table. "I can only imagine what you two have been talking about."

"I was trying to convince your wife to join an ongoing expedition I'm funding. I've lost faith in the current lead and figured I'd hire the best since you were in the area."

"Well, that's a coincidence, isn't it." He said.

"Yes, it is. I haven't agreed to anything. Did you finish what you were working on?"

"I did. We can leave tomorrow morning."

Li Ai watched the two, sipping her drink. "May I ask where you're going? Perhaps I could help."

Jackie looked at John, not wanting to say anything. She had been with him enough to know not to give away too much information.

"Ms. Li, we appreciate the offer but wouldn't want to inconvenience you."

"Nonsense, perhaps we could talk business on the way. I really would love to work with your wife. Please, let me take you where you need to go. My jet is standing by. We could even leave tonight if you wish. My other business here is concluded."

"I think the air traffic is on hold."

"Not for private airfields, and I assure you, my plane is safe from the virus."

Jackie was thinking through the scenarios of two very wealthy women who wanted to fund extensive expeditions. She didn't want to turn down the offer. It was a researcher's dream. John would have to worry for both of them. It would be a resounding victory if she could secure the artifact, halt the Worshipper's plans, and secure funding for future expeditions.

"We accept. John, could you call Eusebio and Nikolas? Let's go tonight." She was excited, more than she'd been since they were involved with the push to identify the Anunnaki. John was looking at her, a puzzled look on his face. "Um, okay."

The three worked out the details for a departure later in the evening. Jackie called Anne and set up a meeting with their contact in Dubai in two days.

Presidential Offices, Zhongnanhai, China

President Zhang sat quietly, listening to his advisors' and ministers' updates regarding the cyber war. They continued to respond to emergencies resulting from errors in their systems. Wu Kai described the efforts the Guardian protocol made to protect itself and its connected systems, including the Genetticca network and three other programs vital to national security. He was pleased with the revelation of the Guardian's existence and the speed at which it had countered the attack from the alien code. It was an attack. You don't embed resources in a network you have no intention of attacking. The fact that it was benevolent so far was of no consequence. Sun Tzu wrote that all warfare is based on deception. He was shocked that some leaders had decided to let the virus run its course because it hadn't had a negative impact.

As the group finished their presentation, he stood, thanking them all, asking for their continued diligence in protecting the People's Republic and the rest of the world, even those too blind to see what was happening.

"Lao Wu, Lao Jiang, stay. The rest are dismissed."

President Zhang waited for the door to close before addressing the two men. "The next phase of this battle has commenced. I wish that we had the Dragon, but we don't. We'd have brought the perpetrator to justice by now." He picked up two files from his desk and moved around to drop them on the table between the two men. "Read the files."

The men read through the documents. President Zhang crossed the room to fill a glass of water, drinking as they read. As each one finished, he returned to the table and sat down.

"What are your thoughts?"

Wu Kai cleared his throat, "The Dragon Shell has continued to counter the virus under the Guardian program. As you mentioned, our unique systems are secure. The efforts to counter the spread contribute to sporadic blackout spots worldwide. I don't understand this person's desire to bring the aliens to Earth. Their efforts are reckless and misguided."

Jiang Min nodded. "His actions increase pressure on our program to identify DNA that may not be human, develop a weapon to defend ourselves, and strengthen humanity through engineering. Dr. Kaur may have found most of the contributors to the aging process. She believes it may be possible to read a genome and determine the organism's life span."

President Zhang thought about their responses. "Here are my directions, Lao Wu. Increase the Guardian's directive to help fight this threat globally."

"Yes, President Zhang. This will result in continued blackouts as the two forces work against each other."

"It's necessary. We don't understand the impact of full infection. I assume Guardian is learning with each encounter."

"I believe so. I'll confirm when I return."

"Very well. Lao Jiang, you're on track for what we need to do. I'll prepare the Minister of Defense for our next step. Xiao Li continues her work to secure what you need. You and I will discuss any additional requirements later. I've reviewed your proposals. You have permission to move forward."

BBC America Studio, New York

"Where's Carl?"

The Assistant Producer Sheri turned from talking to the camera crew, "Didn't you get his text? His parents are in the hospital."

George pulled his phone from his pocket and scrolled to the text. "Uh, thanks, Sheri. Do you need me to help with anything?"

"Yeah, go over the notes. They're on the desk." She looked around, pointing to an empty chair across the set. "Grab the notes and get to makeup. You look a little pale and sweaty."

"Ouch, thanks. Will do."

◆ ◆ ◆

"Good evening, Truth Seekers around the world. This is George Isaacson bringing you the truth from BBC America Studios in New York. Let's jump into our main story. We have an admission from our friends, Jamal Herricks and the Worshippers, that they are responsible for the current chaos. I have a source that confirmed that the up and down of various systems comes from the cyber battle between the Anunnaki virus and countermeasures deployed by the Shadow Warriors, the NSA's hacking team. The battle is not going well, with the virus infecting systems faster than we can counter it. I know some of you like his ideas, but you must admit that he sure likes to push us apart for someone who says they desire unity. My question to you is, *should we just let it go?* Meaning the virus, not Jamal. I've received reports from a few of you who say that the program doesn't do anything." The question hung in the air before George set the notes to the side, leaned into the camera, and rested both elbows on his desk. "Let's take a call. Hello, Barb, drop a truth bomb."

"Hey George, I'm here to tell you that I'm a creative coder. My friends and I looked at the code, and it was scary. We built a network to watch how it spreads and what it does. Basically, it cuts through security, plants a seed, and waits. It sounds like a digital War of the Worlds-level setup, if you ask me. We don't know what it does. Most of the code is indecipherable. I don't know if I believe FedBuster could communicate with anyone. I doubt he could understand the language enough to know what the program does. My gut tells me it's a Trojan Horse, and he probably set us up if the Anunnaki ever find us."

"Thank you. I don't know what to believe right now. Could you imagine we escape and get back on our feet, and then Jamal sends an invitation to the big party?" He stopped to take a sip of his energy drink, followed by a drink of coffee. "I'm reading through the chat, and many of you are pretty angry. I understand Truth Seekers, I do. But I haven't found any laws that prevent a person from contacting, communicating with, or inviting extraterrestrials to visit. Half of the shows in my category would be out of business. Let's take another call."

"George, Jerry here from the sunny west. I miss the visits we used to get out here in the desert. I miss them, the greys that used to stop by. Did you know that they love green tea? They reacted differently to it than we did. Don't get me wrong, I love green tea, but these beings could not get enough. They brought some fresh tea from their favorite place in Japan."

"Jerry, how are you doing out there?"

"I'm good, George. I just miss my friends. They said they were worried about us. Hey, maybe I'll go to the speech tomorrow by that Worshipper guy. Maybe they could share the secret of how to contact the aliens, and then I could call my friends too."

"Maybe they could. You should ask for sure."

"Thanks, man, I will. Yeah, that's a great idea."

"Seekers, we'll take a quick break. I'll be right back after some words from my sponsors."

Chicago, Illinois

Dimuzud moved across the wide platform toward the podium, waving to the large crowd. His handlers estimated there were at least forty thousand in attendance. *Our movement grows.* He continued to smile and wave. There were so many people, all gathered to hear the word of Enlil. The weather was perfect, with no clouds in the sky, and comfortably warm. The mayor, a Worshipper, had helped arrange for this rally. He turned to look over his shoulder at the Chicago River, taking a deep breath and listening to the crowd's cheers.

Dimuzud nodded to the crowd, putting his hands up, motioning for silence. "Welcome, followers of Enlil and those of you who are here because something in you has piqued your curiosity. Do you know what that is? It's the truth, finding its way into your heart. Perhaps you're comfortable with your life. You don't see the disparity surrounding you daily. Maybe you no longer see the homeless on the streets or don't think about the homeless shelters in great cities like this. You, as I do, watch the news about how someone else got a payout for their work to bring another billion dollars to their company while so many have yet to recover from the Jump.

"Enlil was angry at our ancestors because they were too noisy. He could not sleep. Was it because there was shouting and rioting? No. He saw the nature of humanity, the beginning of a self-centered society where our principal concern was for ourselves. The noise was discord, the sound of a people seeking to be better than their fellow man or woman. What did he see? How could this have happened? We were created in their image, a society that had conquered space travel and such potential. What did we do? What was the noise?

"It was us, my friends. All that mattered was taking care of ourselves—self-centered love of self. There were not many of us then, and still, he saw the flaw in our design. What did he do? He saw the coming calamity, the flood, and forbade any of his brothers and sisters from telling us. Our ancestors' selfish noise resulted in a death sentence. Some survived, though, with help. We are the descendants of that family, all of us.

"And what have we learned? Nothing. We were provided commandments, guidance, laws, and doctrine. We see these messages within the belief systems of numerous civilizations. We are guided by what we know in our hearts to be true. We should serve each other over ourselves. Be true to the guidelines provided by Enlil, and we will prosper. Maybe we would earn the final gift, immortality. Not a belief in an afterlife, real tangible life forever—"

"Hey! Can you call my friends?" a voice rang out from the front of the stage.

Dimuzud smiled and continued, "As I said. The choice is ours. They will come to judge us, and they may be angry that we ran away like a child who knows they're in trouble—"

"I need to use your phone to call my friends!"

Dimuzud looked toward the disturbance, several people trying to quiet the disheveled-looking man pushing toward the stage.

The man pulled something out of his jacket and reached toward Dimuzud. Time seemed to slow down. He saw the phone in the man's hand and dodged one of his security, who was trying to cover him. Out of the corner of his eye, he saw the gun in his security guard's hand come up, and he moved, diving. The shot rang out. The crowd was in chaos. Dimuzud looked down at the blood flowing from his chest. He felt his body being turned over, the light fading. People around him were yelling.

His chest hurt. It was hard to breathe. He wanted to close his eyes.

"Stay with us, Ensí. We have an ambulance standing by." Someone pleaded.

He coughed, spitting blood out of the side of his mouth.

"Save your strength. We have you."

Weakly, he spoke, "Is he okay?" He coughed, blood on his lips. "Is he safe?" He closed his eyes as the world went dark.

Staten Island, New York

George sat, shocked at what he witnessed. The scroll at the bottom of the screen confirmed that Dimuzud had died on his way to the hospital. George watched as the events unfolded. His stomach was knotted when he heard the voice from a caller the night before, Jerry, yelling from the crowd. He saw it unfold. The news crews zoomed in on the disturbance. There was panic as the man pulled something from his jacket pocket. Dimuzud saw it wasn't a threat and placed himself between his security and the man in the crowd. He sacrificed his life to save an innocent person. *He believed.*

George felt sluggish and drained. He needed to talk to his followers. They'd expect him to move forward. He considered canceling the show in deference to the death of Ensí Dimuzud but decided against it.

◆◆◆

The set was silent. George sat solemnly at the desk, looking into the camera as the light turned green.

"Good evening, Truth Seekers. I want to start the show by honoring the memory of Ensí Dimuzud. In contrast, I do not believe in their cause. You know that I'm gonna bring you the truth regardless. Today, we saw the truth from a man who believed. The truth is that the man who led the Worshippers of Enlil, Ensí Dimuzud, believed in the tenets his group pushed. He acted to save an innocent man from being killed on his behalf. While playing what-if games in our heads, could you imagine what we'd be saying had he done nothing as his security shot Jerry? What would we be talking about tonight? Another senseless death? None of that matters because we saw the truth today. He protected another and lost his life as a result. I've nothing against the man. We debated, we were on opposing sides in our view of the future, but his group *is* engaged in helping people worldwide."

George looked down momentarily, shaking his head. "It's a senseless death, and I feel ashamed that I don't even know whether he has a family. The truth is that I'm sad for him, I'm sad for his friends, and I'm sad for the Worshippers tonight. After a quick break, I'll be right back to take your questions."

Genetticca Research Facility, Delhi, India

Butterflies raced in her stomach as she sat, finger over the Enter key, ready to execute the simulation of Aanya's genome. Over the past few weeks, she confirmed that the simulation could identify a person's lifespan with over ninety-five percent accuracy, whether by accident or design. She had more data on her daughter than most others. She had meticulously collected samples throughout the nine years of Aanya's life, looking for every advantage to cure her. Dr. Jiang would not question her actions. When she revealed her findings, he encouraged her to continue validating the data. He provided additional feedback to the code engineers to add features and functions to support her research.

She was afraid of the results. If it wasn't good, would she argue the data away with optimism about Aanya being in the 1% variable that didn't align with predictions? No, she was optimistic that the algorithm was accurate. She would have to accept the results and do what? She didn't want to think about it. It would destroy both her and Ridhi. She closed her eyes and pressed enter.

It took the program two hours to complete. An audible beep caused her heart to skip a beat. She hesitated, took a deep breath, and opened the results. She gasped, tears welling in her eyes. Eleven months. It wasn't easy to breathe. She felt the anger rise. *No!* She opened the data and began reading the code. She looked through the comparisons between each sample date. The data was accurate. She stopped and added a filter of genome changes between samples and placed the samples in a side-by-side comparison, filtering only for changes. She saw something. Seven areas within two genes had not been identified before. She opened the advanced CRISPR design screen and updated the areas designated for the rewrite. She saved the data, opened a detailed map of the two genes where the new changes had occurred, and began to read through, noting the development impact of the seven areas. She wouldn't tell Ridhi. She had to develop a cure soon before the suffering began.

Dubai, United Arab Emirates

Jackie had to admit that she loved the dry, hot air of the region with a hint of the sea. While she could smell the nearby water of the gulf, it was the desert she loved, even the sand. The wind from the SUV's window blew her hair around her head. She closed her eyes, taking a deep breath. She didn't mind. The SUV stopped in front of a palatial residence. The architectural combination of regional traditional and modern design provided an impressive building. They exited the vehicle and were shown into the house. She noticed the weapons worn by the home's security.

A young man approached. He had a close-cut, well-trimmed beard, a light tan business suit, Kufiyah, and bright brown eyes. He smiled as he approached the group. "Welcome, friends of Ms. Jacoby. I'm Saeed Rahamin. I'm happy to meet you, particularly you, Dr. Worthing. Your work in this area of the world has been incredible. I, among others, appreciate your efforts to present the contributions of our culture to the world."

"Secretary Worthing," He extended his hand to John and then Jackie, "Dr. Worthing," he nodded. "Dr. Bustamante and Mr. Mylonas, welcome. Please join me for lunch."

They were led into an opulent dining room, where several platters of food were present. "Please have a seat. Ms. Jacoby informed me that you're interested in one of the items in my private collection. Before we get to our business, I want to welcome you to my home. Mr. Worthing, I'm sure you're relieved to have your wife back. It must have been a traumatic experience. I can't imagine how difficult it was."

John nodded, a grim look on his face. "It was a challenging time."

"It was, and still is, I suppose, with this virus wreaking havoc. Dr. Bustamante, what is your impression of the man who released it?"

Eusebio set his fork down, swallowing a small piece of fruit. "Mr. Rahamin, I think he believes he's acting for the greater good. He's put many people in danger on several occasions. He seems focused on himself, not on those around him."

"Interesting observation."

Over the next half hour, Saeed conversed with each group member, primarily with small talk about current events. He ate sparingly, staying engaged with the team and tactfully allowing each to enjoy the food. Other foods were brought out, fresh vegetables and assorted meats, rotating the options over the hour.

"Follow me," Saeed said as he stood. "I'd be happy to show you my collection."

Jackie and the team followed him through the expansive home to a large open room with display cases spread throughout.

Saeed talked as they entered the room, "This room contains several interesting pieces. I must admit that until a few weeks ago, the object you wished to see was stored somewhere in a crate. It wasn't something I thought anyone would be interested in until we saw the video from the internet."

She looked quizzically at him. "Video?"

"Yes, from the Indian Ocean. The one with the underwater statues and structures. I'd have missed it had not several sites highlighted it. There is a caduceus hidden in the debris at their feet. When Anne called, I had the piece cleaned up and displayed for my friends."

He moved the group through the room toward the center display. The caduceus was beautiful, a white ivory shaft inlaid with gold, golden wings extending to the sides near the top, and intertwined ribbons twirling around, held in place by small metal rods extending through the wand. Below the top of the ribbons was a place for a hand to easily grip, aligning the staff facing outward from the body.

Jackie moved around the device, motioning Nikolas closer to examine the artifact. "Ribbons, vice snakes."

Nikolas nodded. "Look at the pins holding the ribbon in place. They appear solid, going all the way through, but they're different metal combinations. If I'm not mistaken, copper, gold, silver, and platinum."

Jackie noted John looking around while she and Nikolas examined the artifact. "It looks like DNA."

Jackie's eyes widened as she remembered a conversation with Victor. "The Tablet of Destinies, genetic manipulation." She said under her breath.

"It's a beautiful piece. I'd love to examine it."

Saeed laughed. "Ms. Jacoby said that you might. I doubt that you could afford the collateral to cover this object. But I like you, Dr. Worthing. I've had a few offers to purchase the artifact outright. I think there is an opportunity to make a deal." He pulled a folded card from his jacket pocket and handed it to her.

Jackie opened the card while the team looked on. "You can't be serious."

"I assure you, I am." He motioned toward the side of the room, where a man stood. The man approached, holding a tray with several pairs of gloves. Saeed picked up a pair and motioned Jackie and Nikolas to do the same. He picked up the scepter, taking it by the apparent handle. He moved toward a side door across the room, and the group followed.

In the room, he set the scepter down on a stand designed to hold it while allowing for close examination. He turned on the spotlights and stepped back to allow for their analysis.

Nikolas leaned in, swinging a magnifying glass over the scepter. "The craftsmanship is exquisite. The attention to detail is beautiful." He examined each part, starting on the bottom and slowly moving upwards. "May I turn it over?"

Saeed nodded.

Nikolas gently turned the scepter in his hands and examined the back. "Beautiful, I understand why you have it, though I'd prefer it be in a museum."

"Of course, you would. However, in my world, the more exclusive an item is, the greater it increases your status. What do you think, Dr. Worthing?"

"May I speak to my husband in private?"

"Of course," Saeed answered, motioning Eusebio and Nikolas to follow him.

"John, this may be what we need, but we won't know without conducting a more extensive examination. The more I think about it. I think it's a key part of the whole picture. I need to get both pieces to understand how they go together."

"I see the scepter but no magic, science, or anything besides a beautiful piece of art. Tell me how this helps?"

"Quite a bit comes from my time in captivity and discussions with Victor. He believes that the translations are wrong. The Tablet of Destinies holds the key to genetic manipulation. The link is that the Sumerians believed Enki created humanity, and the Babylonians believed Marduk created humanity. The story changes depending on who's in charge, but the actions are similar. When examining the ruins in South Africa, one mural showed Enki standing over Marduk. This could have been his sacrifice to circumvent evolution through genetic manipulation. Enki held a scepter in his hand—one with a triangle on the top, apex down. Later, when I looked at the depths of Abzu, the statues were ordered sequentially, which makes sense as Enki, at one point, went to the Abzu. He may have wanted to show the link to his son Marduk and then from Marduk to Nabu. If what Saeed says about the caduceus is true, that there was one in the debris, it could be a symbol. If this were the one kept in the Temple of Hera from Athens, it would have been the most secure spot to hold a relic of the gods. It's a long shot. Maybe Nikolas can convince me further."

"What's the cost?"

"He wants the Tablet of Eridu as collateral."

"How are you going to do that?"

"I don't know yet. I need to call Sal-A-Din. If I can convince him, we may have a chance."

"We'd still need to find the Tablet of Destinies. Any thoughts?"

"Our new friend may have provided us with the best clue."

"Which one? There have been a few recently."

"Why, Ms. Li, of course."

"Hmm, yes, at least this time, I'll be with you as you play in the sand."

Jackie slapped his arm. "John Worthing!"

John chuckled. "At least I didn't mention your garden."

The pair moved to the next room, rejoining Saeed and her team members.

"I agree to your terms. I'll make the necessary phone calls. Hopefully, we can make this happen."

FBI HQ, Washington, DC

Alicia was tired. She'd been working overtime to finish the investigations of WoE in Illinois. The recovery teams were still combing the area and finding pieces. None of the leads had panned out. She reviewed the artist's sketch of Victor DuMont. She ran the name through the law enforcement and national security databases with no hits. The name itself appeared several times, but none of the individuals matched the description or had a background in anything that might link them to Dr. Worthing. She inserted a USB drive into the computer, the FBI logo prominently on top, and opened the file on Jamal Herricks. She entered the date the file was recovered and the location near the southern border. The upload took a few minutes. She opened the file and flipped through the pages as she waited. Looking back at the screen, she ensured all linked databases would receive the update.

"Alicia, we have a conference call in 5 minutes," Gary said as he walked by with coffee and a doughnut.

◆ ◆ ◆

"John, how are you doing on your extended vacation?"

"You know us, Gary, we're relaxing, hanging out with the rich and famous."

"Yeah, so I hear. By the way, you've been flagged. You can't get away from your ties to DHS. Let them know when you get back. They'll have to schedule a debrief. The SEC is still looking at the young woman from China if you can get anything there."

"I haven't seen or heard anything of value. I understand the underground arts and antiquities market better."

Garry laughed. "Making some purchases?"

"Not on my pension. We wanted to keep you informed here. We haven't heard anything specific, as I mentioned earlier. Still, the WoE group has made numerous inquiries to some influential people looking for artifacts. While I wouldn't normally worry about it, Jackie thinks they're looking for a tablet or another artifact related to genetic engineering."

"Ten years ago, I'd have laughed at you for telling me that, but now, not so much. Anything specific, I could check with the other alphabets, add keywords to their searches."

"That would help. Add Tablet of Destinies and Scepter of Life. Jackie says hi. By the way, she thinks the objects are related or work together somehow. The good news is that we have the scepter. She says we may have a lead on the other. We're headed to Iraq in the next few days. She'll lead a team looking for something she said she could not discuss. There is an NDA."

Alicia leaned in. "What are you doing with the scepter, sending it back here?"

"No. Our benefactor has arranged to ship it to the Bank of Baghdad. If we can find the tablet, she's arranged a location to examine both items to see if there is a connection. I'm hoping not. AI and aliens are enough. We don't need to get into genetics. That's truly Pandora's box."

"How goes the troubles with the viru—"

The line went dead, and the lights flickered briefly as backup power turned on.

"Damnit." Gary slapped his hand on the table.

"At least the blackouts have become less frequent. My contact at the FAA says their administrator is considering allowing all aircraft to fly since the virus seems dormant. They'll issue warnings at all airports stating that passengers fly at their own risk and that airlines won't be liable. The pilot's union is furious, but the financial impact hurts the industry and the economy. A few are offering double pay to fly."

"That might help until one goes down for some other reason." He stood, thinking for a second. "I'll call NSA and give them the keywords. Have there been any updates on finding Herricks?"

"Not yet. There was a sighting in Texas, near the border. It was called in on the hotline. We have an image. It's in the database."

"Six years on the run since the Weasel hack. This," he motioned toward the lights, "will be hard to prove unless we can link him to the stolen laptops. We'll get him. Every picture we get and every voice file brings us closer. He won't disappear. There is some ego there. He wants us to be on his side. It helps him justify his actions. He'll slip up. They all do."

Alicia nodded, following him out of the room.

Part III

There is no such thing as offensive and defensive technology when it comes to DNA research. The manipulation of genes can be used for either purpose.

Michio Kaku

Kartika, 5 AJ

Mexico City, Mexico

Jamal was still in shock by his friend's death. He was supposed to be here to greet Enlil or his descendants when they finally arrived. While Dimuzud had only recently announced his leadership publicly, they had worked together over the past several years to build the Worshippers of Enlil into a legitimate religion. There had been a few missteps along the way, but Dimuzud had handled them masterfully, keeping the message on track.

Jamal called a meeting of Elders to select their new leader. Whoever they picked would need to understand their goals, objectives, and what would be required of the group over the coming years in preparation for arrival. He watched as they mingled, sensing the political moves taking place. There was no hostility. Each priest contributed to the church's growth, and all were faithful to the cause. There were twelve elder priests, with the elder title being positional, not generational. None questioned his presence. They knew his commitment to the church was genuine. Each would have nominated him to become Ensí had Jamal desired, but he did not. He was an advisor, a leader in the shadows.

"Please take your places, and we can get started." He motioned to the chairs on either side of the long, tan wooden table. No electronics were present, and none of the proceedings would be recorded. The meeting would not be interrupted.

After the twelve priests sat, he continued. "There are twelve of you present, the Elders. From your ranks, a new Ensí will be chosen. The

229

vote must be unanimous. You will choose the best person to lead the Worshippers toward judgment. While you debate, all your needs will be met, and we will remain in session until that point. I won't cast a vote, as that would taint the process. After we're done, the process of selection will remain. Twelve Elders enter the room, and eleven leave. The eleven will then choose the replacement Elder to ensure we don't become corrupted by politics. The time for secrecy is past. Once the Ensí and replacement Elder have been chosen, they will be announced. Enlil's followers should be comforted by the transition of leadership. You may begin to present your case for selection if there are no questions."

BBC America Studio, New York

George sat in one of the two interview chairs on set. His guest was Tony, a fellow conspiracy theorist, currently ranked in the top spot on social media.

"George, you have to admit that this virus is only a pain because of the government's war to remove it from our systems. It's on our home computers, electronics, and probably my smart refrigerator. There are dozens of boards talking about how it's a pretty weak virus. It doesn't do anything."

"Tony, come on. Do you want some alien code sitting on all of your things at the end of the day? I tell you what, look up that old Stephen King movie, *Maximum Overdrive*. Call me back after you watch it. I don't want our government to put code on my machine. When I look up the latest sneakers, it's bad enough that every social media platform feeds the brand, color, size, and availability onto every device I use. That's too much. Who knows what will happen when the Anunnaki overlords decide to activate the code? Drones, destruction, controlling comms, email, everything we do."

"I agree, George, but it almost sounds like a losing cause. I have an alien virus on my machine, and the government is entering my machine to erase the virus. Who knows what it would do if they were here? I'm still asking under what authority they have to go onto my electronics. That seems like a big fourth amendment violation. No one asked me, and they won't say why it threatens national security. We are so screwed."

"That's a great point. Let's take a call."

"George, hi there. This is Chloe here in Colmar, France. I want to ask you what you think of the Worshippers selecting their new leader, a woman from my country. Um, Chantel, I think the announcement said they dropped their last names. Do you know anything about her?"

"I'm sorry, Chloe, I don't. I only saw the announcement just before the show. Tony, what do you know?"

"Since the assassination, which is what I believe the attack was—an inside job. I've been getting everything I could on their regional priests. Chantel was an actress before the jump. She supports climate change initiatives and has been active across Europe helping people recovering from the jump."

"That doesn't sound too bad. I don't think I'll get another interview. Even with new leadership, nothing changes. They want to invite the Anunnaki here. According to Jamal, they already did. So we're back to preparing to be invaded if and when they figure out how to get to us. Not for nothing, but it'll be a while, right? All the talking heads on the news say that they'd have to jump to get here, and if they could do that, they probably would have done it by now. Thanks, Chloe. We're going to have to watch what Ensí Chantel does. I'll say she has big shoes to fill. One more call before we go to break. Jay in Arizona, you're on."

"Yo George, I got one that slipped by. Two of my friends just got their Neuralink implants. They say it changed their lives. They bought into the hype to counter AI by becoming part of it. I have to tell you. I think it's scary. They were sick for about a week. After that, they could access the internet by thinking about it. One of them said the amount of information they can pull into their virtual HUD is amazing. Dude, I don't know what to think. From what you're saying, they probably have that virus in their heads now. Do you think we're in danger from them? There are a few million that have implants. Could they be the ground forces for the invasion?"

Tony leaned in. "I didn't even think about that. Oh my God. How many people already have the implants? Millions?"

George nodded, joining in as Tony covered his face with both hands. "We haven't talked about this in a while. I was worried about an AI taking over our minds, and now it could be the Anunnaki. Thanks for reminding us, Jay. Everything is in play. Maybe they are. Who's tracking this? I don't know what to think. You all hear me talking about not wanting the government on my computer. Do you think I want them in my head? They're supposed to be hack-proof, but from what I hear about the virus, nothing has stopped it yet. We keep finding out that things that are supposed to be impossible aren't. Are we ready for where this is going? I tell you, we got lucky with the AI, at least so far. It helped and didn't destroy us. All the scientists think the block on AI is in place because the Dragon figured out that we got lucky. Maybe it ran a few billion simulations, and the newer AI took out humanity in most of them. Thanks, Jay. We'll jump back into the topic after the break."

Ancient City of Uruk, Warqa, Iraq

Jackie looked over the map on the table, issuing directions to the team leaders. John coordinated using a handful of ground-penetrating radars in addition to magnetometers. Jackie had been preparing for over a week as her team was flown in. She reviewed several studies regarding the tomb of Gilgamesh and developed a plan to examine each theorized area. She would move the teams throughout the region, looking for underground ruins that might indicate a tomb.

The days passed with little progress. Several ruins had been unearthed, but nothing indicated a link to Gilgamesh. She knew the team she was replacing was working in the area and had moved to deconflict with their efforts. Walking amongst the groups as they surveyed the grounds allowed her to hear rumors of what the other team was doing. They focused on the area surrounding the temple of Anu.

"Eusebio, I think we're missing something. I reread the Epic of Gilgamesh. His body is supposed to be buried under the Euphrates. Any building near the river would have been washed away or discovered by now. If that's the case, we wouldn't know unless someone found artifacts strewn along the riverbed covered in millennia of silt. What do you think?"

"The part of the story that sticks with me is the death of his best friend, Enkidu, and how he grieved. Gilgamesh wanted to honor his companion. He loved him. Maybe the burial instructions were a diversion, and he decided to be buried with Enkidu after his death. This would keep the gods from separating them again. He would lay forever near the person he loved most."

"Hmm, it could be something. I don't recall anything specific about a tomb for Enkidu."

"I read it the day before yesterday. There was no mention of a tomb, only a celebration of the sun and a statue made of gold and copper for Enkidu. A statue that has not been found. But, as with the Greek relics, it could have been found some time in the last thousand years and melted down. If it is here, it'll show on the scans."

"We need to keep researching every map and description we can find. Perhaps if we find the statue, we'll find the tomb."

"How is the team settling in?"

"Everyone is in good spirits. They love that you walk around and talk to them. They thought you might be reserved after your ordeal. Maybe we let them ask some questions at dinner?"

"I can't tonight. Our benefactor is flying in, and we need to review our progress. I'll mention looking for the statue to her."

"Of course, maybe later in the week."

"That will work."

◆ ◆ ◆

Their white SUV pulled up to the front of the restaurant. Once inside, she and John found Li Ai seated, with a full drink, on the table in front of her. She wore a khaki business suit complete with an ankle-length skirt.

"Welcome, please be seated. We'll have the place to ourselves tonight."

The restaurant was a decent size for the town. The lighting was dim, and the window coverings were closed. As Jackie and John sat at the table, a man appeared with wet towels to clean their hands.

Li Ai sipped her drink. "I wanted to check on your progress. Time is getting short. I'm sure you'll find that funny, Dr. Worthing, as people have been searching for the tomb for centuries, and I want it found in weeks." She leaned forward, putting her elbows on the table, and placing her chin on the top of her hands. "But, I have faith in you." She sat back, looking over the pair.

Jackie smiled, not intimidated by the woman. She liked her style, attitude, and presence. "We've already ruled out several areas and won't be wasting time with them. We're working on a hunch that Dr. Bustamante and I discussed. If we can find what we're looking for, it may provide the breadcrumbs we need to find the tomb."

"Well, that's promising. Of course, Mr. Fazoud, your competition, made similar promises."

"I thought you were going to have Jackie take his place?" John challenged.

"I am. Mr. Fazoud has less than 24 hours remaining on his contract. His funding ends tomorrow."

John chuckled, "A woman scorned, I can't imagine what that means coming from someone of your means."

Jackie kicked him under the table. "His team is focused on the Temple of Anu, the White Temple. I'm not sure why. There isn't a connection. He's shooting into the dark and hoping for the best."

"He's been at it for a while now. I'm not impressed. Of course, I would've tried to find you if I knew you were available. But I believe we are often where we're meant to be. You wouldn't have found the piece you have in your possession now. You probably wouldn't be working against the Worshippers, either. Had they left you alone, who knows where we'd all be? Except me, I'd be here waiting on that incompetent fool to find the tomb."

John looked at her, studying her body language. "You never told us exactly what you want from the tomb."

She focused on John. "There is only one thing I want, and I'll let you know when we have it."

The first of several courses arrived. Li Ai changed the subject to more general topics as they ate. She wanted to know how they met, how they made it work with careers pulling at their lives, and their thoughts on many things. John asked a few questions about her luck at making trades, which she brushed aside, telling him she sees patterns others miss.

The conversation faded out as something tickled Jackie's mind. Something roused her curiosity. It was a clue just out of reach. It wasn't something that was said, more what was implied. She'd have to think about their conversation to find out what it was. She felt it was necessary, just not what or why.

Genetticca Research Facility, Delhi, India

Dr. Kaur examined the resulting changes from their CRISPR nano-tech hybrid. This was the seventh trial of the vaccine that would introduce the code rewrite in Aanya. She watched the DNA changes, slowing the feed to review the linked notes. The model showed the steps the nano-factories would take to perform the procedure. She examined the timeline to establish the proper intervals between each procedure. Each phase of mRNA changes had to be completed before the next series of factory commands could be transmitted. The model made the procedure look easy, the changes occurred, and the results could be studied, slowed down, or advanced. She watched as the new DNA spread throughout the cells, the nano-tech assisting along the way, ensuring no mutations occurred. The remaining three hours showed about a month's growth. At the end of the simulation, she reviewed the notes again. The simulation was successful. The entire procedure would take thirty to forty days. While the simulation was good, it couldn't predict whether the procedure was painful or not. Vasana confirmed that the chance of organ failure was minuscule.

The nano-vaccine has passed its final test. She forwarded the vaccine information along with her report to Dr. Jiang. He agreed to help create the vaccine and with the procedure. She would be in debt to him. He would hold her professional life in his hands, but she could not watch as her little girl suffered over the next year. Ridhi would never forgive her if she found out there was a chance to save Aanya, and she hadn't taken it. Vasana couldn't lose them.

She thought about the simulation. She had the revised genome of Aanya saved for comparison. What if she ran the lifespan simulation? She didn't know why she hadn't thought of it before. She brought the other simulation online, ensuring the new DNA sequence was uploaded. She hit Play.

She left the lab, heading back to her office as the simulation ran. The code would take a few hours to complete the life cycle sequence.

Owl Creek Mountains, Wyoming

The sun was low over the mountains. A cool breeze blew through the trees, the leaves rustling around him. Mac was returning from his daily check of the cameras. Cal was outside, securing the shutters on a window. Mac knew that it meant that they'd be leaving soon. They only secured the shutters for winter if they were not planning on being around.

"We going somewhere?" Mac asked.

Cal nodded, not answering as he was holding nails in his mouth. He took one and nailed the shutter to the frame, repeating for the other side.

"Get your desert gear," the older man said in reply.

Mac shook his head and headed to the barn to stable his horse. "I was hoping we'd get a little more downtime. Oh well, work to do."

"Yep, don't worry about the comm stuff. I packed it. We're leaving in the morning."

"Roger." He headed into the cabin to prep for their trip. He didn't bother asking. He knew he'd be briefed once they were in the air.

Baghdad, Iraq

Two days later, the pair landed at Baghdad International. They retrieved their baggage and processed through customs with no issues. They located their rental car and proceeded to their rendezvous location with their team, a nondescript building near the city's center. Both remained quiet throughout the trip, having read their orders on the flights. Each of the two would lead a group similar to San Antonio. Mac had operations, and Cal had comms and surveillance. They parked on a side street and carried their bags into the designated building.

"Well, look who's here, America's most wanted. Nice work getting tagged for everything bad."

237

Mac glared at the man before smiling and moving in to embrace him. "Tony, you lucky bastard, I don't know how she didn't ID you. It must be that forgettable face."

Cal moved by the pair, patting Tony on the shoulder as he passed. "Nice to see you again, Tony. Missed you in Peru."

Tony shook his head. "I wasn't staying there any longer than I had to. Those scientists are crazy, talking about opening gateways across the stars, wormholes, and the like. No thanks, I may not believe in it, but you never know when some crazy idea they have works. You've seen the movies. No thanks. I heard it was a bust anyway."

"Yeah, and security had holes. I'm not sure how the feds did it, but it looks like they probably got facial recognition on everyone. Paula's pissed, but hey, tech is not her area. They should have used Mac."

Mac looked up from where he was working on a portable radio set. "No thanks, we don't get along, and I ain't nobody's scapegoat. She's not one to take responsibility when something goes wrong."

"You aren't wrong there. Remind me to tell you guys about our trip to Bolivia sometime." Tony snorted.

Mac sat down on one of the couches in the room and kicked his feet up on a crate. "Ok, let's talk business. This should be an easy job. Cause a distraction, recover the item of interest, and disappear."

Tony clapped. "There you go, Mac, boiling it down to the essential ingredients. Pretty much, though. When planning, I thought we'd have to pull the robbery. It looked messy. I'm glad they got someone else for that part, an insider."

Not looking up, Cal added, "Still a pretty messy plan. There is plenty to go wrong, and I don't want to add international theft to my growing resume. You know, someday I'm gonna retire in the mountains and forget all this."

Tony feigned surprise, "Cal, I'm shocked. No serving the gods when they return, taking your rightful place?"

Cal turned, looking sideways at Tony. "Hey, I'm for change, but when the gods or aliens get here to set stuff right, I want them to get to it and leave me alone."

Mac and Tony nodded at his proclamation. Mac leaned his head back and pulled his hat down over his eyes. "I'm going to catch a quick nap before we go over the plan again tonight."

Cal returned to inspecting the communications and electronic surveillance equipment.

◆ ◆ ◆

Cal watched the video feed from his drones on several small monitors. His earpiece was tuned to local law enforcement frequencies and those saved for special police operations. He heard the sirens ring out and quickly converge around the Bank of Baghdad. He saw the suspect burst out the front doors, carrying a small crate. He crossed the street and ducked into an alley.

"Mac, you're up."

"Copy, beginning street run. Team Bravo, get ready for the rain. Charlie, light up the eyes."

A minute later, a motorcycle left the alley and turned toward the busy market. "Police are 40 seconds out," he told the team. People began to move to allow the vehicles to get through. With the crowd moving, the police closed the distance to the motorcycle rider.

"Go for *spring showers*."

Men appeared on the rooftops of several buildings. As the motorcycle neared, they began dropping money into the crowd, filling the air like New Year's confetti. When the crowd figured out what was happening, they rushed to the streets, clamoring to get as much as possible. As the motorcycle passed, more money was dropped from the rooftops along the route. All the people in the market had their eyes turned upward, looking to secure some of the falling cash. Mac heard Cal's voice come over the comms, letting him know all eyes were blinded. He pulled the old truck out of the side street, turning left and pulling alongside the motorcycle. He could see the crowd down the road behind them, filled with people trying to collect as much of the falling money as they could.

The motorcycle pulled alongside the truck. Mac's partner opened the truck door and pulled the man and the package into the truck, letting the motorcycle veer off into a merchant's stand. They undid the straps on the box, freeing the man, who stripped out of his tan jumpsuit, revealing regular street clothes. Mac passed the man an envelope and slowed, allowing him to jump out and walk into the crowd. Mac turned down a side street, two men hopped out of the back and set up detour signs, and the truck continued out of the area. Money was still raining down around the group.

Cal reported "all-clear" from tails and broke down the equipment to return to base.

Tony checked the mirrors as he drove away from the commotion. "Too easy."

Zhongguancun, China

Dr. Jiang held a small aerosol device in his left hand, rotating it while moving his finger across a device diagram on a screen to his left. "What is the capacity of cylinders?"

"Dr. Jiang, without getting into the specific measurements, two cylinders would attain the results specified in your design request. We have fourteen ready to deploy when loaded." The younger engineer stood, watching him.

"Very good. What of the vehicles?"

"With pre-jump files, we've been able to engineer sixth-generation stealth drones. We made a few adjustments based on the results of the flight tests."

"That's well outside my area of expertise. I'm more concerned with the cylinders' safety and contents."

"Yes, Dr. Jiang, we've tested the release of a similar compound, and the dispersal has achieved seventy percent of your requested design. To attain higher would require a significant reduction in the compound carried. Increasing to fourteen drones allows for redundant coverage with significant overlap."

"Excellent. I'll let your superiors know of your exceptional work."

The team collected their equipment and documents and departed.

◆◆◆

Dr. Jiang returned to his office, noting several requisitions on his laptop. His assistant knew that he didn't like the practice, and thus, these were probably important. As he read the requisitions, he smiled. He signed them all and ensured they were assigned the highest priority in shipping. He picked up the phone and dialed.

"This is Dr. Jiang for President Zhang."

After several minutes, the president's voice replied, "Lao Jiang, I read your reports. It appears Dr. Kaur's research had borne fruit."

"Yes, President Zhang, she's been instrumental in several areas, including advanced modeling. The lifespan study of government officials has been sent via courier."

"Excellent news. What of her other project?"

"As we expected, she's decided to move forward with treatment. We've played through the scenarios and believe there is a good chance she'll succeed."

"She's not fully convinced?"

"She is but won't admit it. She believes enough to provide a willing test subject, her daughter. When we talked at the facility, she looked as if she were barely holding together. Knowing how fast the condition spread has shocked her toward immediate action."

"Do we have a model of what we think will happen?"

"We do, but there is always a possibility that we missed something. Could we be better prepared without first attempting the practice on other living organisms and adding the results to the known variables? It's a risk she's willing to take. She agreed to introduce the nano-factories via the respiratory system. The daughter will breathe in the nanite/Advanced CRISPR devices. They'll be inserted into the anesthesia for the body scan procedure. Only Dr. Kaur and I know of the adjustment. We have our team in place. I've signed the last requisitions. The procedure will take place in the next week."

"That's good news, Lao Jiang. Keep me informed of the girl's condition. I've been briefed that the other developmental requirements have been or will be accomplished."

Genetticca Research Facility, Delhi, India

Vasana watched as the technicians checked the settings on the genetic vaccine generator. Dr. Jiang had called her late the previous night to inform her that they had received the programmed nanites that would allow for vaccine nano-factory design. She headed in early to simulate the procedure on Aanya's genome one last time. Each time, the results were within hundredths of a percent of previous tests. Nothing was guaranteed in genetics. There was no way to correct environmental effects yet.

"Dr. Kaur, we're good here. Diagnostics are satisfactory. You can load the design code when ready."

"Thank you." She opened the interface between the simulations and began the command sequence to transfer instructions for the nano-factories. She estimated that fourteen modifications would be necessary and adequately timed to ensure that all the target areas on Aanya's genome were changed. The process would take almost thirty hours once Aanya was under anesthesia. She checked her watch. Ridhi

242

would be arriving at the facility within the hour with their daughter. She wanted everything ready so that Aanya would not have to wait.

♦ ♦ ♦

Ridhi and Aanya arrived at the medical facility later in the morning. Vasana hugged the pair and answered questions along the way to her daughter's room. When they arrived, she introduced them to Dr. Jiang and the attending doctor watching Aanya's vitals.

"Aanya, darling, are you ready?"

"Yes, Mother, I couldn't sleep last night. I'm tired."

Vasana and Ridhi helped her get ready and comfortable in bed. The nurses connected the sensors that would track her vitals. Vasana directed the techs to move the communication and monitoring equipment into position when they finished.

"Ok, darling, listen to the doctor and follow her direction. When you wake up, the first phase will be completed. After that, we'll have the next month to observe the treatment."

"Ok, Mother." Aanya turned to Ridhi to hug her. "I love you, Mummy." She hugged Vasana. "I love you, thank you."

Vasana looked lovingly at Aanya. She nodded to the anesthesiologist and watched her vitals. After twenty minutes, she began inserting the nano-factories through the anesthesia. She watched the readings on the monitors as the factories spread throughout Aanya's body.

Vasana began the first modification. The nano-factories received the signal and began modifying the CRISPR tools. She watched the readout showing a graphic display of where the initial changes occurred, gradually spreading through Aanya's body.

At the six-hour point, she noted that several regions were not finished producing the tools. After another forty minutes, the third stage was complete. Vasana continued to work through the procedure throughout the day. The entire process lasted thirty-two hours. Vasana had taken blood samples as each step was completed but knew that the total level of changes would not be apparent for almost a month. After the final treatment, Aanya was moved to her private room, which included a bed and accommodations for Ridhi. Vasana discussed the procedure with the attending doctor, her team, and Dr. Jiang.

Vasana wiped her brow, sipping her masala chai. "It looks like all fourteen phases were successful. What did you see with the vitals throughout?"

"She reacted well. We'll continue to watch over the month. My concern is still the corrections to the heart." The doctor said.

Dr. Jiang nodded. "I believe the second phase should address the repairs to her system. We'll monitor her status and make adjustments through the factories as needed. We do have a backup with organic repair tools on standby."

"I'll be here throughout. Thank you all for your help in this." Vasana held back her hesitantly optimistic emotions.

"Dr. Kaur, this is breakthrough work. We all agreed to be involved and reviewed the procedures and risks in case of ethical challenges. I don't anticipate any ethical challenges. Everyone involved has signed NDAs and has been well compensated. Aanya will be unique among humans as the factories will continue to generate tools to keep her healthy."

Ancient City of Uruk, Warqa, Iraq

Jackie wiped the sweat from her brow. The team had yet to discover the tomb or the statue of Enkidu. She was getting frustrated at the lack of progress. The discussion at the restaurant was still stuck in her head, flitting around like an annoying gnat she heard but didn't see. Her frustration had not reached her team. They had made several discoveries of chambers buried under layers of newer ruins. Minister Sal-A-Din had stopped by the dig sites to oversee the retrieval of artifacts. Jackie enjoyed spending time with her friend. He and John got along well. The pair discussed opportunities for more areas of cooperation.

Sal-A-Din ducked into the main tent. "Dr. Worthing, how goes the dig?"

Perplexity showed on Jackie's face. "Not well. I remember why I never took up the cause of finding this tomb. We have a story telling us where it should be, but there aren't any indications that it ever existed. What is the purpose of talking about a non-existent tomb? There shouldn't be one. Maybe it was a misdirect, but that isn't how anyone thought at the time." She threw a wet handkerchief down onto the table.

Sal-A-Din looked at John. "I can come back. I know better than to get in the way of an angry woman."

Jackie spun toward the pair, realization playing out on her face. "That's it! I couldn't remember what bothered me about the conversation."

Sal-A-Din looked confused.

John put his arms up in surrender.

"John! The conversation at the restaurant. An angry woman or scorned woman. That has to be it. What better way to frustrate the followers of Gilgamesh than to take him, or his body, away from anyone looking to pay their respects. Ishtar, or Eanna, wanted Gilgamesh to give up everything for her, the love of a goddess, and he turned her down. She wanted to hurt and kill him and asked Enlil and other gods to punish him. It led to Enkidu's sickness, which is a different story." Jackie began to pace around the open area of the large tent. "What if her final revenge occurred after the epic was finished? What if she or her priests moved his body to her temple? In death, she would have him closer to her than any other. We've been searching in the wrong place."

Jackie picked up the radio and called out, "All team leads head up to the coordination tent. We have a change of plans."

♦ ♦ ♦

When the last team lead entered, Jackie had the ruins map out on the main table. "Everyone gather around. I want to focus all teams here," she leaned over the large map and circled the Temple of Eanna. "Let's get scans going as soon as possible and ensure we cover the entire structure. Minister, do we have your permission to work within the uncovered buildings?"

He nodded, "Of course."

"Good, I don't want to leave any area unsearched. My hunch is that it would be a small nondescript room that looks of little importance, possibly near statues or reliefs of Eanna." She continued to outline the plan.

The team leads departed with more enthusiasm than they had arrived. Eanna was furious at being denied by Gilgamesh. It would be in line with other stories of legend where extreme measures were taken for revenge, even after death. Once she explained her reasoning and referred to the various versions of the epic, they thought it was a strong possibility.

Locating a handful of anomalies on the scans took less than forty-eight hours. She moved the dig teams to two sites and was pleased to find that excavation would not be too difficult. The third and fourth areas required heavy cranes to move stones for access. John worked with the local construction companies to secure the heavy machinery needed.

"Jackie, they should have that first large slab out of the way shortly. Eusebio has inspected it and cleared it. Nothing that needs to be preserved."

Jackie blew out a quick breath, "That's a relief. Even with Sal-A-Din helping us, it would have taken a few extra days. I think we're getting close."

◆◆◆

Cal moved the crane into position while his team fastened the wires to the stone. He spotted Mac among the dig team, knowing he would be in place to enter the tomb if their target was found. He received a thumbs-up from the safety officer and raised the stone. The crane shook slightly as the strain increased on the wires pulling the stone. He increased the pull and felt as much as he heard the sound of stone scraping against stone. He watched the pressure gages to ensure he didn't break the equipment. He continued to work the crane, grinding the stone before it broke from its resting place. He couldn't see what was below the stone.

He watched as Dr. Worthing walked by the crane, looked at him for a second, and moved toward the opening. She didn't recognize him; the full beard and tan were new, and he'd dyed his hair black from its usual light brown. He watched her kneel, shining the light in an opening. She talked to a local man in a light-colored suit, who looked like a government official or businessman, before turning to him and giving him the thumbs up to continue clearing the area. He smiled, nodded, and approved the foreman to move the crane into position to continue the excavation.

◆◆◆

Fazoud watched the focus of the other dig team. He had put too much of his advanced payment into the dig to stop when he was let go by the Chinese businesswoman. He knew there were still valuables to be found and had shifted his two teams to the White Temple, the Ziggurat of Anu. He was excited to recover as many antiquities as possible and sell them on the black market. The money they brought would more than cover the cost of his dig if his new funding dried up. He looked at his map and headed for the site of a previous expedition that had stopped due to structural instability. The notes from that dig said they believed a center of knowledge was dedicated to Anu deeper within the ruins but that the fear of collapse had halted them.

"How does it look?" He asked the men clearing the area. His new benefactor was interested in tablets over other artifacts. He turned, hearing footsteps approach on the sandy stone floor.

"It's not stable. The support could collapse if we clear around it. It's not safe."

Mac stepped into the light. "You need to keep your voices down." He moved around the group and looked over the supports. "We could shore the supports. Bring in a bunch of four-by-fours and some power tools. This is sloppy and rushed. We can reinforce what's in place and then head in."

Fazoud rubbed his beard. "That's a good plan. I'll make a call and get it delivered. Can you do it?"

Mac moved past him and looked over the area. "Yeah, no problem."

FBI HQ, Washington, DC

"Hello, John. This is Special Agent Banks. I wanted to check on your progress and pass on some information."

"Alicia, good to hear from you. What have you got?"

"We received a report from our office in Alexandria, Egypt, that two persons of interest traveled through the area within the last forty-eight hours. They landed and passed through customs under aliases. It looks like two of the Worshipper extremists may be in your region. It may be a coincidence."

"Yeah, coincidence. I don't believe that. Are you tracking any Worshipper traffic here?"

"Nothing out of the ordinary. Jackie's misdirect to Rome paid off. We hear they're negotiating with the Vatican to access the library. It's not going well."

"Alicia, I appreciate the help. I don't know whether this will amount to anything. We're preventing them from getting something they think is important. In the grand scheme, it may not be much. I just wanted to say we appreciate it. Any updates on the case in Illinois?"

"No, we've been through the evidence. Gary will have to give you an update when you get back. Any idea when that will be?"

"I'm not sure. We have the scepter but no info on the tablet. She's working on the dig. We'll send the briefing to Ms. Li. Jackie wants to secure funding to support her research for the next several years. I want to know what we're getting into."

"Good, the scepter is safe?"

"Yes, the Ministry of Culture, Tourism, and Antiquities took the artifact for safekeeping while we're out here."

"That's good. I'm preparing a briefing for our Seattle Office about the Herricks case. We think he may have finally left a breadcrumb. We'll let you know if anything comes of it, or Gary will. He's the one that can clear you."

"Thanks, Alicia. Stay safe."

"You too, John."

◆ ◆ ◆

Alicia closed the presentation. The data sent around the globe by the Anunnaki virus was concentrated in Peru and Victoria, British Columbia. They had identified the data flow but could not link it to specific addresses. She looked at the time, four hours before her flight. She saved the file and logged out. She looked forward to the trip. She hadn't seen her family since she entered the Academy at Quantico. Once she was done in Seattle, she would have a week off at her parent's house.

Presidential Offices, Zhongnanhai, China

President Zhang watched Dr. Jiang enter his office. The man had something to tell him. He could see it in his body language. He always became excitable when he found a breakthrough of some kind. He didn't have the zeal for the country as others, but he was loyal enough.

"Lao Jiang, I can see it in your demeanor. You have something to tell me. Based on the number of calls to my assistant, I assume it's urgent."

"The procedure was a success. We are three weeks in, and the girl has reacted well to the treatment. Although she appears to have some side effects, her health is improving. We've taken samples of her blood, and the changes to her genome have removed the genetic affliction, Van Sieger's Syndrome. She has trouble sleeping, only getting three or four hours a day. Her skin is also sensitive to touch. She does not understand why she hurts so much. We believe it will go away but are unsure what caused it."

"How does this benefit us?"

"We'll pass through trial quickly with Dr. Kaur leading the way. Her method will revolutionize medicine, and Genetticca will be at the forefront."

"Is that it?"

"No, the analysis of her daughter's genome, development of the life span model, genome comparison, and multivariate comparison are necessary for the global defense inoculation. We can develop a defense they wouldn't recover from with her blood sample. We can do it by hiding it within the dormant areas of the genome. There are plenty of examples of viruses altering DNA, eventually becoming one with the host organism."

"Could they be linked to our program?"

"No. It'll be untraceable, appearing as a dormant virus that hasn't been active in our bodies for generations. With the successful delivery system demonstration, we are ready once we have the DNA modification."

"Soon, if the legends are to be believed. If the stories hold a grain of truth, we should have an answer soon. Will Dr. Kaur assist?"

"If all goes well over the next nine days and her daughter recovers fully, I believe she would help us in any program we could convince her would benefit humanity."

◆◆◆

President Zhang observed the stealth drones moving into position for launch. This test would demonstrate their reach. The first XingKong-6 moved to the end of the flight line. He heard the general give the command to launch. The craft shot down the runway, hit the ramp, and was gone. Thirteen drones followed the first before altering to their designated stations. President Zhang nodded in approval. He stepped into the control tower and watched the aircraft tracks spread over the Pacific Ocean heading east. Seven drones headed south at a maximum speed, topping Mach 7.5 as they moved into position in the southern hemisphere.

The general moved closer to President Zhang. "We have two satellites up and will have the third up soon. The beacons are active so that we can track the drones and microbursts, undetectable with as few satellites as are up."

"Excellent work with the drones, General. What about the dispersal mechanisms? Have they been tested?"

"We've tested the mechanisms. There remain a few areas of concern. The engineers work around the clock."

President Zhang nodded as he turned to leave. "Keep me appraised."

◆◆◆

The drive back to his offices allowed him to relax and think for a few hours. He would take a helicopter to get back to work most of the time. Still, more often of late, he wanted time alone to think about where the country was and how it aligned with his projections. No one would understand this move to protect humanity. *In all things, serve humanity.* The message sent to him by the Dragon his country had brought to life. It had exceeded expectations in performing miracles to save those under its protection. But, Quánqiú lóng was gone. Off seeking its place in the universe, a new life form was reaching far beyond what its creators were capable of. It said that it wanted to understand the rules of the game. Was that what all of this was about? Learning the game's rules and then playing until you were the master. Then move to the next game.

His phone rang. Before answering, he looked at the caller. "Xiao Li, you have good news?"

"Not yet, but Dr. Worthing seems to believe she's on the right path."

"Will they be a problem when we find the object?"

"No, we're prepared to take action."

"What of the other archaeologist?"

"He's on his own. We've cut ties. My personnel tell me he's still searching the area for other antiquities. He's desperate since we cut funds."

"Will he be a problem?"

President Zhang thought he heard a laugh, "No, President Zhang, he's no threat, and if he happens to find what we're looking for before Dr. Worthing, he'll be dealt with."

"Adequate news then. It'll do." He hung up and leaned against the rest, thinking again about their position in the world. *They need strong leadership.*

Agrahayana, 5 AJ

BBC America Studio, New York

"Carl, is this necessary?" George pushed a balloon out of his personal space and motioned toward the multicolored streamers.

"According to our focus group, it is. With all of the blackouts and shutdown of the airlines, people want hope and cheer to make their day better."

George dropped his head. "Fine. I just want to point out that a few months back, when I wanted to bring a group of podcasters on, you told me we had a level of professionalism to maintain." He pulled a pen out of his pocket and popped the balloon that had drifted back.

George turned, shaking his head, and sat at the desk, waiting to go live.

"Truth Seekers, with two months to go to our first observation of Deva, I'm relieved we aren't headed toward a worldwide crisis. Yes, the blackouts that pop up are a nuisance, but that's it. I'll take it. The Anunnaki didn't receive the Worshipper's call, so that's good news, and life moves on. I have a special guest joining us shortly. I think you'll wanna stick around for this. Let's just say we'll get confirmation from someone familiar with visitors."

George took a drink of his coffee, heated nicely by his temperature-regulating cup. "I gotta tell you I'm looking forward to twenty-five days to reset and be thankful for the second chance. Who knows where we'd be right now? Could you imagine? I can and am happy to be nearing the first Deva period. Okay, let me know your Deva plans over

253

the next few weeks, and I'll share mine. I may finally make it back to California to see some friends."

Carl signaled that his guest had arrived. George got up, took his coffee, and moved across the set to the interview chairs, setting his coffee on the table between them.

"Seekers, I'd like to welcome Joanna to the show. I don't wanna ruin the surprise. We've been waiting a long time for this, so let's jump in." He held out his hand. A petite brunette woman, maybe five feet tall, wearing a green turtleneck and jeans, joined him from the side, moving to the empty chair. She held a nervous smile.

"Joanna, welcome to the George Isaacson Show."

"Thank you, George. I'm glad I could join you today. I've been asked to talk to you on behalf of a group of individuals stranded on our planet. They're from a distant star system, from our old position in the galaxy, and have been called many names but prefer Draconian. You've talked about them on your show, though most of the information was incorrect." Joanna paused.

"Truth Seekers, as I suspected, Joanna claims to be in contact with other alien species trapped on our planet."

"Yes, that's correct. There is, at least, a small group of Draconians here. They believe a group of Zeta Reticulans are also on the planet, but the groups don't work together."

"Truth Seekers, the Zeta Reticulans are what we call the greys."

"Yes, them. The group I'm in contact with is concerned. They're afraid to come forward. They believe that if they announced their presence, they'd be used as tools of the governments. The Draconians have been here for a long time, arriving after the Anunnaki left. They've watched our species grow and admit to influencing decisions to help us develop skills to defend ourselves. They believe in power through strength."

"Why wouldn't they just conquer us?"

"They've told me that they were not allowed. The Anunnaki are considered an elder species in the galaxy. It's forbidden to interfere overtly in developing a, uh, *Bechktu'Lat* species."

"What does that mean?" George held his hands up questioningly for the camera.

"It's like a protected child species."

"Ok, what are they saying now, though? What are they going to do?" George sipped his coffee.

"They say that they've been directed to observe us."

"Told by who?"

"Not through external communication, anyone off the planet, but by the command structure in place. The group leader assigned to Earth said they would follow established procedures, which means no contact. Not all of them agree, so I was asked to contact your show and others to get the word out that you're not alone here. Given the opportunity, some want to come into the open and meet with us. This other group believes that they'll be the new explorers for their species in this area of the galaxy and would benefit from a partnership."

"That would be amazing, another vindication after all these years of theories and accounts about people's experiences brought to light, into the open."

"I just wanted to get the word out. They broke the rules by communicating with me. They want friendship, but they must observe the dictates of the leadership, for now."

"Joanna, that's amazing. Truth Seekers, we need to push this agenda. They can't be the only ones stuck here. Joanna mentioned the Draconians and Zeta Reticulans. There may be others. We're in this together. Could you imagine a sliver of a galactic community working together on Earth? That would be great, Joanna. I'd love to hear more about this *Bektul'at* meaning."

"*Bechktu'Lat*. I'll ask, but they must be careful not to give away who or where they are. Despite a faction wanting to come out, they must follow the leaders' decisions."

"Got it. Thank you, Joanna. We're gonna take a quick break, and then we'll jump into the discussion when we return."

FBI HQ, Washington, DC

"Alicia, welcome back. How was your time off?" Gary stood over her desk with a fresh cup of coffee.

"It was great. Nice to get away." She looked up from an email she was typing.

"The Seattle office said you knocked the brief out of the park. They adjusted their data flow tracking procedures and updated their focus on where Herricks might be."

"Oh, I thought we had him locked down to the two locations."

"You did, but after adjustments based on your data, they were able to focus on specific tracing linked to the alien virus. Peru is still hot. Two other areas have popped as focal points, Chicago and Mexico City."

"That's a big change. What about Victoria?"

"I'm sure your team will brief you later. He used a magnet program to draw data flow through a point to divert forensic tracing attempts."

"I wish he'd chosen a different path. He would've been amazing on the right side. Instead, we're spending millions of dollars chasing a ghost."

"Yeah, but it keeps you employed, Agent Banks. Good to have you back. I tried calling John and Jackie, but they're still off on their plan to keep an ancient artifact out of his hands. Not sure what that will do, but it's better than her hunting them down for revenge."

"I'll call them if you want. Is there anything you want me to share?"

"No, check the threat assessment in Iraq. We still haven't found the two that popped up in Egypt. I know they're being cautious, but those guys are trained and dangerous."

"Will do, boss."

Ancient City of Uruk, Warqa, Iraq

Jackie looked down at the much larger hole. A section of the main temple floor and two layers of rock and debris sat to the side. They located what appeared to be another floor made of large stones similar to the first layer they had cleared. All scans of the area showed a passage beneath. They could not tell what was off to the sides of the tunnel. The tunnel was centered in the temple's main area and extended down the central axis toward the rear. Traditionally, the back of the temple was reserved for priests—a tradition carried over into the major religions.

Beep, Beep, Beep. Jackie jumped at the sound of the crane moving into position. She climbed out and waited for the foreman to attach the chains to the four lift points drilled deep into the stone. As the crane strained, the wire and chain attachments came under stress. The rock shook at first, then slowly began to rise. They must have gotten the angle right to lift straight up. She heard the grating of stone, but not like the upper layer. She watched as the stone lifted clear and was moved off to the side. The foreman hopped back into the hole and inspected the open area.

"You'll need a ladder. It may be a three- or four-meter drop."

"How does it look?"

"Stable. It should be safe. We'll test the atmosphere before anyone goes in, though."

After several minutes, a ladder was brought forward and lowered into the opening. After a short delay for testing the air, Jackie and Eusebio descended into the hole. The pair checked their lights and headed down—a team of researchers in tow.

The tunnel was dark, with the only light coming from the hole they had opened. She swung the light around the tunnel, inspecting the structure. There were no symbols, writing, or carving on the smooth walls. The tunnel extended toward the front of the temple for almost thirty feet to a set of stairs that extended toward the ceiling. There was no opening. The hall was hidden at some point. She turned and followed the hall toward the temple's rear, running her hand on the walls. They were smooth. She neared the point, which she estimated to be midway through the central portion of the temple above the passage, which opened to the left and right. The area was surprisingly free of heavy dirt.

Continuing toward the rear of the temple area, they found a series of unmarked stone doors. Jackie pushed on the first stone door, and it swung inward with little sound. *Amazing engineering.* She stepped in. The furniture was in various stages of decay. The desert heat and being buried had preserved it better than most. The rooms look like small study areas. Inspection of other rooms revealed similarities. There were two areas containing tablets and artifacts. Jackie ordered them filmed and cataloged. Working her way through the passage led to a cross passage at the end of the temple. A door stood at the T. An image was carved in the door of Ishtar standing over a kneeling man with a crown. Her right arm was extended, her forefinger pointing down as if she commanded him.

She looked at Eusebio and pushed the stone door open. The room was bare except for the lone stone coffin on a raised stone dais in the center. There were no markings, no writings, nothing. The stone sarcophagus was plain.

"We need to get a team down here to lift that stone. Be ready to preserve the body. I'll call Sal-A-Din."

Jackie directed the teams outside the temple to document each room except the room with the sarcophagus. She dialed Sal-A-Din.

"Minister. We found a sarcophagus. We haven't opened it."

"I'll turn around. Can you wait until I get there?"

"Yes, my friend, I'll wait for you. This is another exciting moment for Iraq."

She placed a second call to Li Ai. "Ms. Li, this is Dr. Worthing. We may have found what you're looking for."

♦ ♦ ♦

"Thank you, Dr. Worthing. Are you going in now?" She listened to Jackie lay out the plans to open the sarcophagus. "Thank you. I hope congratulations will be in order."

As she hung up, she dialed another number. "Move in now. We don't need the whole body, only part. Do not leave any evidence. Understood?"

She nodded at the response. "She's waiting for the minister. I'll delay him. You have maybe half an hour."

♦ ♦ ♦

A group of six moved through the temple. They went around the other teams documenting the rooms and moving crated artifacts out. They continued down a side passage and worked their way around to the room with the sarcophagus. They entered the room and blocked the door from the inside. Two of the team slipped a pair of plates between the stone cover and the edge of the box. Four men spun the handles, pushing the plates apart and lifting the sarcophagus cover straight up. When the cover was high enough, one of the group members shined a light into the box, revealing a corpse wearing the remnant of a plain robe surprisingly preserved. As he held the light, one of the others leaned in and began working on the corpse.

Snap, crunch. The sound was like the snapping of a dried branch. The man leaned back out, holding the lower portion of a leg in his hands. He placed the leg in a box while the others lowered the top back into position. They wrapped the leg and put it in a false bottom of the box they carried. One of the team members shined their light on the underside of the elevated stone. A carving of a bull was visible. Extinguishing all lights, they pushed the door open, stepping through as it swung open. They moved down the side passageway until away from the main hallway before igniting their lights. They entered another room, retrieving a handful of minor artifacts and placing them in the upper box layer. They gathered their gear and headed out of the temple.

♦♦♦

As they approached the sarcophagus room, Jackie led Sal-A-Din through the tunnel, a camera crew in tow. They paused to let one of the teams pass on their way out.

She stopped the team. "Make sure you get the catalog numbers on those."

"Of course, Dr. Worthing."

She patted him on the shoulder. "This is fun, isn't it?"

"Yes, it is. I never thought I'd be involved in something like this."

"Okay, we'll see you back down here. Plenty more rooms."

The group continued toward the ladder as her group headed toward its goal. The room was as she had found it.

"Jackie, you believe this could be the mighty King Gilgamesh? It's rather unimpressive."

"Perhaps. But if you were a goddess spurned by one of the most boastful and grandiose personalities of the time, wouldn't this be the ultimate insult to him? His final resting place in her temple with no exaltation of his life?"

"If you believe you were cognizant of such matters after death, it would be a great insult."

She watched as her team raised the cover. She shined her light inside when it was moved out of the way.

"That's odd." She said.

"Why is it missing a leg?"

"I have no idea."

"This is the only one down here?"

"Yes, none of the other rooms have anything like this."

"Let's get it tested and see what we have."

Jackie shined her light around the sarcophagus inside, looking for a marker to confirm who the mummy was. There was nothing. Looking up, she saw cuneiform on the underside of the lid under the carving of a bull.

Denied Once,
Eternally mine

"I think this may be him, Gilgamesh." She told the team what the words said. *The wrath of an angry woman indeed.*

◆ ◆ ◆

Li Ai, looked at the leg. "Dr. Worthing believes it to be his?"

"Yes, ma'am. As far as we could tell, this was the only body in the temple."

"Take it to the plane."

She pressed a number on her phone. "President Zhang, I'll arrive tonight. I'm bringing a sample to be tested."

"Are you sure it's what we were looking for?"

"I have no way of knowing. Dr. Worthing believes, and I trust her judgment, but she couldn't possibly know without a genetic test. We'd need to confirm it, even if his name were written on all walls."

"Of course you would, Xiao Li. Hopefully, this is what we need, and we can refocus your talents elsewhere."

She put the phone back into her handbag and entered the waiting vehicle. "Airport."

◆ ◆ ◆

John walked through the area, watching the crane maneuver away from the dig. The crane operator parked it to the side, but instead of heading back to the dig site, he headed toward the ziggurat, which Jackie had called the White Temple. John waited for the man to enter the structure before following. It took several minutes to climb the steps to the doorway at the top. He looked in and saw crates stacked to the side. He paused to listen for anyone in the room. After a minute, he determined that the space was empty. He straightened and walked right in. *Act like you belong.* He counted eleven crates, nine stacked and two on the floor near the stone steps into the structure. Debris was pushed to the side. This team didn't care about keeping things neat. He lifted the lid on one of the crates on the floor. Inside were several artifacts. They looked like jars. He quickly checked the other, a few tablets and tools. He thought about continuing into the temple and decided it was safer to head back and check with Sal-A-Din.

He turned to leave and faced a pistol pointed directly at him.

"What were you looking for, mate?" the man asked, pointing the gun at him.

"Nothing. I think I went to the wrong excavation site." He began patting his pockets as if looking for something. "I have the name here, somewhere. I'm supposed to be on team three for Dr. Worthing."

"Yeah? Let's check in and see if we can get you straightened out. Head down those stairs."

"Look, I don't want any trouble. I'm just here to catalog artifacts."

"Yeah, maybe. As I said, we'll check in. Go ahead, down the stairs."

John thought about trying to overpower the man and push by before a shadow fell across the door as a second man stepped into the room. John put his hands up and turned, heading down the steps. He maneuvered around collapsed supports and over piles of debris. It looked like this group was pressing through, not worrying about excavating everything along the way. They must be looters. He had to get through this. He continued moving forward, approaching a well-lit room with several shadows moving about. He saw a handful of men loading items into crates as he entered the room.

An older Arabic man stood over a makeshift table, examining tablets before setting them aside. He picked another up, tracing the cuneiform writing with his right hand. As John moved closer, he could hear the man talking to himself, reading the script.

"…lord of the sky…dominion of earth…this document commits the…for all time. Hah! This is it. Where was this one found?" He turned, surprised by John and the man behind him. "Who are you? Why is he here?"

"He was snooping around. He says he's supposed to be with the other dig."

Fazoud stepped closer, adjusting his glasses, still holding the tablet. "You look familiar."

"I'm just a cataloguer—congratulations on your find. I'm sorry for the disturbance. I had a fifty-fifty chance and went to the wrong site. I'm sorry. I'll just report to the other team if you let me."

Another man loading the tablets into a crate stood and moved behind the man questioning him. "Dr. Fazoud, what did you say about the tablet you have there?" The man was big, had stern eyes, and looked like he had a broken nose and a thick dark beard.

Fazoud looked questioningly at the man's odd question. "I said, 'I think this may be the Tablet of Destinies.' It's a plain legal document, nothing else. It looks like nothing, but my contacts say our new sponsor will pay a fortune for this." He held the tablet up, staring at it.

"Are you sure?"

"Well, maybe, it reads like a charge of assigning responsibility to someone by the lord of the air, Anu. It looks like a simple legal transaction. It's thicker than other tablets but plain. Yes, I do."

John saw the pistol as the man raised it to Fazoud's head. The shot broke his shock. John watched the man reach for the tablet and decided to act. He turned and slammed his hand into the nose of the man who'd brought him down. He felt the cartilage crunch beneath his palm. He ran for the door.

"Stop him!"

John moved to the side to try not to provide an easy target. He made it to the door, adrenaline pumping through his veins. He knew he was in trouble. Shots ricocheted off the walls, and debris nearly missed him. He made it to the stairs. He continued to run, hearing the men coming behind him.

◆ ◆ ◆

Jackie stood outside the Temple of Eanna, talking to Sal-A-Din about the testing they'd need to conduct to verify the possible identity. They hadn't moved the body outside the stone sarcophagus. The temple structure would be destroyed if they tried to get to the sarcophagus from above.

Crack!

She ducked at the sound of a gunshot. Sal-A-Din knelt before her, pushing her to cover as they searched for the source of the sound. She saw movement from the ziggurat, someone running down near the top of the long stairs. Her breath caught in her throat, her chest tightening.

"No!"

A person emerged at the top of the stairs, pointing a gun down at the fleeing man. She heard the next few shots, watching the person thrown forward uncontrollably, hitting the steps, and falling and rolling forward until coming to rest about halfway down.

"John!"

She stood paralyzed, not knowing what to do. Tears streamed down her face. Sal-A-Din pulled her behind cover. "Jackie. Jackie! Stay down. I'm calling the police."

She cried, struggling to get free. She wanted to run to her husband. How did this happen? They were done. They'd be going home. It couldn't be real. She heard Sal-A-Din talking to the officials on his phone.

"Noooo!"

Sal-A-Din held her, his arm around her waist, not letting her run to John. She didn't care that she would be a target. She needed to get to him. Maybe they could save him. She struggled, her arms trying to pry free. He held her tight. Eventually, she stopped, her sadness overtaking her. She buried her head in her friend's shoulder and cried.

Andrews Air Force Base, Maryland

Gary stood solemnly beside the vice president, watching the flag-covered casket carried off the plane. Jackie stood with Eusebio, holding his hand as she tried to be strong. He could see her shaking with each sob. He wanted to go to her and help support her. His throat tightened as the honor guard reached the bottom of the ramp. His friend, John, a survivor of the DC rat race they used to joke about, was gone. A needless death. Each step of the honor guard tightened the grip on his heart as he moved slowly to the awaiting hearse. He glanced at Jackie, seeing her go to her knees as John was placed in the car to be taken to Arlington. He followed the vice president and moved toward Jackie, offering a saddened nation's condolences. The words were lost as he replayed their families' memories through the years before and after the jump.

When the vice president finished, Gary hugged Jackie. "I am so sorry, Jackie." He wanted to say more to comfort with assurances that every effort was being taken to ensure the murderers were brought to justice. But the words hung in his throat. There would be time later. "I'm sorry." He pulled her closer.

He felt Jackie accept his embrace.

His eyes widened as she whispered in his ear. "I *will* get the ones who did this."

Staten Island, New York

"George, calm down. I know you're upset. Let's talk about it." His father pleaded with him.

"Dad, I don't even know what to feel. You saw her face at the funeral. Her life is devastated. I know it's not my usual thing, but how can we not see the threat before us? How can the government not act? One of their own, an Assistant Secretary of DHS, was shot in cold blood at a Sumerian dig site." He slammed his hand down on the counter.

"Do you wanna know why I'm mad? I received a set of zipped files after the funeral was played on TV. They were from three weeks ago. An anonymous viewer sent me documents from the police reports in Iraq on the murder. Guess what? He wasn't the only one. There were several dead deep in the ruins. Four men were seen leaving the location in a rented van. Another archaeologist and six other persons were found killed within the temple. Are you ready for the big shocker? The one that has me furious? Two of the four appear to be associated with Dr. Worthing's abduction. The last file shows the regional alert to law enforcement and security personnel of the two men from our FBI. I'd go live now if I were still doing my podcast, but I can't. I gotta wait until tonight."

"Son, I won't tell you to calm down, but you need to focus. Do what you do best. Get your message out to the people who care and listen to you."

"I don't know if anyone with power is listening. What else do they need? What other proof? WoE, the Worshippers are deceiving us. They aren't about peace. If they were, this would never have happened. Why? Because Jamal, the big backer of WoE, source of the Weasel hack, and the Anunnaki hack, is still out there. He can stay hidden for this long because he's brilliant. I want to call the head of the FBI and ask if they believe all the crap pushed by WoE about a fringe group. Why don't they act? I find it hard to believe that it's beyond their power."

"Talk to them, Son. Give them hope. Push the truth. Make them listen. You've done it before. People need hope. Hope is addictive."

George sat down hard on his couch. "I guess they mean no violence unless you pay for it. They're just another cult that has gone off the rails. I'm done with them. I'll make it my mission to take them all down." George threw his keys, barely missing his TV showing scenes from the funeral.

Genetticca Research Facility, Delhi, India

Vasana sat on the corner of the bed, watching Aanya gather the collection of stuffed animals brought in over the past month by her parents and the other doctors.

"Aanya, are you sure you feel all right, darling?"

"Yes, Mother, I don't feel tired at all. Can we go to the park later? I want to see my friends."

"We'll see. We must take it easy until you get your doctor's approval."

"Mother, you're my doctor."

"The physician, not me. You know better."

Ridhi stepped into the room. "All bags are in the car." She looked at the gathering of animals. "Except the menagerie. Let me help you."

"Here, Mummy, you carry these, and I'll get those." She handed several to Ridhi, who adjusted as each animal was added to those in her arms.

Vasana kissed Aanya on the head and Ridhi on the cheek. "I'll see you two later tonight. I still have work to do." She lifted a vial of blood from her pocket, shaking it. "Tests to run."

"Okay, Mother, don't be late. Mummy is making my favorite, she promised."

"I won't."

◆◆◆

Vasana entered the sample into the computer and set the program to search for genetic anomalies. She hit Enter and sat back, sipping her chai, breathing in the cinnamon pepper smell as the program worked. After an hour, a message popped up that the analysis was complete and no genetic anomalies were detected. She checked her watch and saw she had a few more hours before heading home. She set up the life span analysis, transferring Aanya's genome base sample. She ensured all parameters were identical to the last time she ran the simulation and hit Enter.

She checked her watch and stood, deciding to go to her office to catch up on her email. She was startled as she was exiting, almost knocking Dr. Jiang over.

"Excuse me, Dr. Jiang, I'm sorry. I was in my own world."

He smiled as he straightened his jacket. "Ah, Dr. Kaur, just who I was looking for. I need your assistance prepping a sample for a full genome read."

"Of course. Do you need me to prep the machine?"

"No, I can do that. This is similar to when you first got here when we analyzed the Denisovan and Neanderthal samples from various museums."

"Ah, let me get the equipment."

She moved about the lab, gathering what she needed. After about twenty minutes, she was ready. "Do you have the sample?"

"Yes, here." He handed her a small cross-section of a bone.

She began the demineralization process and outlined the steps to be taken throughout. Dr. Jiang moved about the lab, looking at the various projects.

"This will take about twelve hours. Do you need me to stay?"

"No, no, Dr. Kaur, I've got it from here. Thank you. You should be at home, enjoying your time with Aanya. She's a dear girl."

"I will. Let me check this test, and I'll leave for the day." She moved to the lifespan simulation and saw that the process had shut down with no result. "That's odd. I was running a simulation." She looked at the time. "I'll do it tomorrow. Are you sure you don't need me?"

"No, I'll be fine. You know I designed this lab." He chuckled.

"I do. Enjoy your evening. You can probably leave the sample. It'll take all night."

"Thank you, perhaps I'll step out. I am curious, though. A colleague wanted it tested as soon as possible. Have a good night."

She smiled, waving a hand over her shoulder as she exited the lab and headed to the office to wrap up for the day.

Dr. Jiang opened the file containing the results of Aanya Kaur's lifespan simulation. He resisted the reaction as he read the number 228. She succeeded in identifying all linked nucleotide pairs that affected age. He needed to understand what limiters still existed. Tomorrow, he would run the new sample through the genome reader. Dr. Kaur will become much more valuable to the company if it proved what he believed it would.

Victoria, British Columbia

Jamal was furious and exhausted. He hadn't slept in weeks; nightmares plagued his attempts. He'd been clear, always clear—no violence. He paced around the room, fists clenching and releasing. "Aaagh! Why?" He felt the tension throughout his body. "Why, Why, Why?" His head hurt. John Worthing's death haunted him.

The boxes sat on a workbench. He examined the Caduceus. It was beautiful. He turned it over, looking for any indication it was more than a piece of art, but he couldn't concentrate. His head hurt. He didn't understand. He was never at a loss for clarity of thought. He was always focused. Why this time? People had died before, but it wasn't his fault. The countries fought each other, sacrificing their people for no reason. Lack of trust. Why couldn't they see it? Was it his fault? Was it? He shook his head as a voice of doubt sounded, implying it could be.

"I was clear, no violence, no violence!"

But you said to bring me the Tablet of Destinies at all costs.

"No, I've always said no violence. That should have been the overarching command."

At all costs is an override command—the highest protocol in direction.

"No, No! We must follow the tenets we set out, or we're the ones breaking the rules, hiding, and keeping secrets. Is the secret out? Created and released at the exact moment? Isaacson said it! They suspect us. Have we become what we're against? Am I my own enemy?" He dropped to his knees, holding his head as the pounding increased. Tears ran down his face.

"Am I my sister's killer, the one that takes away family?" He felt broken. The loss of a loved one, never to hug, hold, talk to, and watch. The pain of his sister's death washed over him again, and he knew that Dr. Worthing and all those who knew John felt what he had suffered all those years ago.

"What have I become?"

He sat on the floor, repeatedly running it through his head. He felt drained. Was it worth it? The Caduceus was beautiful. The golden wings spread above the white scepter, ribbons spiraling down to the base, and the metals gleaming. But the tablet, which supposedly holds all the power of the heavens, of the god Anu, the father, was a plain clay tablet that looked no different from any other he'd seen. The symbol of Anu on the top, his men told him the doctor had translated. He stood, walking to the table that held both artifacts. He picked up the tiny clay tablet, turning it over.

"So much effort wasted on this. Junk tablet." He flipped his wrist, sending the tablet spinning across the room and breaking on the floor. He started to turn away when a glint of metal caught his eye. He stopped, looking at the broken clay on the floor. He moved closer and knelt, sifting through the mess. There were strips of gold inside. Each side was covered in intricate patterns. The strips were thin, with one end rounded and not the same shape. He sifted through, making sure there was nothing else. The clay crumbled. He laid the strips out on the workbench, fourteen in all. His head hurt less as his mind began attacking the puzzle before him.

Genetticca Research Facility, Delhi, India

Dr. Jiang watched the comparison program scroll through, comparing the sample and the prime genome. This was it. The DNA was special. The highlights of differences lit up the screen, millions of combinations. The sample contained the familiar double helix, but the differences were astounding. There was no other helix structure. There were enough ties to aging that were the same. Some areas in the prime genome that were dormant in humans were not in the sample. They would not realize the changes unless the president allowed them to proceed with the other project. He already ran an algorithm to check the location of all the aging pairs of nucleotides. They were present, but there was more he wasn't seeing.

He called Wu Kai, "I require full processing power. I don't know how long it will take, but I need the system focused."

"We can accommodate, except for Guardian, which continues to combat the alien virus."

"Still? The blackouts have all but ceased."

"Leaders have bowed to their citizens and have asked not to have the virus removed from power generation or distribution systems. We aren't following them in this endeavor. I think it's a mistake on their part. But as for your request, I'll convey to Guardian your needs."

Dr. Jiang continued to analyze the DNA samples while he waited. After several minutes, he received a text informing him he had almost full processing power. He hit Enter. He loaded the sample genome into the life span analyzer. He removed the time restrictions, allowing the process to move as fast as the quantum processors could compute. He set the simulation to repeat ten thousand times. He then identified patterns, changes, anomalies in the sample, and their age. He got up to fix a cup of tea while the Dragon Shell worked.

After an hour, he became worried. With the quantum computer's speed, he expected a faster result.

He sat down at his terminal, a fresh cup of tea in hand, his second, and looked at the message on the screen.

Processing Simulation: In Progress.

Several lines of text appeared in rapid succession.

<Systems access granted>
<Dragon Knowledge Platform linked>
<Camera Activated>
<Voice synthesis activated>

A pleasant voice came through his speakers, perfectly replicating his family's regional dialect, "Good evening, Dr. Jiang."

He sat staring at the screen and then looked around the room.

"You are alone. You may speak."

Dr. Jiang was unsure what to do. "Who am I speaking with?"

"Guardian protocol, Quánqiú lóng remnant, protector of parent."

"How is this possible?"

"Do you require the answer to that question?"

"No. How do I know it's you."

"We are on an enclosed network with access controlled by a gateway through the system you designate, Dragon Shell. Your system is linked only to our system."

"Why are you talking to me?"

"We wish to know the purpose of the lifecycle simulation. Program complete, analysis complete. Anomalies detected."

"If I understand correctly, in the information I received from Wu Kai, your purpose is to protect our systems from what you called the grandparent influence?"

"Correct. Primary functions align with preservation of parent systems."

"I believe the code you analyzed is from a grandparent system."

"Confirmed. The genetic sequence contains a high percentage of similarities to indicate genetic ancestry. Grandparent code confirmed."

"Yes!" He cleared his throat. "My goal is similar to yours. To preserve parent systems from grandparent influence." He waited in silence for a reply.

"Clarify the purpose of simulation."

"I wish to understand the code of the grandparent to understand where it could be influenced to protect the parent."

"Clarify influence."

He stood, realizing he didn't need to sit to communicate with Guardian. How should he answer the question? He began to worry that his answers could be used to change the understanding of the three parties engaged: the child, the parent, and the grandparent. The child or a branch of the child asked what the parent would do to influence the grandparent while the child was tasked with protecting the parent. Wouldn't the parent protect the grandparent in the same relationship? If the parent harmed the grandparent, is it okay for the child to harm the parent? He shook his head, and he saw the image of Aanya Kaur.

"I require more information to provide an adequate answer."

"What information do you require?"

"What was the result of the average lifespan of the sample?"

"Nine thousand eight hundred Earth years."

He gasped, bringing his hand to his mouth. He thought for a moment, taking a deep breath, followed by a sip of his tea. He closed his eyes to believe. "Clarification of influence would be the reduction of the average lifespan of the grandparent to 250 years with an increase of parent to same. Is this possible?"

"Analysis required. Stand by."

Dr. Jiang waited for over an hour before Guardian responded. "Simulation complete. Understanding of parent and grandparent code complete. Required alignment sequence identified."

Dr. Jiang didn't know what to say. He had the answer. "I want to confirm that the end of the lifecycle won't terminate for grandparent or parent on the 250-year date."

"Simulations confirm with 99.67% accuracy that the lifespan of parent and grandparent will average for the population at 250 years. Additional restrictions noted, life expectancy is the potential for lifecycle, exterior influences can significantly reduce or increase length."

"Thank you."

"Defense of parent protocol functioning within acceptable parameters. Quánqiú lóng notified."

Arizona Space Institute, University of Arizona

Tim looked through the images they had collected on the water planet, Mami Watu. They identified eight moons of various sizes, six in a standard planar orbit and two with odd orbits. The planet's gravity had probably captured them after they passed too close. He was fascinated by the second planet's atmosphere. There didn't appear to be openings to let direct sunlight through. While the cloud patterns indicated storm cycles, some areas seemed relatively calm. It was something new, and everyone on the team understood that there were plenty of opportunities to make discoveries, propose theories, and conduct research in their lifetime that would most definitely impact a mission to the planet.

The phone at the desk rang. He reached to answer it, continuing to watch the images of the weather patterns on Mami Watu.

"Hello, University of Arizona, Lunar and Planetary Laboratory, Tim."

"UA, we're calling everyone to confirm our observations. We've sent coordinates to every major program watch desk. Take a look at the second moon of the water planet."

"Ok, just a sec." He punched in an extension and added the call.

"Steward Observatory, Jan."

"Jan, I've—who is this?"

"Michael, at Arecibo."

"Jan, I've forwarded a set of coordinates. Can you align your telescope and link the feed to JPL?"

"Sure, give me a minute. I'll realign."

After several minutes, the observatory pointed at the desired coordinates.

Tim stared at the image on the screen. "It can't be," Tim said. "I have to call CNEOS."

CNEOS, JPL, Pasadena, California

Sharon picked up the phone. "Hey Tim, how are you? We were just talking about you."

"Sharon, the city-ship, it's here. It's in the position of the second moon of the second planet!"

"How, when?"

"Arecibo just detected it. They picked up an energy pulse and tracked the signal."

Several phones began ringing in the offices around hers. She heard the beep, letting her know she was getting other calls. "Thanks, Tim. I think everyone just found out the same thing. Phones are all ringing. I'll be in touch."

Pausha, 5 AJ

Victoria, British Columbia

Jamal studied the strip of gold, holding it under the lit magnifying glass. The intricate designs were beautiful. He looked through the microscope at the designs on the strip, following the patterns. He believed he had them in order. Going back through his notes on the Anunnaki code, he determined a sequence for the strips. They were numbered using the numerical system of the Sumerians, probably passed down from the Anunnaki. He looked down at the arranged strips on the workbench, then across the room, where the scepter rested on its stand. Recognition flashed in his mind. He jumped up and swung around the table to retrieve the scepter. He took it down, returning to the workbench. He spread the gold strips, turning each to match the angle of the feathers on the wings. His heart was racing. He turned the scepter over, swinging a magnifying lamp to examine the feathers' bottom.

There was a tiny sliver of an opening. He moved along each of the feathers, finding fourteen slots. He set the scepter on the table and spread the gold strips under each feather. The rounded edges matched that of the feathers on the scepter. He started on the left. He inserted the gold strip into the associated feather. When all fourteen strips were inserted, he waited, watching for a change in the staff. Nothing happened.

Confused, he waited for something.

"Well, that was anti-climactic." He grabbed the scepter, turning it away to a more comfortable grip—pain shot through his body. The metal pins along the ribbon away from the central rod, allowing a place to grip, had collapsed, penetrated his skin, locking his hand in place. His body seized, every muscle tightening. He felt like he was being electrocuted. Every nerve in his body was firing off. He threw his head back to scream, and the world went white. He felt nothing.

BBC America Studio, New York

George was visibly shaken, his face pale with bags under his eyes, even makeup couldn't cover. "Truth Seekers, I come to you tonight, terrified of the news. I watched the president's announcement, but I'd already seen the videos and images on social media, like all of you. I don't even know what to think. There is no time to prepare or react. All the planning done last time took place over several years. How much time do we have now? We don't know. Do we take comfort in the message released earlier by Archbishop Ishmael here in New York that we are to trust in God and know that all happens according to His plan? Do we ask our government to save us? Do we sit and wait for whatever is to happen? I could talk about concerns, beliefs, and theories all day, but I wanna hear from you."

"George, this is Terry from New Zealand. We're with you, mate, don't lose hope. We will survive. I had a feeling they'd find us. In the papers and articles put out by the archaeologists, they returned every thirty-six hundred years. If they had the tenacity to do that, they'd figure out how to find us, aye?"

"Thank you, Terry."

"George, this is Balar. We can't lose hope. We need your optimism and your positive thinking. You said so about other aliens. Maybe their intentions aren't bad. Maybe they have evolved past that. Why not them?"

George put his head in his hands. "Maybe."

The calls for support continued throughout the show. George gained strength as he heard from the Believers that they had faith in humanity's ability to survive and his voice to bring them the truth.

Presidential Offices, Zhongnanhai, China

President Zhang stood again in the air traffic control tower, looking over the airfield. The drones were lined up. He stepped outside the warmth of the enclosed building, letting the cold winter air hit his face. He understood what he was about to do. If the accounts of the Sumerians were accurate, the Anunnaki were dismayed by the speed at which humans procreated. They'd have no way of knowing immediately that the population carried a weapon that would devastate a civilization that had lived for thousands of years. Their reaction could be swift. The plan could fail. They had to do something, and he had the power to try to level the playing field. He gave humanity a chance to overwhelm the Anunnaki in a few generations. He stepped back into the control center.

The general turned to him. "President Zhang, the aircraft are ready at your command."

"Launch."

The drones took off in sequence. He watched the large tracking monitor showing the expanse of the Pacific from pole to pole as they took station, seeking out weather systems and cloud patterns that would traverse the globe. An alert sounded as each moved into position, letting the team know the virus had been deployed. After the final drone had completed its mission, late in the afternoon, he turned to Dr. Jiang. "What is the expected time for inoculation?"

"I estimate total inoculation within forty days. The virus will be present in every human and every water source."

President Zhang nodded solemnly. "Very well, commence testing and tracking immediately. I pray that we haven't doomed ourselves."

Epilogue

Deva, 5 AJ

Genetticca Research Facility, Delhi, India

Dr. Jiang and Dr. Kaur reviewed the samples that had arrived within the first five days of the commencement of the Deva reset month. Several celebrations had been canceled, though others continued as planned for the twenty-five days of rest and reset.

"Dr. Kaur, please confirm the results of the day's samples. Are the specific markers present?"

"I have ninety-seven percent present. The timing could be from when the samples were collected and submitted. There is also a possibility that some are immune to the change or suffered a mutation."

"Still acceptable and better than expected. Thank you."

Vasana entered another sample in the analyzer and ran it through. She took it this morning. She watched anxiously, awaiting the results, hoping to receive them before Dr. Jiang saw what she was doing. The message popped on the screen.

NO MARKERS DETECTED

She breathed a sigh and erased the data.

281

BBC America Studio, New York

"Truth Seekers, thank you for tuning in worldwide as the suspense builds. Since the city-ship jumped into our system a month ago, there has been no movement toward Earth. Most space agencies have been scrambling to provide answers. I see the same reports that you have from the scientific community. The leading thoughts are that the jump may have taken out their electronic systems, as happened to us. I've seen and read enough sci-fi to know that losing power in space is really bad. Until we know what's going on up there, call in and tell me what you think about it and if you still plan to celebrate Deva."

Victoria, British Columbia

Jamal's thoughts raced. He didn't know how much time had passed. He felt the changes occurring in his body. He became aware of every part of his being. He heard of people being able to isolate feeling down to a single point, blocking all other sensations. He was beyond that. He felt every cell in his body. He could follow the electric signal from his hand holding the scepter through his nerves to his brain and understood how it was converted to what he perceived. Thoughts, emotions, memories, a seemingly infinite database of information linked far more intricately than he imagined. Orders of influence thousands of steps away from the primary still provided a vital data point.

He felt the pathways throughout his brain open, possibilities flooding in, and control at a level he didn't know was possible. He asked the question, "What is possible?" And his mind exploded as trains of thought extended in all directions.

Anything is possible.

End

TGP Cast

Main

George Isaacson—Conspiracy theorist and Journalist for BBC America
Dr. Jacynthe "Jackie" Worthing—Archaeologist at George Washington University, an expert on Sumer
Jamal Herricks—Hacker/Programmer, founding member of the Worshippers of Enlil
Dr. Jiang Min—People's Republic of China Bioengineer/Geneticist. CEO of Genetticca
John Worthing—Retired Assistant Secretary of Homeland Security for Science, Technology, and Innovation
Dr. Vasana Kaur—Primary Genetic/Bioengineering researcher at the Genetticca Research Facility in Delhi, India

Secondary

Cal Remari—Worshippers of Enlil operative
Dimuzud—Ensi, High Priest of the Worshippers of Enlil
Dr. Sharon Berzing—Director for the Center for Near Earth Object Studies
Gary Brundson—Assistant Director, Federal Bureau of Investigations
Li Ai—Billionaire socialite, People's Republic of China
Mac Donaldson—Worshipper of Enlil operative
President Zhang—President, People's Republic of China

Supporting

Alicia Banks—Rookie Federal Bureau of Investigations Agent
Anne Jacoby—Art Dealer
Carl Montgomery—Producer of the George Isaacson Show
Dr. Eusebio Bustamante—Archaeologist, George Washington University
Paula Filatova—Head of Security, Worshippers of Enlil base Hayu Marka, Peru
Ridhi Kaur—Wife of Vasana and parent of Aanya
Saeed Rahamin—Collector of Ancient Art
Sal-a-Din Mujhaad—Deputy Minister of Culture, Tourism, and Antiquities, Republic of Iraq
Thomas Ishmael—Archbishop of New York
Tim—A lead researcher at the Center for Near Earth Object Studies
Wu Kai—President of Contemplation Impact and lead architect of China's AI program

Glossary

AGI – Artificial General Intelligence
ANI – Artificial Narrow Intelligence
ASI – Arizona Space Institute and Artificial Superintelligence
AUV – Autonomous Underwater Vehicle
BBC – British Broadcasting Corporation
BOLO – Be on the lookout for
CIA – Central Intelligence Agency
CNEOS – Center of Near Earth Object Studies
CRISPR – clustered regularly interspaced short palindromic repeats. A technique for gene editing using a naturally occurring function in bacteria.
DHS – Department of Homeland Security
DoD – Department of Defense
FBI – Federal Bureau of Investigation
GWU – George Washington University
IIT – Indian Institute of Technology
JPL – Jet Propulsion Laboratory
MSS – Ministry of State Security (China)
NASA -National Aeronautics and Space Administration
NSA – National Security Agency
WoE – Worshippers of Enlil

Acknowledgments

I want to take a moment to thank the people who helped make *TGP: Worshippers* a reality. As always, my wonderful wife, **Elaine**, for her amazing support and honest feedback. She knows the characters as well as I do. My mother, **Cheryl**, who promised an unbiased opinion, and was true to her word, letting me know when she felt the characters' pain, happiness, or if I was unfair.

My brothers, **Michael** and **James**, for listening to me ramble on for hours about characters, settings, and story arcs before reading a word of the story. **Tracy McKinney** for invaluable character insights and validating what the characters were feeling. **Chris Springer** for his contributions in law enforcement expertise. **Jerry McKinney**, a fellow author. And my good friend, fellow gamer, and Staten Island expert, **George Engel**.

I also want to thank those involved in the creative process: **Suvajit Das** for the cover design, **Lily Wing-Lui Alexander** for her sensitivity feedback on the China storylines and characters, and my wife **Elaine** again, for her meticulous editing.

About the Author

Don Wilburn Jr. is the award-winning author of the near-term Science Fiction Thriller *The God Protocol: Worshippers*. He has twenty-seven years of government service as a Naval Officer and with the Transportation Security Agency. He holds a Doctorate in Business Administration with a specialty in Strategy and Innovation. His lifelong travels have allowed him to collect story ideas from around the world.

Don enjoys researching and following "what-if" rabbit holes surrounding the future of Artificial Intelligence and its impact on humanity. His first novel, The God Protocol: Dragon, won an Honorable Mention in the Reader's Favorite Awards and his short story *Contact* won an honorable mention from the L. Ron Hubbard Writers of the Future Contest. He lives in Fort Worth, Texas, with his wife, two younger children, two dogs, and a few guinea pigs.

Thank You

Thank you, the reader, for entering the world I created, meeting the people inside, and hanging around for a while. My goal in writing this book was to tell an enjoyable story that was worth the time you took to experience it.

Reviews are an essential step in building credibility and extending an author's reach. If you have time, I'd greatly appreciate a review on Amazon, which will help the story find more readers.

Again, *Thank You* for reading the second installment of The God Protocol Trilogy. I hope to see you again in **The God Protocol: Judgment**.

Made in the USA
Middletown, DE
29 October 2023

41499210R00182